A Love for the Ages

A Novel

I G Cummings

Kindle Direct Publishing

ISBN: 979-8-9898826-0-1

Cover design Feb 2024 By Lou Designs @Igr202 Fiverr

To sign up for the author's newsletter visit website: igcummings.com

Praise

A Love for the Ages will whip your head around as it brings America's culture clash onto the page.

This captivating closeup reveals the secrets that undermined the 31 year marriage to Minnie Donaldson's recently deceased husband. Minnie, a middle-aged black woman, makes these damning discoveries on an extended road trip to visit her children and golf friends. She now feels released from any sense of responsibility about her loveless marriage. Guilt free, she is ready to live her life for herself.

It's meeting talented John Dawson --young, white lawyer, half Minnie's age—that is her romantic challenge. This is when John and Minnie's story begins. Cummings serves up fresh answers to questions of interracial loves and striking age differences. The story sparkles with insight and moves swiftly without preaching. A Love for the Ages shows us passion need not end as we age.

HALLIE MOORE

Poet Laurette of Montgomery County, Texas

PART I

Chapter 1

September 2016

On a hot, cloudless early September Friday, Minnie Donaldson told nursing goodbye. She gathered her gift bags and offered her Lutheran Memorial Hospital colleagues' thanks for her retirement party. Minnie felt a slight pang of regret as she got off the elevator and walked through the bright, modern lobby, but it was minute. She wasn't sad she wouldn't pass this way again soon, maybe not ever.

Her co-workers presented her with decks of cards, DVDs of movies and television shows, golf-related items, books, board games, and a tea pot, Minnie's affinity for tea being widely known around the hospital. Nobody bought clothes. Some joked that she owned more outfits in more styles than the rest of the nursing staff combined.

With the DVDs, Minnie could catch up on her favorite British television shows like *Death in Paradise, Doc Martin,* and *Lewis,* along with a full set of one of the few American shows she'd give the time of day, *The West Wing*.

She had plans for the evening. At least she thought she did. A little voice told her she shouldn't get her hopes up, but she felt giddy over the prospect of a retirement night dinner with her husband, then maybe, just maybe, a night in bed with him. She'd planned her wardrobe from the skin out.

Brutal sun and the 80 percent Dallas humidity struck Minnie hard as she navigated the revolving doors. Her brown skin glistened even before she reached her car. She'd lived in North Texas or southeast Oklahoma all her life and hated July, August, and September more each year. Would retirement make them bearable? *One can only hope,* she thought as she started the car.

Turning out of the parking lot, doubts about the evening seeped into her head. At the wheel of her late-model Lexus, Minnie acknowledged her loneliness. She would never have believed she'd feel this way after 31 years of marriage, not with the financial security she had, not with three grown, successful children.

But, here she was, starved for affection, starved for sex, and uncertain of where this life was taking her. Despite some doubts, she'd decided shedding work would help. So, she retired at 54. For an instant, she asked if she'd made a mistake. Would she come crawling back to this place, to the people she'd left, bored out of her mind, unfulfilled, and searching for a port in a storm worse than the one she'd braved the last few years?

Her husband, Bradley, was, pure and simple, preoccupied with his business. Hardly anything mattered except the company's fast-food restaurants and real estate holdings. They brought in more money than she and Bradley would ever spend. What was the point? Making their children and grandchildren rich?

Still, when she turned onto the freeway from the street that adjoined the hospital, she smiled. She previewed the evening she hoped lay ahead. Surely, she could command his attention on the occasion of her retirement. Surely, Bradley would agree they should try rekindling their old magic. Surely, he would hold her hand at dinner, take her home, and ravish her. Surely, this night would turn things around.

At home, Minnie surveyed their too-big house. Two people didn't need six bedrooms or five thousand square feet. Bradley, however, showed no more interest in downsizing than she expected he'd have in her new DVDs, books, and games.

Minnie shook her head as she placed the bags in the corner of the first-floor bedroom she sometimes used as a hideaway. She'd sort things out later. Right now, she could think only of the coming night and the hope it offered for the future. She looked at her watch. It said 5:45 p.m. She should get ready. She expected Bradley home in 45 minutes.

Having stripped, Minnie caught a glimpse of herself in the full-length bedroom mirror. She noted the toned, muscular arms and legs and narrow waist she worked so hard at keeping. Her 34B breasts didn't sag. Gray streaks hadn't invaded her jet black hair. A modest nose and thin lips made up part of a calm, put together look. Not an unattractive picture, she said to herself, not unattractive at all.

In the shower, she let the warm water flow over her. Body wash produced a rich, white lather she worked into her brown skin with a long handled, bristled brush. Rinsing off left her feeling fresh and new. When she stepped out of the shower onto a plush green rug, she grabbed a thick white towel and wrapped herself in its softness. Minnie spent the next few minutes drying every inch of her body.

Now came dressing and make up. She'd planned both down to the last detail. A glance at the black dress hanging on the closet door ramped up her hopes for tonight. On the bed, she'd laid out a black lace bra, a matching half-slip, and the evening's treat – seamed nylon stockings and black garter panties.

During Minnie's college years, her older sister, Mildred, taught her about panties with attached garters. They let her wear stockings rather than pantyhose, yet avoid a cumbersome garter belt. Bare thigh between the stocking tops and the panties always helped pull Bradley into her clutches. Please, God, let tonight be no different.

Minnie slipped the bra around her middle, fastened the back clasp, then rotated it into place, pulling the straps over her shoulders. She stepped into the panties, rolled each stocking up a leg, and fastened six garters. An instant later, she'd pulled on the slip, worked the dress over her head, then smoothed it down. Another look in the mirror told her that if a 54-year-old woman could radiate sex, she did.

Her watch lay on the table in the dressing area just outside the bedroom. It now read 6:22 p.m. She put it on and sat down at her make-up table. Before she could apply the foundation, her cell phone, lying on the dresser, rang. A sick feeling raced through her middle. She scurried into the bedroom and answered on the fourth ring. "Hello."

The deep voice on the other end boomed, "Hey. It's me. I won't be there for another hour, maybe an hour and a half. What's going on?"

Minnie sat on the bed, stunned. "What's going on?

What do you mean, what's going on?"

"Just what I asked. What's new?"

He doesn't remember! She said nothing for a few seconds, grappling for what words could possibly meet the moment.

"You still there, Minnie? What's the problem?"

She grunted. "What's the problem? You must be kidding. What's the damn problem? You can do better than that, Bradley Donaldson."

"Minnie, don't go off on me. What's wrong with you?"

Her voice rose almost to a shriek. "You don't remember what today is, do you? What tonight is?"

Now he yelled at her. "What the hell are you talking about?"

Minnie stopped and took a breath. She wasn't doing this. "If you don't know what's going on, if you don't know what today is, I sure won't tell you. I'm not doing your work for you. Good bye!"

Minnie threw the phone down on the bed. For a second she sat in disbelief, her makeup unfinished. This could not be happening.

∞∞∞

Forty-eight hours after Minnie's bitter disappointment that Bradley didn't remember her retirement, she found herself in a little restaurant in suburban Detroit sitting across the table from her longtime lawyer friend, Connie Wilson. After half an hour of crying Friday night, Minnie called Connie and asked what would happen if she showed up on her doorstep for the weekend.

"Oh, at least three rounds of golf and four or five bottles of wine," Connie had replied.

She found a 10:35 p.m. flight to Detroit. Minnie traded the garter panties, seamed stockings, cocktail dress, and stilettos for an everyday cotton hipster, white half-socks, khaki shorts, a green polo, and running shoes.

With the time zone change it was 3:10 a.m. when her head hit a pillow at an airport hotel, but she happily crawled out of bed four hours later for the start of a two-day golf adventure in central and northern Michigan. Frank Withers, a former Air Force pilot, retired heart surgeon, and one-time medical colleague of Connie's wife, Gretchen Downs, made things easy by flying them around in his twin engine plane.

Chapter 2

Minnie arrived home Monday glowing from 54 holes of golf, enthralling company, and the sense of freedom that went with a day of no work. Bradley wasn't there. She found a note asking if she could "spare a few moments" Tuesday morning before he left for the office.

Still seething about Friday, she wrinkled her nose, wondering what he wanted. Minnie slept in the spare bedroom and didn't notice when Bradley arrived home Monday night. She rose at 6:30 a.m. Tuesday, threw on shorts and a t-shirt, and headed for the kitchen.

She saw him at the island in the spacious, remodeled room, pouring coffee. Bradley Donaldson stood six-feet-three inches tall and weighed over 240 pounds. His bulging belly annoyed Minnie. She silently berated him for not exercising and for his fried food habit. The fact he often ate late at night didn't help.

In their brightly lit kitchen, his coal black skin stood out against the stainless steel appliances and cream colored wallpaper. He still had black, closely cropped, tightly curled hair. As she watched him, Minnie remembered when she thought Bradley Donaldson the most graceful, handsome man in the world. Now, he looked tired, awkward, and ill at ease.

He turned to her. "You're up, I see. What're you doing today?"

She clenched her jaw, annoyed by the question. "I'm retired, something you obviously didn't remember Friday. I'm not sure I'm doing anything. Why?"

He ignored the Friday reference. "You could help me with some things at the office."

She bit her tongue and balled up her fists. "I'm not doing

that."

"Not doing that? What's that about?"

"I've been working at the hospital all these years. You've gotten along fine without me. I'm retired."

"You could help me get a handle on changes we're making in our inventory control system."

She crossed her arms. "Somebody has done inventory control all this time. Why do you need me now?"

"It's our family business and I – "

"You think you can save money by having the wife provide free labor, right?" Minnie asked him through a tight frown. "No thanks. I earned my retirement and I'm taking it. Hire somebody who can get a handle on inventory control. I have other fish to fry." She walked out.

∞∞∞

For the next four weeks, Minnie and Bradley said little to each other except "good morning." They never said "good night" because they never retired at the same time and never slept together. Bradley arrived home from work at about 7:45 p.m., gorged himself on burgers and fries, watched Sports Center on ESPN or a Dallas Mavericks basketball game, then fell into bed about 10:30 p.m.

Minnie read or watched recorded episodes of British TV shows. More nights than not, she pulled out her vibrator and gave herself the orgasm that brought sleep.

During the day, she ran and worked out, practiced her golf game, or played rounds by herself or with this or that friend. Before or after golf, she took in movies, sometimes alone, sometimes with others. Plays and concerts occupied her an evening or two each week.

One night in October, as Minnie put on her makeup before heading off for another play, she looked up and saw Bradley in the mirror, standing in the doorway between her dressing area and the bedroom. "Did you want something?" she asked as she powdered her nose.

"Do you have any idea what you're doing? You're aimless."

"That's the point," she said, unscrewing the cap on a bottle of eyeliner and shaking her head. "I'm retired."

"I barely know what you do with yourself."

"I'm sure you don't. You have no interest in anything about me if it doesn't involve making you money."

"Making us money."

She continued applying eyeliner. "You don't need my help. I know the bottom line. I see tax returns. I read financial statements. The company's doing fine."

"It's not just money."

Finally, as she turned toward him, she shook her head. "You could've fooled me. That's all you talk about."

"It's the principle of the thing. We should help each other."

She tilted her head and sneered at him. "We're not a struggling young couple, Bradley. We're mature people who set our course a long time ago. You ran the business. I worked as a nurse and raised the kids. Both are over for me. I want a different life."

"But, Minnie…."

"Now, if you'll excuse me, I'm out of here. Don't wait up."

She turned back to the mirror, checked her makeup and hair one last time, then closed her compact and dropped it and a tube of lipstick into her purse. She rose from the table, grabbed her bag and keys, and walked past him. Perfunctory pecks on the cheek or ritual brushing of lips ended a while ago.

Before she reached the kitchen, she thought of something

she'd seen while driving home that afternoon. She returned to the bedroom, where Bradley stood by the closet door, unbuttoning his shirt. "Didn't I see you heading east on Northwest Highway today? And didn't you have a kid with you?"

He averted her gaze. She noticed his chin quiver. "Wasn't me," he said. "Must have been somebody with a car like mine."

Her eyes widened. "I know your car."

"Lots of blue cars in Dallas."

Minnie wrinkled her brow. "Sure looked like your car. And why would you be going that way? That's the opposite direction from the office."

He blew out a series of short breaths, as if trying to control himself. "It wasn't me."

Minnie looked at her watch. She should go. Something wasn't right, but pursuing this seemed pointless. Friends and a supposedly enthralling play beckoned. She turned and walked toward the garage.

As Minnie opened the overhead door with the remote on the car visor, her cell phone rang. "Carol? Carol Robbins?"

"Hello, Minnie. Did I catch you at a bad time?"

"I'm heading for a night of theater with friends." Minnie started the car's engine, but didn't back out of the garage.

"This won't take but a second. I'm inviting you for around of golf at my club next week. Are you up for that?"

Minnie blew out a long breath and grinned in the darkness. "You know my answer. When?"

"I thought Wednesday, the 19th. Let's play early and have lunch there."

Minnie widened her grin. "Sounds like a great treat."

"Your retirement present. See if your friend Cynthia McFadden can play. I'll find somebody else and we'll make it a foursome. If the weather keeps cooling off, we'll get caddies and walk. I know how much you like that."

"Sounds wonderful. I'm seeing Cynthia tonight."

"We'll have a memorable day."

∞ ∞ ∞

Carol Robbins was about the wealthiest person Minnie knew, yet maybe the fairest. The suggestion she include Cynthia McFadden demonstrated that. Most white women Minnie played golf with would never have asked that she bring a black friend. Private club invitations usually meant a one-blackat-a-time rule. Aside from adoring the Jackson Creek course, Minnie relished the invitation because Carol let her bring her own guest and didn't care if that person was black.

The game Minnie cherished remained mostly white, especially among women her age. Despite a rich history in amateur golf, black female participation in the sport remained flat. Barely a handful of her black women friends played and only a few of those played well enough that she enjoyed playing with them.

Word got around that Minnie Donaldson played golf especially well, so black women's social clubs introducing younger members to the game asked her for advice and instruction. That was well and good, but when Minnie played for personal enjoyment, she had little patience with sprayed and topped drives, flubbed chips, and five tries at getting out of a bunker. Yes, she was a golf snob.

She found Dallas-area tournaments for black social and charity groups frustrating. In individual women's events, she always won her age group, often with a better score than many younger players. Eight years ago she began playing against men in tournaments, from their tees. It wasn't uncommon that she finished ahead of male players 10 years younger. Even if they out-drove her by 30-35 yards, as many did, her deadly short game and deft putting stroke often let her finish among the leaders and once or twice the winner.

Minnie thought for a second about Bradley. What had she expected when she retired? As the years rolled by, the more paranoid he got. He reacted defensively or became confrontational when she tried engaging him about his attitudes. He stopped taking vacations and became hypervigilant about everything in the business. It was as if something bad would happen if he wasn't there all the time.

Perhaps memories of the 2008 recession fed his insecurities. In fact, though, Bradley made that downturn work for him. He acquired fast food restaurants in suburban areas and small towns near Dallas at bargain prices, refurbished them, and hired better managers. Now they thrived and turbocharged the company's bottom line.

Minnie wasn't interested in getting involved in the business. She needed time for herself before taking on a divorce fight or working at repairing the marriage. If she gave in now, for a while, Bradley would express his gratitude by doing things she thought he should do anyway – share her activities, show affection, maybe even get interested in sex again. She feared, though, he'd quickly resume his old ways.

As she wheeled her car into the theater parking lot, she pressed her lips together, more determined than ever she'd live her own life. Bradley wasn't getting control over her.

The striking, unflappable Cynthia McFadden waited out front. Little flustered the tall, light-brown skinned woman with curly hair. Tonight, she wore a green pantsuit and a beige blouse revealing a hint of cleavage. The wife of a wealthy black lawyer, she'd retired last year at 60 after a 38-year career in real estate sales. For a time, she'd been the top selling black residential real estate agent in Dallas. "You're the first one here, Cynthia," Minnie said. "I have a modest proposal I'll give you before the others arrive."

She tilted her head to the side. "A modest proposal?"

"You and I have a golf invitation at Jackson Creek Country Club next Wednesday."

Cynthia's face beamed. "I'm in!"

"What about checking your calendar?"

"So I can play golf at Jackson Creek, whatever I have I'll reschedule."

"It's a date," Minnie said, noticing the approach of the three other women attending the play with them. "I'll call you with details."

"Deal," Cynthia said and turned to greet that group.

Chapter 3

W ednesday, October 19, 2016, dawned clear and pleasant for mid-October in Dallas. Minnie had slept in the spare bedroom, so she only heard Bradley leave at 5:30 a.m. While retrieving the *Dallas Morning News* from the driveway, she glimpsed his taillights when he turned the corner on the next block.

Getting to Jackson Creek in morning traffic took 45 minutes. She looked at her watch and targeted six o'clock for departure. After a light breakfast, she brushed her teeth and dressed. Minnie preferred shorts for golf, but she'd play today in a skort that ended mid-thigh. A skort let her comply with Jackson Creek's preference that "ladies" wear skirts, yet eliminate worry about someone gawking at her panties as she lined up putts or retrieved a ball from a cup.

Today, she slipped into a blue skort that included matching shorts beneath the skirt, covered her black sports bra with a bright yellow polo shirt, and topped her head with a red straw hat. The hat wasn't part of her standard golf uniform either. She usually played in a baseball cap or a visor, but the Jackson Creek membership frowned on baseball caps and visors for women, so she wore a narrow-brimmed straw hat.

∞∞∞

It wasn't Magnolia Lane at Augusta National, but the tree-lined entrance at Jackson Creek gave the place the feel of old money, haughtiness, and racial exclusion. Minnie had seen and played at her share of such places, in tournaments and as guests of white women friends. She often felt conflicted. Sometimes she experienced tightness in her chest upon arrival. Was she betraying other black people and the cause of equality by indulging herself at such places? When she made it about the golf, her reservations receded.

She'd tried, without success, to get Bradley to join a private club near their home. Though they could afford it, he saw private club memberships as a waste. He could pay the freight at any daily fee course in town. That was enough for him. Minnie, however, liked the idea of a place she could regularly play, practice, eat, work out, and socialize. A private club membership would make life easier for her, but Bradley wouldn't hear of it.

Because she'd played Jackson Creek with Carol four or five times, she had less trouble putting aside her misgivings today. She wondered how Cynthia, a Jackson Creek rookie, would react to the Old South feel of the place. That feel appeared immediately, from the moment a guest entered the grounds. The servants – valets, caddies, maids, maintenance people, food service workers – were mostly black or brown. They wore black and white uniforms that fit a 1950s movie.

Carol said the club began hiring white attendants only five years ago. Some members objected, almost as much as they'd objected when the club relaxed its rules against black, brown, and Jewish members a few years before. That happened because members who held or sought public office and couldn't remain in racially discriminatory clubs threatened, they'd leave and take a big group with them.

This club had one thing Minnie wasn't uneasy about – a spectacular golf course unlike any other in Dallas-Fort Worth. Minnie had seen and played great courses around the world – Pebble Beach and Torey Pines in California, Medina in Chicago, Pumpkin Ridge in Oregon, Bethpage Black in New York, and golf's holy grail, the Old Course at St. Andrews. She'd attended the Masters at Augusta National, a U.S. Open at Wingfoot, and a Women's British Open at Royal Birkdale. Not one had anything on Jackson Creek. Whatever her misgivings about the club's culture, Minnie decided she could deal with the unease in exchange for playing, every once in a while, as good a golf course as existed.

Jackson Creek did what great courses do – reward good shots and penalize bad ones. It included no tricks that massaged the designer's ego. "Tweener" holes that played as long par fours, but were really par fives, didn't muck up the scorecard. Bunkers served a real function, like protecting otherwise easy pin placements. Water hazards and swampy areas created forced carries that generated justifiable tension, not agony. Elevation changes made holes more attractive, not more difficult.

At the pro shop counter, Minnie saw Carol standing behind three men. She always first noticed Carol's raven hair, thin waist, and broad shoulders. Three inches shorter than Minnie, she wore a green skort topped with a white polo and a brown straw hat.

Minnie looked at her watch. It said 6:59 a.m. "I knew I couldn't beat you here, Carol, though I tried."

Her host turned and they embraced. "I planned on being here half an hour ago," Carol said when she stepped back. "It's so good to see you. I've been looking forward to this. We should have a great time."

"I know we will. Who's our fourth?"

"Ginger Goodman. She called and said she'd be here by a quarter after seven. And Cynthia?"

"I spoke with her on the way. Said she wasn't far behind me."

"Great."

"Tell me about Ginger."

They reached the front of the line at that instant,

interrupting the conversation. From behind the counter, a 50-something man wearing a smile on his weather-beaten face and the obligatory white Jackson Creek polo shirt, greeted them. "Good morning, Mrs. Robbins," he said, brushing aside his sandy hair. "I take it all your group isn't here yet?"

"They're not, David, but I'll tell you who they are so you can check them in now."

"That's fine, Mrs. Robbins. You can meet them outside and go straight to the range. Your caddies will meet you there. Tell me their names and I'll let outside reception know they're coming."

"Cynthia McFadden and Ginger Goodman. They're not together, but both should arrive any moment."

"I know Mrs. Goodman. I believe she's played here with you. Ms. McFadden will be with us for the first time, right?"

"Yes. Thanks for whatever the staff can do that makes her feel welcome."

"My pleasure," he said when he handed her a receipt. Minnie knew not to offer to pay for anything, though she'd make sure she generously tipped her caddie – perhaps $150 to $300 if he performed well. Cynthia had played at enough private clubs that she knew the drill, but Minnie wasn't sure if she understood just how rich the blood was at Jackson Creek. She made a mental note to give Cynthia a heads up before the round ended.

Carol and Minnie walked out the door together and stood at the front of the elegant, ornate clubhouse complete with massive white columns and bronze statues of horses. While waiting for their playing companions, Carol said, "Our fourth is Ginger Goodman, a charity board colleague. She played at LSU in the late 1980s, so she's a little younger than we are. She's very good, though she doesn't shoot below par very often these days. She doesn't play or practice enough. She'll shoot 75-76 today."

"You've played with Cynthia haven't you?" Minnie asked.

"I played with the two of you in a tournament at Bear Creek, that great daily fee course near DFW airport. She was good that day."

Minnie scanned a Jackson Creek scorecard. "She should shoot in the low 80s on this course. You and I are about the same, just like we're the same age. How should we pair up?"

Carol turned and grinned. "You and I are not the same. I never beat you. You won by three strokes the last time we played."

"You have the advantage of local knowledge."

"We played here."

Minnie laughed. "I guess we did."

"I'll play with Cynthia. Otherwise, somebody will say it's a color thing."

"Yeah, Cynthia and I probably shouldn't be partners."

Minnie often told people playing golf beat anything else she could have been doing at a given time except sex. Never had that been more true than that October Wednesday. Visions of the hours between their 7:55 a.m. start and the 12:07 p.m. finish stuck with her for years, blotting out other memories of 10/19/2016.

Above all, there was how she played, a three under par round of 69, fueling the two up win she and Ginger took over Carol and Cynthia. She couldn't forget the way the course, the cloudless sky, low 70s temperatures, less than 20 percent humidity, and calm winds embraced her. There was the easy camaraderie among the four of them – laughter, jokes, gentle putdowns, encouragement. As she told Cynthia near the end of the round, "I couldn't have written the story of today any better if I were Ernest Hemingway."

Nothing eventful happened on the first two holes except Minnie's 15-foot par-saving putt that halved No. 2, leaving the match tied. Ginger exclaimed in a loud voice, "I won the partner picking contest!"

"You wait," Carol said as they ambled toward No. 3. "I did okay. I've seen Cynthia play."

That hole presented a greater challenge than the first two. "I have more trouble making a birdie on this hole than any other on the course," Carol said.

Minnie looked at her playing companions as she took the tee. "It's really simple," she said. She took an easy breath and relaxed her shoulders. She went through her pre-shot routine, beginning with a practice swing behind the ball while she looked down the fairway. Once she addressed the ball, there was one more practice swing before she fired away. Her Titlist Pro V1 flew high and long, bending left with an ever-so-slight draw. It landed in the fairway, shy of the deep rough, 240 yards out from the tee. She turned and looked at her three playing companions again. "See, I told you it was simple."

"You're full of it," Cynthia said through a frown. "This'll be a long day if we have to put up with that the whole round."

Ginger, Cynthia, and Carol placed their shorter drives on the 470 yard, par five hole on the right side of the fairway, leaving more difficult second shots than Minnie's. Her angle took out of play an array of deep bunkers 75 yards from the green. A perfectly struck second shot rolled to within 20 yards of the putting surface.

"Ten years ago, I might have reached this green in two," Minnie lamented as she walked beside Carol and took the club for her next shot from her caddie, a young black man with dark skin, white teeth, and a toothpick in his mouth. He wore the Jackson Creek caddie's uniform – black shorts, white polo shirt, ivory-colored caddie's apron, and green cap.

"Ten years ago that shot might have gone anywhere," Carol replied. "I played with you in those days. You hit it farther, but you are vastly more accurate and more consistent now."

"Lessons and practice have benefits," Minnie said with a sly smile. She deftly swung through her chip shot, sending the ball past the edge of the green. It stopped a foot from the pin.

"Somebody made a birdie on this hole," Ginger said, the putt having been conceded. "Might be my partner."

"Might be," Minnie said, high-fiving Ginger when they walked off the green.

With Minnie's birdie on No. 3, her team took a one up lead in the match. They moved two up on No. 5, a 140-yard par three with a forced carry over a pond. Minnie carded her second birdie of the day, when she coaxed in an eight-foot downhill putt that died at the hole and barely fell.

The lead grew to three-up on the 361-yard par four No. 8 when Ginger rolled in a chip from 15 feet off the green that eliminated the effect of Minnie's only bogey of the day.

Cynthia had her moment on No. 9, a long par four Minnie thought she'd birdied herself when her sweetly struck approach shot landed six feet from the pin and stopped. But she missed the putt and Cynthia drained a 25-footer for a birdie. That left Robbins-McFadden only two down at the turn.

"Want anything from the grill?" Carol asked as they walked past the clubhouse toward the back nine. "Drinks? A snack?"

Everyone shook their heads. "I'll pass," Minnie said. "There are lots of things I love about this golf course. Having cold drinking water on every hole sure is one of them."

"I'll second that," Ginger said, gulping from the tumbler she filled on the last hole.

"What's next, Carol?" Cynthia asked. She would hit first because of the birdie she made on No. 9.

"Might be my favorite hole on the course. They have the tee up today, meaning it's only 325 yards. It might play like 275. It's downhill, so you can get a good roll and have no more than a sand wedge into the green. There's a creek just right of the green and a deep bunker left, so hit that wedge straight. The green slopes front to back. Ideally, hit the approach shot past the pin so you have a putt back up the hill. It's a short hole, but it's not easy."

"Show us the way, Cynthia," Minnie said, for the moment caring more about her friend's success than the effect of the upcoming shot on the match. She watched as Cynthia hit her best drive of the day, a towering shot that landed on the downslope and didn't stop until it reached the bottom of the hill.

Minnie grinned and ran over to Cynthia, still eyeing where the ball rested, perhaps 50 yards from the green. Minnie held up her hand, inviting a high five. "I'm not supposed to do that, since you're on the other team, but that was spectacular. Well done, my friend."

Carol, Minnie, and Ginger matched Cynthia's effort. "I guess it's game on," Carol said as they headed down the fairway.

All of them put their second shots within birdie range, but only Carol made her putt. Ginger, who hit her shot closest, groaned when her five-footer lipped out. That kept Donaldson– Goodman from halving the hole. They sat one up as they moved to No. 11.

"I hate this hole," Carol said, pushing her tee into the ground.

"I thought you hated the third hole," Minnie replied. She folded her arms over her chest.

"That's the hole on which I have more trouble making a birdie. I like that hole. I just don't play it well. I dislike this hole."

"It is diabolical," Ginger said. She smoothed out wrinkles in her blue polo shirt. "I made seven the last time I played here."

"You guys are scaring me," Cynthia said, tightly gripping her driver and scanning the 346 yards that lay ahead. "It doesn't look so bad."

"That's because you haven't seen the green," Minnie replied. "Just wait."

As they reached their drives, the reasons for Carol's disdain became obvious. Deep, unforgiving bunkers surrounded the left side and center of a kidney-shaped green that sloped right to left. Those bunkers suggested going right, though an approach shot hit in that direction but short, would leave a dangerous chip the most skilled players could have trouble stopping.

Minnie, who outdrove the others by 15 yards, said with a straight face, "I have a solution for the problems on this hole."

"What?" Carol asked with a smirk, as she took a practice swing.

"Just watch."

With a six iron, Minnie ran through her pre-shot routine. Her free and easy swing propelled her ball over the bunkers and onto the green, where it stopped six feet from the pin. "Just hit the green," she said. "If you hit the green, there's no problem."

Cynthia's smirk would have filled a good-sized room. "I hate you."

"So do I," Carol said, tilting her head away.

"I don't," laughed Ginger. "She's my partner."

They didn't know it at the time, but that shot, which set up Minnie's birdie, her third of the day, turned the match to Donaldson – Goodman for good. That put them two up with seven holes remaining.

Minnie played the next four holes cautiously, helping protect her team's two-hole lead. She didn't fire at difficult pin placements but instead dumped the ball into the middle of greens and two-putted for pars. That worked until No. 16 when Carol holed another birdie chip, suddenly leaving the outcome in doubt. The teams halved the next hole when Minnie's long birdie try, carrying a touch too much speed, lipped out.

As they climbed stairs to an elevated tee, Carol said, "You're one up and if we win the next hole, we'd halve the match. The last hole means something."

"It often does when we play," Minnie told her.

"You usually save some magic for this one." "I do love this hole," Minnie acknowledged.

"What do you like about it?" Cynthia asked. She stood beside Minnie as Carol talked with her caddie.

Minnie's face, shielded by her hat, lit up. "If you don't hit a long, straight drive and a solid approach shot, you won't hit the green in regulation. The deep rough on the right in the landing area makes me think about leaving the driver in the bag. If you keep the ball in the fairway, drive it past that bad rough, and hit the approach shot well, there's lots of reward, because the green is flat and you can make a birdie here. I like holes like that. Hit a bad shot, pay for it. Hit a good shot, get rewarded."

Carol held the honor because of her birdie on No.16. She hit a long, low drive down the left side of the fairway, which produced a good chance of reaching the green on her next shot. Cynthia's shorter drive likely left Carol on her own in trying to tie up the match. Minnie drove past Carol, but by only five yards. Ginger pushed her shot into the right rough. The match became a contest between Carol and Minnie.

"Poetic justice, I guess," Carol said.

"Something like that," Minnie replied, as she surveyed her

approach shot.

Carol, because she was away, hit first. Her shot with a fairway metal soared high and landed in the middle of the green, but didn't release. It ended up 20 feet from the flag. She had a birdie chance, but only a chance.

Minnie continued looking over her shot. She checked her GPS watch. It said 161 yards to the hole, but only 138 to the front of the green. "How does this pin placement work?" she asked her caddie while rubbing her chin. "That doesn't look like 161 yards."

"Trust the number, Miss Minnie," he said. "Most people, men and women, make that mistake on this hole. That pin is farther back than it looks. That's all of whatever you hit 160 yards."

"I'll take your word for it, my man." Minnie grabbed a hybrid club from the caddie, lined up the shot, and let it fly. The ball landed past the middle of the green and rolled toward the flag. Initially, neither Minnie nor her caddie could see exactly how close she'd gotten, but both soon knew the shot left her with a putt their opponents would concede. Minnie turned and received the caddie's high five. Out of the corner of her eye, she saw Carol, standing next to Cynthia, shake her head.

"So much for that," they said in unison.

∞∞∞

Sitting in the Jackson Creek grill, lunch behind them, Minnie turned to Carol, as a warm feeling spread through her body. "Thank you for one of the best days of my life. I can't imagine a better time."

"You're so welcome. And thanks for bringing Cynthia."

Cynthia flashed a huge smile. "Thank you. This was

wonderful. And thanks for being a great partner. Didn't you shoot even par – 72?"

"I did. Thank you. Your 83 is very respectable on this course for someone who'd never played it before." She stopped. "Minnie and I often shop a little after our round."

"We sure do," Minnie said, nodding and remembering the backpack she'd brought.

"Like to join us?" Carol asked.

"I can't," Cynthia said as she rose from the table. "Tomorrow is our 33rd wedding anniversary. My husband's taking me to dinner tonight because he has a business trip tomorrow. I should get home and get pretty, at least as pretty as I can these days."

Carol turned to Ginger. "How about you?"

"I'll pass. I have a family party tonight celebrating my son's promotion."

"You told me about that. Please congratulate Donnie for me. Thanks again for playing. What'd you end up with?"

"I shot 76, which for me these days is good. I'm pleased." She looked at Minnie. "Thanks to my partner, I have a great memory of winning our match, two up."

As Ginger and Cynthia left, Carol turned to Minnie. "Looks like it's just us."

Minnie followed Carol home and, after a hot shower in her guest bathroom, changed clothes. They spent the afternoon cruising stores and rehashing the round. As day became night, Carol suggested dinner at a jazz club near their shopping haunts. Drinks, food, and live music led inevitably to Carol's gentle, but persistent probing about Minnie's marital situation.

"Things aren't better than the last time we talked," Minnie said between sips of white wine. "Actually, they're worse. Since I'm retired, Bradley wants my help in his office."

"What's that about?"

With a shake of her head, Minnie responded, "Controlling me. He's afraid I'll do what I want, not what he wants."

"Will you just put up with it?"

Minnie told Carol of her belief that after a year of relaxing and indulging herself she could better decide between ditching Bradley and working at repairing the marriage. "I'm just not up for a fight right now," she said with a sigh.

They took in one more set by the band and called it a night. Standing by their cars, they embraced. Minnie teared up for a nanosecond, then said, "Thank you, Carol. Today meant so much to me."

"After tonight, I understand why."

Getting home took Minnie 40 minutes. She pulled into the garage and closed the overhead door with the remote. Her dashboard clock read 9:53 p.m. In the kitchen, she retrieved a glass of water from the refrigerator ice maker, then walked to the master bedroom.

Bradley wasn't there. The bed, made up by the housekeeper during the day, appeared untouched. He's in his game room, she thought, and briefly considered just getting ready for bed herself and not worrying about him. No, that's needlessly rude, she decided. I should say hello.

Nearing the game room, Minnie heard the ESPN Sports Center theme music coming from the television set inside. She opened the door on a room lighted only by the glow of the TV set. She looked toward the recliner where she expected she'd see her husband. He wasn't there. She flipped a light switch. Her eyes adjusted and dropped to the floor.

There, Minnie Donaldson saw something she knew well. Death.

Chapter 4

Nurses know a dead person when they see one. The man on the floor was dead. Bradley Donaldson lay on his right side, his left arm outstretched as if he'd been reaching for the recliner when he fell. His head rested on the floor, inches from the chair.

Minnie knelt beside him and felt for a pulse. She found nothing. She rolled him over on his back and lifted his eyelids. She saw no response to light, a telltale sign of death.

She kept several stethoscopes in the laundry room, artifacts from her nursing career. She found a dual head model, fitted the ends into her ears, and placed the bell over Bradley's heart. Nothing. Her husband was dead.

After putting the stethoscope back in the laundry room, she picked up her cell phone and dialed 9-1-1. "What's your emergency?" the operator asked.

"My name is Minnie Donaldson," she said, speaking flatly and taking slow, even breaths. "I just arrived home from a day and evening out and found my husband dead in his recreation room. It's likely he had a heart attack."

"How do you know he's dead, mam?"

"I'm a nurse. I took his vital signs. There are none."

"What's your address?"

She gave it to the operator, then repeated it when asked for confirmation.

"Someone's on the way."

∞∞∞

While waiting, Minnie wondered if she should call the children. She looked at her watch again. 10:26 p.m. Better to get the body processed first, she thought.

Paramedics showed up five minutes later. Two uniformed Dallas police officers arrived 10 minutes after that. As the paramedics worked, one of the officers asked that Minnie meet with them at the kitchen table. "I'm Officer James. This is my partner, Officer Richardson. We have a few questions, Mrs. Donaldson. Just routine."

The two burly officers, middle-aged white men with short haircuts, ruddy complexions, and small mustaches, made Minnie nervous. Like many black people, she regarded white cops warily. This seemed a benign enough situation, but she still wanted the meeting over as soon as possible.

Both men wore dour expressions. After James took basic personal information about Minnie and Bradley, he asked, "Can you tell us what happened?"

She gathered herself and smiled and wondered if the officers saw her suspicion of them behind the smile. "I'd been out all day and evening. I arrived home just before 10 o'clock. I went into my husband's game room. I heard the television. The lights were off. At first I didn't see him. After I turned on a light, I saw him stretched out on the floor. I was quite sure he was dead."

"Why were you so certain?" Richardson asked, a forefinger touching his parted lips.

"I've been a nurse for over 30 years. I know a dead person when I see one, and I found no pulse."

The officer shifted in his chair. "Can you tell us where you were today?"

"Playing golf with friends."

"Where?" James inquired. He fiddled with a button on his uniform.

"Jackson Creek Country Club."

"Pretty ritzy place, right?" Richardson asked, his eyes widening.

Minnie assumed neither white man could imagine a black woman playing golf there. She ignored her agitation at the demeaning question. "I can give you the names and addresses of the people I played with."

Richardson nodded. "We'd appreciate that."

Minnie got up from the table and took a notepad and pen from a cabinet drawer. She scribbled contact information for Carol and Cynthia and handed Richardson the single sheet of paper.

"What time did you finish playing golf?" James asked, his cold eyes boring in on her.

"Around noon. We ate lunch at the club, so I left there at quarter of two."

Richardson, sitting with his back to the wall, seemed the more aggressive of the officers, and the most suspicious. Lifting, almost rolling, his eyes, he asked, "Where were you the rest of the day?"

Minnie clenched her teeth. "Carol and I went shopping, then had dinner."

"Where?"

"Jacob's Place, a jazz club and café in Arlington. I can't remember the address."

Richardson stared at her again. "Did you talk with anyone there except Ms. Robbins?"

"Just the waiter who took our orders."

"What time did you leave the restaurant?"

"A quarter after nine."

James broke in. "Did you talk with your husband during the day?"

"No."

"Any reason why not?"

Now, Minnie didn't mind the officers seeing her scowl. "I was busy. I assume he was busy."

"And you found him on the floor when you got home?"

"Yes."

James frowned and threw open his palms. "You don't seem broken up for a woman who just found her husband dead."

Minnie looked up again at the wall clock above the table, behind where Richardson sat. She stared at him, then at James. "You think I poisoned him or something? Well, I didn't. As I told you, I'm a nurse. I've seen almost everything. I will grieve at the appropriate time. Right now, I have a lot of things on my mind, including calling my children about what's happened with their father. Is there anything else?"

"That's all for now," Richardson said, closing his notebook. "We may contact you again. We'd appreciate it if you didn't leave town."

Grimacing, Minnie replied, "I have no plans for that, but I've had enough of your insults. The medical examiner will find that my husband died of a heart attack or a stroke or some other medical condition I didn't cause. Now, if you gentlemen will excuse me, I have things to do. Good night."

Just after the police left, a team from the medical examiner's office arrived and removed the body. Despite the late hour, Minnie then called her children. Each reacted with shock and hurt, but agreed they should focus on supporting one another during the coming days.

∞∞∞

Moving around the kitchen the next morning, Minnie found

herself perplexed at her feelings. Dressed in white shorts and a green polo shirt while sipping tea and nibbling wheat toast, she felt sad, not distressed. Had she let the distance that grew between her and Bradley destroy what she'd once felt for him? Was it all gone, washed away by his preoccupation with the business and her anger and disgust with his neglect of her?

When she found him, not even an audible gasp escaped her lips, much less an anguished cry. Despite her scorn for the police officers, they'd been right about one thing. She wasn't broken up about her husband's death.

Bradley's demise made her sad but, that morning, tears didn't fall. Would they as she comforted their children and received condolences from other family members and friends? Would those people see through her and whisper behind her back? Would they search the mourners at the funeral for a secret lover at the root of her lack of visible grief? For a second, she regretted there wasn't one.

On a conference call that morning, Minnie and her children targeted Monday, the 24th for the funeral, assuming the medical examiner released the body in time. Jerry agreed he'd drive to Dallas from his home in Norman, Oklahoma Friday and help Minnie with arrangements. Crystal and Sandra said they'd arrive Saturday.

After talking with the children, Minnie dialed Christopher Maxwell, their family attorney. He said he'd begin working on Bradley's finances. Minnie told him, "The day after the funeral, I want to see where I stand."

The location of the funeral presented an issue. Church had become a sore point between Minnie and Bradley. She dreaded contacting Bradley's pastor about using his church. She knew Bradley had said derogatory things about her there. She hoped Jerry could run interference and keep the situation from degenerating into a nasty, unpleasant mess.

Bradley and Minnie attended Rock of Ages Baptist Church

together for the first 18 years of their marriage. The children experienced Sunday school there and participated in the church's youth programs. As her theology evolved and the children became teenagers, Minnie decided she'd give them options about church. They could keep attending Rock of Ages, go somewhere else, or go nowhere. That clashed with Bradley's notion of how the world worked. As long as Jerry, Crystal, and Sandra lived under his roof, if he said they were attending Rock of Ages, they were attending Rock of Ages.

The battle left scars that didn't heal for years. Ultimately, Jerry stayed at Rock of Ages until he left for college. He attended there with Bradley when he came home for visits, which mollified his father. The girls defied Bradley and opted out of church altogether while in high school. Crystal still didn't go to church, though Sandra now attended a Methodist church. Bradley fumed for years about how Minnie "corrupted" their children.

Minnie became disillusioned with Rock of Ages in particular and the Baptist denomination in general. She tried other places and styles of worship. She experimented with different denominations and different churches in the same denomination. For a while, she attended no church.

Four years ago, she joined Dodge United Church of Christ. Later, she asked Bradley to attend services there with her. He went once and labeled the place a cult because it welcomed gay, lesbian, bisexual, and transgender members and visitors. He declared Minnie would rot in hell. She heard he'd bad-mouthed her to the minister and congregation at Rock of Ages. She wondered if they'd shun her at his funeral.

∞ ∞ ∞

Minnie notified family members Thursday evening and Friday morning. With both sets of parents and her one sister long dead, she needed to call only her cousins and Bradley's siblings, two younger brothers and an older sister. They all lived in Texas and agreed on a Monday funeral in Dallas.

After lunch Friday, the medical examiner's office called and asked where she wanted Bradley's body sent when they released it that afternoon. The George Robertson Funeral Home would pick it up, she told the man on the phone. That left the matter of securing Bradley's church for the funeral service. Minnie dialed Jerry. "Hi, Mom," he answered. "How're you holding up?"

"I'm okay baby, putting one foot in front of the other. I need your help with something."

"Anything, Mom. Just ask."

"Please call Reverend Johnson about using the church."

Jerry sighed. "I'll do it, but you can't avoid him and his congregation at the funeral."

Minnie felt her mouth go dry. "I don't want a scene. If I call him, he'll be nasty or get in my face about not staying there with Bradley or whatever. He may even blame me for Bradley's death. The police wanted to."

Jerry let out an audible gasp. "What?"

"Two officers gave me the third degree after I found him."

"You'd been out all day, right?"

"I had, but they still asked that I not leave town."

"That's insulting."

"I was annoyed." She fidgeted with a button on her shirt and paced the kitchen. "Anyway, the medical examiner concluded it was a heart attack, as I thought. We can have the service Monday. So, will you call Reverend Johnson?"

"I'll do it, because you're asking. Still, I think you're being silly."

"Just call him," she said, a scowl crossing her face.

"I'll call before I leave this afternoon. I should get there at half past seven."

Minnie sagged against the kitchen counter. "Thanks so much. You're such a great son."

"I'll see you tonight. We'll get through this."

"Yes, we will." Minnie hung up, knowing 'getting through this' probably meant something different to her than to Jerry.

∞∞∞

Saturday, Minnie and Jerry planned the funeral program while awaiting the arrival of Crystal and Sandra. At 3:15 p.m., Jerry left to have the programs copied.

Crystal, who drove in with her husband Michael from Alexandria, Louisiana, showed up at four o'clock. Sitting at the kitchen table, Crystal picked up a copy of the program and blinked. "Mom, why's there nothing about burial in the program? Don't people usually want to go to the cemetery after these things?"

"We're doing that at eleven o'clock in the morning, before the service. It's family only."

"Did you get that idea from your new church?"

Minnie crossed her arms over her chest. "No, the idea didn't come from my church. Most people there prefer cremation, which is what I would have liked, and what I want for myself."

"Dad wouldn't want that," Crystal said, standing up and pacing the room.

"It's how I want it done," Minnie said, shaking her head. "I respect your father's wish for what he'd call a Christian funeral and burial, but I have a say in this."

Crystal rolled her eyes. "I still don't understand. Why do the burial before the funeral?"

"I know why," Jerry said as he walked into the room. He

dropped two boxes containing the programs on the kitchen table, hugged Crystal, and shook hands with Michael. "You do?" Crystal asked, entwining her fingers.

"Mom doesn't want a fight with the people in the church over having Dad's casket opened at the service."

"What?" Crystal asked, now standing beside the table, hands on hips.

"Mom doesn't want that. When I called Reverend Johnson about using the church, he asked if we'd include time in the service for viewing. Mom said no. The best way of avoiding conflict about it was having the burial first. Hard to view a body already in the ground."

"How do you feel about this, Jerry?' Crystal asked.

He yawned. "It's Mom's call."

"If people want to see him, shouldn't they see him? I stopped attending that church, but people there loved Dad and they should get to say goodbye the way they want."

Minnie inhaled deeply, then exhaled. "This matter is closed. We're not having an open casket service and that's that. If you want to engage in the morbid practice of looking at dead bodies, have the funeral home arrange it for you."

Crystal's nostrils flared. "Mom, what's this about? Why are you so adamant? You seem so certain, so defiant."

Holding her chin high but lowering her voice, Minnie said, "I was traumatized at age seven by seeing my grandmother lying in a casket. My parents made me walk by it at her funeral. I hated remembering Granny that way. I had nightmares for a long time.

"I decided if I ever had a say, I wouldn't allow it. Well, I do now and it's not happening at your father's funeral."

Crystal dropped her head. "I didn't know about that." With a shrug, she reminded her mother, "You're a nurse. You've seen many dead bodies."

"That was part of my work. This is about how we remember a loved one. I don't want my memories of your father ruined by seeing him lying in a casket."

Crystal sat down. "Won't people at the church still be upset about this? You can't explain all that to everybody."

Now standing, Minnie shook her head and said, "It's not the only thing they're upset with me about."

"It seems weird we're having this turmoil about Dad's funeral. Jerry told me you wouldn't talk to the minister about using the church."

Minnie approached the chair where Crystal sat. She put her hand on her daughter's shoulder. "People think what they think. A lot of things got said over the last few years, most not nice, many untrue. We just have to get through this.

"Now, if everybody will excuse me, I have friends I haven't told." She grabbed her cell phone and headed for her sanctuary, the spare bedroom.

Chapter 5

"Let us pray," Reverend William Johnson intoned, raising his arms as he stood in the pulpit of Rock of Ages Baptist Church at Monday's funeral. He bowed his head. "Heavenly Father, grant that your faithful servant, Bradley Donaldson, enter into everlasting rest; give his soul its rightful place at your side; provide that his children find peace as they live their lives before they join him in heaven; assure that those of your flock at Rock of Ages shall live righteous lives and find the Kingdom of God through their dedication to your Word. We ask these blessings in your name and in the name of our Lord and Savior, Jesus Christ. Amen."

When the organist struck the first note of the recessional, the Donaldson family rose from the front pews and filed out. Congregants followed, spilling into the church lobby before moving toward the fellowship hall for the reception.

Minnie seethed inside. Jerry offered his arm when they left their seats. She first wouldn't take it, but latched onto him a few steps down the aisle. In the lobby, she released her son's arm and burst through the front door, ignoring those headed toward the reception.

Despite wearing heels, she ran down the church steps, into the parking lot, and looked for Jerry's car, the one they'd all taken to the service. "Why didn't I trust my instincts and drive myself?" she asked out loud. "At least I have his keys."

"Mom, come back!" Jerry shouted. Heads turned and congregants detoured from their route to the fellowship hall. Some stepped outside so they could watch. Why was the bereaved widow fleeing the church?

Minnie slowed her trot as she neared the car. Jerry caught up with her. "You should come back inside, Mom."

Sandra had now joined them. "Jerry's right," she said. "Come back inside." Briefly, the three of them stood beside the car, clad in dark dress clothes, each pleading with their eyes for a break in the standoff.

Minnie bared her teeth. She glared at her children. "Why should I go back in there? I've been insulted in a way no person mourning a spouse should be, certainly not at the spouse's funeral. That was beyond the pale. You both know it."

"Not everybody here feels the way he does," Jerry said. "He and Dad were close. I'm sure Dad said things he shouldn't have."

"Don't make this harder, Mom," Sandra warned.

Minnie planted her feet wide apart. She jabbed a finger into her chest. "I'm not making it hard. It was bad enough Johnson ignored me when we gathered before the processional. I should have gotten in his face and made him shake my hand. Then he left me out of the closing prayer. How tacky is that?"

"We understand," Sandra said, clasping her hands together. "It was tacky, but has nothing to do with you going back in there and thanking people who came here for Dad. This is about him, not you."

"Johnson made it about me," Minnie snapped.

Jerry tapped his mother's arm. "I'll stay with you when we go back in and mingle. Say a few hellos, shake some hands, and we'll leave. You can claim you've had a long day – which you have – and you're tired – which you are."

Sandra leaned in. "Do what Jerry says. He can take you home. Crystal and I will stay and greet people. Several of my high school friends showed up. Somebody will give us a ride home."

Minnie paced around the car. Her feet hurt, a consequence of how seldom she wore heels these days. She felt confined by her pantyhose, something else she seldom wore anymore.

Her head spun. She remained angry, but what if her children were right? Was she being selfish? Wasn't it best she made a brief appearance, beat a hasty retreat, and never gave this church or these people another thought? "Mom, please?" Jerry begged.

"Okay, baby. I'll do it, for no more than 20 minutes. I'm watching the clock."

∞ ∞ ∞

As Jerry drove them home, Minnie grabbed her mobile phone and called Connie Wilson, who gasped when she answered. "I thought the funeral was today."

"We just finished. Jerry's driving me home." She turned to him. "It's my friend Connie Wilson in Detroit." He nodded.

"Tell that handsome son of yours hello for me, okay?"

"In a minute, you can tell him yourself."

"Fine. What's up?"

"I'm taking a road trip starting Wednesday. Can I land on you and Gretchen for a few days?"

Minnie heard a giggle on the other end. "Assuming you bring your golf clubs, of course. When would you get here?"

"Next week, maybe the week after. I'll see friends and family in the East, then the Midwest. I'll call you with more details. I want out of Dallas for a while."

"Probably what you need."

"It is. I'm packing tonight. Now, talk to Jerry." She handed her son the phone.

When they turned into the driveway at home, Jerry gave his mother a dazed look and asked, "What's this road trip deal? And what family are you going to see?"

"I'll stop in Alexandria and visit with Crystal and Michael, head for North Carolina and spend some time with Sandra, then go north for a week to ten days, maybe more. I'll stop in Norman on the way home. I hope I can get back by Thanksgiving, but other than that, I have no schedule."

Jerry rubbed his chin. "You just saw us. Not that I ever mind seeing you, but so soon?"

"When did we talk? We planned and attended your father's funeral. I need real time with my children now. I'm retired. There's nothing keeping me here."

He nodded. "You're right about that. Maybe we can talk about things we didn't talk about while we got ready for the funeral."

"Yes. We need that."

Jerry twisted the Big 12 football championship ring he wore on his right hand. "That's a long trip. Are you up to it?"

Minnie fixed a defiant stare on her son. "Of course I am. We put your father in the ground this morning, not me."

∞∞∞

Initially, Minnie's Tuesday morning meeting with Christopher Maxwell went as she expected. She would inherit five million dollars in real estate, cash, and liquid assets like stocks, bonds, and other securities, plus the company. Bradley left each child $500,000.

Christopher estimated the company's value at $12-14 million. She'd already decided she'd sell it, requiring a full valuation, something that might take as much as a month. Christopher said he'd begin working on that and they'd meet about a sale when she returned from her trip. He estimated that after taxes Minnie would end up with a net worth of $15-17 million, including what she'd put away herself and the value of her land in Oklahoma.

Then came the bombshell. They finished covering the schedule for probating the will and Minnie rose from her chair in Maxwell's plush, suburban office. He said, "You should know you dodged a bullet."

"I did what?" she asked. Even to herself, she sounded fearful and uncertain.

"Bradley called a few weeks ago about changing his will. I asked that he think through the changes he outlined. I saw legal problems with them and thought they would cause a family upheaval."

Minnie frowned and shifted uneasily in the chair. "What kind of changes?"

Maxwell, a tall, dark black man with short hair and probing brown eyes, hesitated, then said, "I told him he should proceed cautiously. Some of what he said he wanted to do would run afoul of Texas community property law. He said I should find a way. The changes in any form never got made. He died first."

Minnie collapsed back into her chair, but pressed Maxwell again. "What kind of changes?"

The middle-aged lawyer, wearing a crisp, white buttondown dress shirt with a dark red tie, took a deep breath. Suddenly, to Minnie, the room felt small and cramped. "Bradley asked about cutting you out of his will almost altogether. You'd have gotten money through the insurance policies, of course, but directly inherited only a few thousand dollars. Crystal and Sandra would have received $5,000 each. Bradley still planned on giving Jerry $500,000."

She tilted her chin down and swallowed hard. "Didn't I own part of the company?"

"Technically no. That was structured so he had complete control. You had community property rights, but he seemed bound and determined to find a way around those."

For a long moment, Minnie said nothing. She ran a hand

through her hair, then folded her arms over her chest. "Suppose he found a way. Where was what I didn't get, or the girls didn't get, going?"

"He wanted to leave as much of his estate as possible, including proceeds from selling the company, to Rock of Ages Baptist Church."

Minnie bit her thumb and held back the scream that almost came out. "Did Reverend Johnson know about this?"

"He knew at least the broad outline."

Inside, Minnie felt lightheaded, a sensation that almost immediately gave way to stomach cramps. Just as quickly, everything cleared. It all made sense now. The reverend had almost hit the jackpot. But, it didn't happen because Bradley died too soon. For all she knew, Johnson thought like the police officers – that she somehow engineered Bradley's death, depriving Rock of Ages of millions of dollars. No wonder he didn't greet her before the funeral and left her out of the closing prayer.

She looked up at Maxwell. "And you stopped him?"

"I wouldn't say that. He still might have done as much as the law allowed. I told him he should go slow. He could change whatever he wanted, of course, but I wouldn't be a party to it. I said if he did it, I'd withdraw from representing him. I've always considered myself the family's attorney."

She teared up. "Thank you, Christopher. Thank you very much."

Minnie left Maxwell's office shaking, feeling as if someone had cut her heart in half. Still, by the time she reached her car, she had dried her tears and was more determined than ever that she'd live the life she wanted. She hurried home and finished packing.

∞ ∞ ∞

An unplanned excursion like Minnie decided she'd take meant going into overdrive for a time. That was her fate from noon Tuesday until she pulled out of the driveway at a quarter after four Wednesday afternoon, her car stuffed with clothes, golf clubs, shoes, books, and her CD collection. She'd do this her way and she planned on enjoying it.

She'd first visit Crystal and Michael in Alexandria, Louisiana. Aside from Detroit and the cities in which Sandra and Jerry lived, Minnie knew her other destinations only vaguely.

The calendar had reached October 26, meaning she might encounter bad weather at some places she'd considered playing golf along her still-fluid route. She looked in the back seat. She'd brought rain gear and umbrellas. Warm clothes packed in her suitcases and stuffed into corners of the trunk should get her through. Her course guide sat in the passenger seat.

Tuesday's news confirmed that she needed talk time with her children. Heading east on I-20, she contemplated what she should tell them about Bradley's will-changing scheme. His plan would have hurt both daughters. They were doing well professionally and financially, but a huge difference existed between what Bradley left them and what they would have gotten had he made the changes Christopher described.

How would what he cooked up have affected them emotionally? They'd feel a terrible blow from realizing their father cared more for that church than for them. Had something happened between them that triggered his plan? Minnie assumed Jerry benefited because he stuck with the church. Bradley, however, planned on throwing his daughters under the bus. What happened?

Was it her fault? Bradley may have hatched the plan because she abandoned Rock of Ages and approved of letting the children do the same. She'd picked for herself a church he despised and she didn't follow his post-retirement work plan. Had her desire for managing her own life so enraged him he'd exact such a punishment?

"Lots to think about," Minnie said out loud as she rolled along I-20. "Lots of things I must figure out." But not now, she thought, slipping her *Temptations Greatest Hits* disc into the CD player. The haunting opening bass line from "My Girl" filled the car. "Tonight, Motown, country the day I leave Alexandria, and jazz the day after that." She looked at her CD cases, satisfied with the variety of genres and artists. "I spent a lot of time and money on this collection," she said. "I knew it'd come in handy one day."

Chapter 6

A s Minnie drove through the night and grooved to her favorite Motown artists, she focused on her children, beginning with the one in the middle. Crystal Jean Donaldson arrived early on June 22, 1990, after an easy pregnancy. They went home following a two-day hospital stay.

During the months after Crystal's birth, Minnie often gushed with gratitude for the family life she lived every day. Bradley shared the housework and took a real interest in the children's lives. Jerry had been an easygoing toddler before Crystal's birth and didn't change. Crystal was crankier than Jerry had been, but a far cry from the horror story some of Minnie's friends told about their children.

Bradley and Minnie had Jerry two years after their June 1985 wedding. Though Minnie got pregnant with Crystal sooner than they expected, they could still say she was planned. They'd put aside most of the money Minnie made from her nursing job as a cushion in case Bradley's fledgling business went south while the children were infants. Both parents felt Minnie should stay home with them during that phase of their lives, so she put her career on hold.

Their plan worked perfectly, at least at first, but things later got complicated. Minnie and Bradley resumed having sex three months after Crystal's birth. Since middle-of-the-night connections occurred from time to time, before bed each evening Minnie checked the drawer in the night stand beside the bed for her diaphragm and tube of spermicide. For some reason, one time she didn't.

Bradley worked late that night and Minnie dozed off before he got home. She usually slept in a short nightgown and panties, but that night she didn't put on her panties before falling asleep. With the heat turned up higher than it should have been, by the time Bradley arrived home, she'd kicked off the covers, leaving her exposed from the waist down. Before she knew it, he was in bed with her, lifting the night gown, fondling her breasts, stroking her legs, and running his fingers into her.

For years, Minnie believed she'd tried pushing him away and that she told him they should stop because her diaphragm wasn't in place. Bradley claimed she did neither. Whatever the truth, he slipped his erection into her and she responded to his thrusts. She experienced an intense orgasm, just as he ejaculated.

While feeding Crystal later that night, she felt telltale wetness between her legs. In the bathroom she saw her diaphragm in a drawer where she'd left it. "Oh, my God," she said out loud. "I hope I'm not pregnant."

Minnie didn't have morning sickness with Jerry or Crystal and she didn't have any with her third pregnancy. Tender nipples and a missed period told her soon enough her fears had been realized. Minnie gave birth to Sandra Diane Donaldson on July 31, 1991.

A third baby made things difficult. Two children two and a half years apart was hard enough. Three within less than four years was really, really hard. Minnie wondered if that unexpected child permanently strained the marriage. For five years she lived a life of perpetual fatigue. Driving along, she gazed at the stars in the clear, dark sky and shook her head. How had she survived?

Then she stopped. As Jerry, Crystal, and Sandra marched toward and through their teenage years, they became her pride and joy. She couldn't help throwing back her shoulders, thinking about the happiness they brought her. She could barely wait each day for the unfolding of a new aspect of their lives.

All three aced school except for a wobble here or there. All three challenged her intellectually. All three behaved well, save Crystal's middle child angst and a dark time in high school when the two of them regularly butted heads, then avoided each other. A dip in Crystal's academic performance kept her from getting the track scholarship she'd wanted. Even that turned out fine as she rehabilitated her grades and track career in junior college.

No, the third baby, inconvenient though she was at the time of her conception and birth, didn't cause the later marital problems. Any thought that was the reason just represented an excuse.

$$\infty\infty\infty$$

It was after ten o'clock when Minnie arrived at Crystal and Michael's house in Alexandria. Michael answered the door, saying Crystal had turned in because she had an early meeting the next day. He situated Minnie in the guest room at the back of the red brick, ranch-style home on a quiet street in a new neighborhood. This was the first time she'd visited Crystal and Michael since they had bought this house in the spring.

Thursday Minnie made a point of getting up at 6:30 a.m. so she could see Crystal off to her job as assistant director of a regional health agency operated by the State of Louisiana and a consortium of local governments. Crystal was a rising star in her field, sometimes mentioned as a candidate for a significant position in the administration of Louisiana's Democratic Governor, John Bell Edwards.

"Hello, daughter," Minnie said, sitting at the kitchen table and sipping the tea Michael brewed for her before he left for his job as a mechanic at a local car dealership. "I thought you had an early morning meeting."

Crystal favored Bradley in her dark skin, large nose, thick lips, and lower cheek bones. She was tall, matching her mother's five-feet, ten inches, something that served her well in her sprinting and hurdling career.

"I do," Crystal said. She fiddled with an earring. "Early here and early in Dallas might mean different things." She looked at her watch. "It's a quarter past seven. My meeting is at eight o'clock. I'm 10 minutes from the office."

The older woman stood up. "Let's start over. It's nice to see you, dear."

"Fair enough, Mom. I'm glad you're here. How was your drive?"

"Good. I easily found the house." They embraced in the middle of the room, near the table. Minnie stepped back and looked over her middle child. Something about her seemed different from even at the funeral Monday. She couldn't put her finger on it, so she said nothing.

Crystal poured a glass of orange juice. "I'm glad you came. I am curious about your reasons. You said you wanted to talk, but we just saw each other."

"We spent Saturday and Sunday preparing for the funeral. We had Monday's burial and church service. You and Michael left right away. Did we spend more than five minutes on anything other than the funeral?"

"No."

Minnie said pointedly, "I'm taking you out for dinner tonight – just you and me. We can talk then."

"No Michael?'

Standing with her chin high, her neck exposed, Minnie said, "We'll do something with him Friday night, since I'm not hitting the road until Saturday morning. Tonight, it's just you and me."

"That's fine, but we can't leave him out two nights in a row.

Now, I should go. Work calls. Make yourself at home."

$$\infty\infty\infty$$

Alexandria didn't boast many top notch restaurants, but Crystal said Miller's was good. "Not fancy, but good food, good service, and a better wine selection than anywhere else in town."

"We'll go there," Minnie said as they got into her daughter's car. "I'll see plenty of fancy places on my trip. Tonight, 'good' sounds fine."

"What brought on this trip? I didn't hear about it until you called Tuesday."

"I decided Monday afternoon. I wanted out of Dallas. Tuesday morning only made me want that more."

"What happened Tuesday morning?"

Minnie described the Christopher Maxwell meeting without revealing how much money Bradley had left her. "Christopher will tell you that himself. You'll be pleased."

Crystal pressed for more details of her father's plan.

"Dad was going to leave most of his money to that church?"

"He was looking for a way, Christopher says."

Crystal spoke through slightly parted lips. "But he changed his mind?"

Minnie grimaced and shook her head. "I don't know that. Your dad put the plan on hold, and died before making the changes. Christopher suggested he go slow and told him there were legal issues that complicated his plan. He still might have done some version of it after more thought."

Crystal's tone deepened. "Why would he? Leaving aside what we each get, you helped him build that business by holding the family together. He had no reason for treating you that way. Did he?"

Minnie stared at her daughter as they pulled into a parking space and Crystal shut off the car's engine. The questions bit. "No, I didn't cheat on him, if that's what you mean. He was unhappy with me."

"Why?"

"I'll tell you inside."

A young black hostess seated them, a young white server took their drink orders, and they each sampled bread and butter he left on the table. Minnie picked up her story. "Your father was displeased with me because I wouldn't work in his office after I retired. He also never got over the fact I quit attending Rock of Ages. It infuriated him that I picked my own church, a place he hated."

Crystal filled a wine glass from the bottle the server left, picked up the menu, then put it back down. She pushed the full wine glass to her mother but didn't pour any for herself. "Those hardly seem reasons for disinheriting you. There must have been something else."

"That's one reason I took this trip, so I could have uninterrupted time for thinking about my life with him the last few years. Maybe I can figure out what happened. I hope talking with the three of you helps."

Tapping her index finger on the table, the younger woman said, "I doubt I can help. Dad lost interest in me." Minnie heard hurt in her daughter's voice.

Crystal picked up another piece of bread, buttered it, and continued. "After I gave up track, I was no longer his child prodigy, the medal-winning star sprinter and hurdler he bragged about. I became just a grown daughter with a husband and a government job in Nowhere, Louisiana. He was more disappointed I didn't make the Olympic team than I was."

"Did you resent that?"

Crystal twisted her mouth into a sour expression. "You could say that. Dad didn't speak 10 words to me while I was in graduate school at LSU. He thought I should stay with track, work at making the 2016 Olympic team. After Michael and I got married and we moved here, I'd call him up and try engaging him. He had no interest in interacting with me at all." She shrugged half-heartedly. "I quit trying. I didn't even call him on his birthday last year. The year before, he hung up after two or three minutes. His attitude was one reason Michael and I did our own Christmas the last two years."

The waiter returned and took their orders. Minnie selected a seafood dish he suggested. Crystal ordered roast beef. For a few moments, they sat in silence, scanning the walls covered with paintings of trees, streams, and flowers. Minnie sipped wine and her daughter nursed a glass of water.

Crystal finally spoke. "Don't take this wrong, Mom, but leading up to and at the funeral, you didn't seem broken up about Dad dying. I never saw you cry."

"You didn't see me cry because I didn't. I'm sad about Bradley's death. That's my genuine, honest feeling. But that's all."

"Did he hurt you?"

As Minnie contemplated her reply, for a moment she felt as if time had stopped. "In his way, yes. He didn't cheat. At least, I never saw that. I became numb from his indifference, his inattentiveness, the way he gave up on the things that defined our life together – playing golf, doing yard work, taking trips, and sex. There, I said it. Your dad and I quit having sex three years ago. That wasn't my idea."

Crystal shifted in her chair. "Did Dad have a, shall we say, problem?"

"You mean erectile dysfunction?"

"Yes."

Minnie shook her head. "I don't know. He wouldn't talk about it. If I mentioned it, he blew me off. When I suggested a medical consultation – I certainly know lots of doctors who treat male sexual problems – he said, 'not happening.' If I touched him, made an overture, he pushed me away."

"I'm sorry," Crystal said as she reached across the table and squeezed her mother's hand.

The food arrived and they ate in silence. Minnie noticed Crystal hadn't sampled the wine. "No wine? That's not like you."

"Not feeling it this evening. Drinking late sometimes keeps me awake."

The older woman checked her watch. "It's half past seven, not late. Have a glass with me. We shouldn't waste it."

"No, you go ahead. I don't feel like it tonight."

∞∞∞

Friday morning, Minnie again rose early and approached Crystal before she left for work. "Let me ask you about something you said last night, something I didn't know."

Wearing a crisp white blouse and dark slacks, Crystal stood at the cabinet, slightly turned away from the kitchen table. She popped two pieces of bread into the toaster and waited. Minnie, sitting at the table, again thought something seemed different, awkward, about her daughter. Crystal yawned. "Yeah what, Mom?"

"The fact your father pressured you about the 2016 Olympics. When did that start?"

"February 2013."

Minnie put down her orange juice. "What happened?"

Crystal buttered the toast and sat across the table from her mother. She dropped her head. "He screamed at me."

"Screamed at you?"

Before answering, Crystal pressed her hands into her temples. "I'd gone back to Louisiana Tech so I could finish my degree. I moved into a three-bedroom apartment with two other girls who'd been Tech athletes and were doing the same thing. Dad showed up one day and barged into the apartment."

Minnie's mouth dropped open. "What'd he say?"

"It was how he said it, what he did, that made it so awful."

"Yeah?"

"I was standing in the living room. I'd been looking for a hair pin. I was wearing just sweatpants and my bra. Dad didn't even knock. He came in yelling, asking why I wasn't training. He said I'd never make the next Olympic team if I didn't. I remember his saying, 'I knew you might be a quitter. I hoped I was wrong. I guess I wasn't.'"

"What'd you do?"

"I told him I should get dressed. I grabbed a shirt from my room, then came out and we talked."

"Did he calm down?"

"Only a little. He had a plan for me."

Minnie noticed Crystal rubbing her fingers together.

"Which was?"

"I'd told him I was thinking about graduate school, probably at LSU. He said if I lived at home in Dallas while I trained, and enrolled at SMU, he'd pay for school."

"Did you consider that?"

Crystal shook her head side to side. "For maybe five minutes. I was done with track. I had my shot and messed it up with that stumble in the finals of the hurdles at the 2012 trials. I wasn't up for more. I'd met Michael and knew we'd eventually get married. He said he'd move to Baton Rouge with me.

"Living at home and enrolling at SMU held zero attraction for me. SMU didn't offer the program I wanted. I hated the idea of school there. I told Dad I'd get on with my life. He was ticked. He stopped talking about it, but our relationship was never the same."

"You didn't tell me about this. I would've understood."

Crystal set her jaw. "I felt I should fight my own battle, stand up for myself. Getting you involved would have only made things worse."

"I could have been support for you."

"I had Michael. I wasn't alone."

∞ ∞ ∞

At a barbeque place Friday night, Minnie could hold her tongue no longer. After they finished their meal and returned from the drink station with iced-tea refills, she blurted out, "Crystal, are you pregnant?"

Daughter and son-in-law looked at each other. Silence reigned. Finally, Michael said, "Come on, tell your mother."

Crystal's face lit up and she and Michael broke into laughter. "Yes, Mom, I'm pregnant. How'd you know?"

Minnie felt quivering in her arms and legs. "Mother's intuition. I was pregnant three times myself, you know. First, you look different – I can't explain it, you just do. Second, last night at dinner you wouldn't drink any wine. That isn't like you at all. You had roast beef, not fish, which you love. I guess you believe pregnant women shouldn't eat fish. Finally, this morning, you kept turning your back on me when I looked at you from the side. I decided that must be it. When are you due?"

"Late April, early May. I'm about three months. My morning sickness is almost gone. Am I showing?"

"Oh, sort of. Your body looks different." Minnie broke into a grin. "So I'll have my third grandchild. This has already been a great trip."

Crystal reached across the table and grasped her mother's hand. She pulled in a deep breath. "Michael and I thought I should get further along before we told anyone. We had such a hard time getting pregnant, I didn't want anybody getting their hopes up, especially grandparents."

"We should tell my folks now," Michael said, his brown eyes blinking as he looked at his mother-in-law. "You're the only person who knows about this other than the two of us and the doctor."

Minnie rubbed her hands, clasped them together, and shook them in jubilation. "I'm so happy for you both. This is great news. Even if I shoot 80 plus in every round I play, I'll consider this trip a success."

Minnie raised her tea glass. "To Crystal and Michael and my new grandchild!"

Chapter 7

The sign read I-12/ Hammond left; I-10/ New Orleans right. Just past the LSU campus in Baton Rouge Saturday morning, Minnie said out loud, "I'm on vacation. I think I'll go see New Orleans today."

She changed lanes and followed I-10 toward the Crescent City. Nothing wrong with spending a few hours in the French Quarter, she thought, believing she could still make Montgomery, Alabama by ten thirty.

An hour and a half after that spur-of-the-moment decision, Minnie parked in a lot between the Mississippi River and the Quarter and walked toward Bourbon Street. "Never been here before," she muttered to herself. "Can't wait to see it."

It was late October, so the summer crowds had thinned out. Minnie still did plenty of people-watching as she strolled the Quarter streets, stopping in souvenir shops and clothing boutiques. "I'll take that," she kept hearing herself tell store clerks. "And that." By three o'clock that afternoon she'd filled four bags with jewelry, blouses, t-shirts, mugs, coffee table pieces, and miscellaneous gifts for friends and family members.

"Have I got time for a beignet at Café Du Monde?" she asked, again out loud, at 3:25 p.m. "I'll make time," she said, lugging her shopping bags and heading toward Decatur Street.

∞ ∞ ∞

Sunday began a different phase of the journey. Golf took center stage. She'd focus again on family stuff at Sandra's at the end of the week. She left time for seeing two old nursing colleagues, Nancy Hicks and her partner Samantha Kindle, Monday in Atlanta. Yes, Minnie thought as she got into the car Sunday afternoon following her round at a Robert Trent Jones Golf Trail course in Montgomery, Alabama, I have a lot of gay friends.

Had that been what turned Bradley off the last few years? He barely acknowledged Minnie's friendships with Nancy and Samantha or with Connie Wilson and Gretchen Downs in Detroit or her numerous lesbian and gay friends in Dallas. He wouldn't socialize with any of them.

Was that the burr under his saddle? She remembered how he disparaged Dodge Church. "Is everybody there queer?" he asked following his only visit.

She brushed him aside, accusing him of looking for anything he could dislike about the church. They never talked about it again. Had she given Bradley's negative vibes about her friendships with gay people short shrift?

∞ ∞ ∞

The gentle rhythm of windshield wipers and old country songs like Willie Nelson's *You Were Always on My Mind* and Alabama's *Feels So Right* entertained Minnie as she tooled along I-85 between Greenville, South Carolina and Charlotte Tuesday afternoon. The rain started after her Clemson University stop.

That visit included a four under par round on the Clemson course and a look at the "Tiger Paw" hole, a green surrounded by bunkers giving the hole the shape of a tiger's paw. She got a campus tour, guided by Jo Lynn Henderson, a Clemson junior and the daughter of one of her mixed-race couple friends, Mark and Brenda Henderson. Mark was about the blackest man she knew, in skin tone and culture. Brenda was blonde and blonder. Yet, they'd made their marriage work for 24 years and raised two confident, accomplished daughters who navigated the black and white worlds.

Sandra and Crystal babysat Jo Lynn a few times. Minnie promised Brenda she'd look up Jo Lynn on this trip. They met at the golf course after her round. Jo Lynn rolled out the red carpet, taking her to lunch and for ice cream at the Clemson student union.

"What's the deal on this ice cream?" Minnie asked as they licked cones. "This is really good."

"It's made and marketed by Clemson students," Jo Lynn replied. "I haven't found any better."

"I'm not sure I have either," Minnie said, grinning and finishing off her serving.

∞∞∞

Including Tuesday at Clemson, Minnie played five golf rounds in four days. Three days at Pinehurst Resort in North Carolina left her exhilarated. With the calendar flipped to November, daytime temperatures ranged between the high 50s and the low 70s and skies turned an exquisite deep blue. Minnie felt she'd escaped the bonds of her world for a never-never land from which she hoped she wouldn't return.

She walked every Pinehurst round, each time assigned a knowledgeable caddie and often paired with accomplished, if skeptical, players. It was the same old story. Men, especially white ones anywhere near her age, expressed shock at how well she played. Few women could match her consistent ball striking or her deft short game.

She confounded her playing partners with her stamina. When she told the New Jersey couple she got paired with the second afternoon she'd walked 36 holes that day, both bowed down in mock adulation. "What planet are you from?" asked the exhausted, dark haired, 51-year-old woman who'd ridden in a cart with her husband, a 59-year-old recently retired corporate executive.

When Minnie stopped Friday for lunch in Durham, North Carolina, she pulled out her Pinehurst scorecards. They said 73, 68, 71, and 72. She released a deep, gratified sigh, then ordered a steak. She figured she'd earned it.

∞∞∞

Old, refurbished dwellings mixed with newer housing make up affluent parts of Winston-Salem, North Carolina. One area west of downtown includes condominiums and modern apartments scattered among new and renovated single family homes. That neighborhood lies south of where Sandra worked, Wake Forest University, an elite private institution of 7500 students loosely affiliated with the Baptist Church.

Sandra gave Minnie directions to her condo in that hilly, heavily wooded portion of the city. Minnie arrived in Winston-Salem at seven o'clock Friday evening, November 4. When she turned off I-40 toward Sandra's place, political signs lined the roadway, reminding her the following Tuesday was election day. She'd put that and other current events out of her mind since leaving Dallas, ignoring newspapers, radio, and cable news. After the visit with Crystal, she'd occupied herself with golf, post-round drinks and meals with people she met, and her CDs.

She had, however, fulfilled her civic responsibility. Part of the intense getaway rush her last two days in Dallas included voting early. She knew Sandra, the most politically aware of her children, would ask if she'd done that, maybe before saying, "Hello."

Minnie approached politics with the moderation that characterized other parts of her life, golf excepted. Her black women friends spent a lot of time on Democratic Party politics. They volunteered in campaigns, organized fundraisers, and wrote checks. Minnie did some of that, but not as much as Cynthia McFadden, Dawn Brooks, and many of her other pals.

True, in Tuesday's presidential race, she wasn't indifferent. She preferred Hillary Clinton because (1) she believed Clinton had paid her dues and earned the job, (2) of the importance she placed on reproductive rights, which Clinton would protect and Donald Trump wouldn't, (3) she thought Trump was a sexist jerk and probably a racist, and (4) she felt it time the United States elected a woman. She couldn't imagine Trump winning, so she hadn't worried about it much.

Feeling disappointed Trump appeared to have won the sign war in Sandra's part of Winston-Salem, Minnie recalled her last political conversation with Bradley. Like many businessmen, even black ones, he instinctively supported Republicans. Still, they usually voted alike in presidential races. Republicans often ran candidates she couldn't stomach. She convinced him he should vote Democratic because Democrats advocated things black people needed on voting rights, health care, and education. But, now she remembered, not this year.

Right after the Republican National Convention, one evening when he arrived home from work, Bradley announced he'd vote for Trump. "You can't be serious," Minnie gasped, covering her mouth.

"I'm serious as a heart attack," he replied, a phrase Minnie now found unfortunate.

Her posture stiffened. "Why do that?"

"He'll make America great again."

She stared him down. "That's a slogan. And a silly one at that."

"He'll shake things up. And he's not a crook like Hillary

Clinton, who should be locked up."

Minnie turned her back on him. "Keep thinking that. You're off your rocker."

"He's going to win. Wait and see."

They never talked about it again. She thought now of how Bradley's support for Trump would have unnerved Sandra. When Minnie turned onto her daughter's street, her cell phone rang.

"Mom, it's me. Are you in town?"

Hands free, Minnie said, "I'm near your place, a block away I think."

"I'm stuck at work. A meeting ran long and there's one thing I must finish before I leave."

"That's okay. I can go drink tea until you get home. I passed a bunch of places on the way here. I can find my way —"

"Go to the condo. Ronnie's there."

"Ronnie?"

Minnie had parked in front of a condo unit with the address Sandra gave her. She heard her daughter take a deep breath after a long pause. "Yes, Mom. Ronnie is my boyfriend. We live together."

"You never told me that, but you're a grown woman. You can live with whomever you like."

"Dad didn't see it that way."

That took Minnie by surprise. She replied, "This sounds more complicated than we should get into right now. Does Ronnie know I'm coming?"

"Yes. I thought I'd be there myself. I called and told him you'd show up soon. You said you'd be there about now and I know how punctual you are."

Minnie scanned the street and double checked the address. "I'm out in front of the unit now. I'll go on in and meet him. I'll see you when you get here."

"There's one thing you should know about Ronnie."

"Oh?" Minnie thought she heard her daughter swallow.

"He's white, Mom."

∞ ∞ ∞

"Did you think I wouldn't approve of your having a white boyfriend?" Minnie asked Sandra Saturday during a lunch break from shopping at Winston-Salem's most popular mall. "You didn't think that would freak me out, did you?"

"After how Dad reacted, I wasn't sure."

Minnie leaned back, then forward in her chair at a table at an Applebee's just off the main mall. Sandra seemed nervous as they awaited their food. It was early afternoon and the place had begun filling up. Clanging dishes and utensils mixed with the buzz of voices and laughter at tables while occasional cheers and groans erupted from people at the bar watching college football games.

Minnie considered Sandra's response while scanning her youngest daughter's thin face and wiry frame. Sandra, who had the lightest skin and straightest hair of her children, wasn't the athlete Jerry and Crystal had been as teenagers. She tried tennis and volleyball in school. She bailed on tennis before she understood the sport. Sandra wasn't tall enough for most volleyball positions, so she became a math whiz who ran rings around her high school classmates.

A Northwestern economics degree and an MBA from the Wharton School of Business put her on track for a promising management career at IBM before she decided she preferred the non-profit world. A brief stint at a foundation in Indianapolis laid the groundwork for her current job as the director's chief deputy in Wake Forest's development office.

Despite her lack of athletic success in school, Sandra became a fitness fiend. She worked out in a gym every other day, did yoga, and ran 35 miles a week. Her passion for fitness matched her mother's for golf. Family friends said Sandra took after Minnie more than any of the Donaldson children in temperament, approach to life, and thoughtfulness.

Minnie intended on assuring Sandra she didn't object to her romance with a white man. First, however, there was the matter of understanding Bradley's problem. "What did your father say and when?"

Sandra grimaced. "The what was 'Why are you with that white boy?' The when was August. Dad stopped through here on his way home from, I think, Washington."

Minnie tapped her forehead and held up a finger. "It was Baltimore. He met with a supplier in Baltimore. I knew he visited you, but he didn't talk about the trip after he got back."

Sandra cleared her throat. "I met him at the airport. As you learned last night, Ronnie is an assistant men's basketball coach at Wake. He was leaving town on a recruiting trip. Before Ronnie went through security, he and I stood in the lobby and kissed each other good bye. Dad saw us as he came off the concourse. He jumped me about it as soon as we said hello."

Minnie raised her eyebrows. "He didn't leave it at that?"

Her daughter shook her head. "He dogged me about it the whole time he was here which, fortunately, was just overnight. I couldn't get him out of town fast enough."

"What else did he say?"

"He called me a traitor."

Minnie noticed Sandra's sharp, defined jaw line. "Really, baby?"

"The meanest thing he said was, 'Don't let that white boy put any blonde, half-breed babies in you.'"

Minnie recoiled at her husband's crudeness. "That cut deep, didn't it?"

For a moment, Sandra struggled for words. "After he left, I cried. I couldn't tell Ronnie those things. That was so hurtful. I said nothing."

"Including to me?"

"Especially to you." She continued after a gulp of water. "I feared you'd see it the same way. I didn't even tell Crystal. You know how close we are."

"You've carried it around with you since?"

"Yes."

Minnie reached across the table and squeezed Sandra's slim fingers. "For the record, youngest daughter, I could give a rat's ass about Ronnie's color. I only care how he treats you, that you love him if that's what you want, and that you think carefully about whether he's right for you."

Sandra closed her eyes and nodded several times. "He is, Mom. We started seeing each other not long after I got here. We moved in together last year. I'm really, really happy being with him."

"That's good enough for me."

Sandra sat up, appearing calm and relieved. "Did Dad hate white people? You and he had white friends when we were growing up. I never thought either of you would have a problem with my dating a white guy. I was shocked at Dad's reaction."

"Your father was a troubled man in his last years. I've just discovered some details. A lot of things, I didn't know. Some I knew, I didn't understand. It's hard realizing I was with him so long yet, by the end, I didn't know him. Now," Minnie said, taking a last sip of water, "let's finish lunch. I saw outfits in department stores we should check out."

"Time at the mall is a terrible thing to waste, right?"

"Right."

$$\infty \infty \infty$$

Breakfast at the condo Sunday morning finished off the Winston-Salem visit. In the living room, ready for goodbyes, Minnie found the tall, blonde Ronnie dressed in a dark blue suit, white shirt, and red tie. Sandra arrived a moment later in a black dress that fell below her knees, tasteful earrings, and dark pumps. Sheer hose covered her legs.

"These are our Methodist clothes," Sandra explained. She fiddled with an earring, then checked her hose for runs. "It took getting used to, but I actually enjoy church now. And I like dressing up."

"Yeah," Ronnie said as he moved across the room and kissed Sandra on the lips. "I straightened her out. She's come around."

"You voted before you left, didn't you?" Sandra asked. She leaned on Ronnie's shoulder and looked intently at her mother.

"Of course I did. I couldn't take the chance of provoking your wrath if I hadn't. Not that it makes any difference. Trump will carry Texas regardless."

Sandra shook her head. "Probably true, but people still should vote."

Standing beside their cars after parting hugs, Minnie surveyed Sandra and her boyfriend. They made a handsome couple. Their children, if they had any, wouldn't have the same dark skin as Jerry's two boys or the likely brown hue of Crystal and Michael's child. But, as Minnie embarked on the next leg of her trip, she felt satisfied with her world. Learning of Sandra's happiness with Ronnie and getting Crystal's pregnancy news confirmed how good an idea this trip had been.

Chapter 8

The next five days brought Minnie satisfaction and despair. A visit with old friends in northern Virginia and spectacular weather Monday and Tuesday for playing golf there and in western Pennsylvania left her exhilarated. She pleased herself with even par rounds on difficult courses and felt a "pleasantly tired" glow on her drive through northeastern Ohio Tuesday afternoon and early evening.

Things came crashing down when she checked into a hotel along the Ohio Turnpike, 75 miles east of Toledo. She turned on election night TV coverage and learned Hillary Clinton might not carry three states – Pennsylvania, Michigan, and Wisconsin – needed for an Electoral College victory. The news left Minnie so stunned she couldn't drag herself to the shower. She stripped and lay on the bed, naked, watching in horror as Donald Trump claimed the presidency.

When MSNBC called the decisive states for Trump, Minnie punched the off button, crawled under the covers, and tried sleeping. The day's grime finally forced her into the shower. Hot water, soap, and shampoo didn't wash away her disgust.

The prospect of three days with Connie Wilson and Gretchen Downs, anticipated with glee since she left Dallas 14 days before, now depressed her. The visit would become not a celebration, but an intense therapy session. How could gay people, women, black people, brown people, every other out group, survive the next four years? How in the world did this happen?

∞∞∞

Connie and Gretchen lived in Auburn Hills, a Detroit

suburb northwest of downtown. When Minnie reached their sprawling, red brick house on a quiet street Wednesday afternoon, the two women, both wearing jeans and sweaters, burst through the front door and greeted her. The three embraced and let their tears flow. Only a few words passed between them until after Minnie dropped her bags in the second floor guest room.

Gretchen, the blonde-haired, blue-eyed maestro of the Wilson-Downs kitchen, made tea and set out veggies and fruits on the living room coffee table. Connie broke the silence. "We live near Canada. If we leave, you can join us."

That morose comment relieved the tension. Minnie couldn't help laughing. "On the way here I started thinking about getting more involved in fighting this clown. People like me have been too passive, which is why this happened."

"We went all in for Hillary, for all the good it did," Connie said, hanging her head. "We gave the household campaign contribution limit."

"You guys weren't the problem," Minnie responded, staring at the floor. She wore khaki slacks and a red, longsleeved polo shirt. "This is on people like me. I did nothing but vote and send Hillary one sorry $250 check. That's why she lost."

Connie, wearing her beloved Detroit Tigers baseball cap atop a short Afro, shook her head. Between sips of tea she said, "She lost for a host of reasons, starting with that slime ball James Comey."

"What'd he do?" Minnie asked, as she bit into a pineapple chunk.

Connie described the FBI Director's letter indicating the Bureau was reopening its investigation into Clinton's e-mail scandal. Minnie's eyes widened, her jaw dropped, and she said, "Beginning with Bradley's death and while I've been on the road, I paid no attention to the news. I didn't know about that."

"Comey wasn't the only problem," Gretchen insisted. "Start with the--"

"We should let this settle and figure out how we make the most of the time I'm here," Minnie said, uncrossing and recrossing her legs. The election post mortem could go on all day. "I'm dying to tell you about the time I've had since I left Dallas. I'm not letting a sorry bastard like Donald Trump spoil that."

"Fair enough," Gretchen said, raising her tea cup and munching on a carrot. "Start at the beginning. You went to see Crystal in Louisiana first, right?"

They spent three hours on Minnie's adventure, including her plans after she left Detroit Friday night. They scheduled their golf rounds, first agreeing they'd again visit the delightful Timber Ridge course in Lansing they played in September. They accepted an invitation from Frank Withers for a round at his club, one of the top private courses in Detroit.

∞ ∞ ∞

After a Saturday of shopping in Chicago, Minnie did something different Sunday. She went to church. Her need for the embrace of a spiritual community in light of the election outcome pushed her that way. From Sandra's days at Northwestern, Minnie remembered driving by First Congregational United Church of Christ in Evanston. Why not spend part of her Sunday there?

It was a big building, a two-story red brick monstrosity with white columns located across the street from a park. The cavernous sanctuary seated over 500 people, Minnie guessed. Fewer than 50 showed up that Sunday, so she sat by herself through a choir's inspired singing and a thoughtful sermon about how Christians should respond in the face of evil in their midst.

Despite the small crowd, the enthusiasm of the congregants provided a lift. Most of the post-service conversation concerned the election. Nearly everyone voiced the same horror at the outcome. Several people said they shared her belief fighting Trump by getting more involved in politics represented the best response.

∞∞∞

Minnie took Monday easy, driving only as far as Des Moines, Iowa as she headed for Lincoln, Nebraska where she'd see Dr. Evelyn Connors, her now 74-year old former nursing professor. Minnie may have looked forward to seeing Dr. Connors – Evelyn, as she preferred – more than anyone on the trip except her children.

Evelyn Connors grew up in Tulsa, earned her nursing degree from the University of Oklahoma, worked for several years in small-town hospitals in Missouri and Arkansas, then attended graduate school at the University of Wisconsin. She was a brand new faculty member at Southeastern Oklahoma State University when Minnie arrived there for college in 1980.

Evelyn surprised no one when she left for the University of Nebraska two years after Minnie graduated. Eventually, she became Dean of the Nebraska School of Nursing and a nationally recognized authority in nursing education. She now held emeritus status on the Nebraska faculty. Despite her accomplishments and position, she kept herself available for former students. Late night calls didn't bother her, or, if they did, she never let it show.

Minnie hoped her former teacher could help her understand Bradley's late-life behavior, including his run-ins with their daughters. Two marriages, one that ended in divorce and one in widowhood, plus numerous boyfriends, gave Evelyn a Ph.D. in men. She'd seen almost everything in her years of working as a nurse, teaching, and living. Maybe she'd seen this.

They met Tuesday evening for dinner at the university's faculty club. Evelyn was a short, wiry woman whose breasts remained a little big for her slender frame. Her pale complexion fit with once blonde hair that had turned white, contrasted with a dark top above gray slacks.

"I doubt you routed yourself through here just so we could reminisce," she said as they settled at a table overlooking the campus. The twilight mix of the setting sun with street lights and building lights offered a comforting glow. "I'm delighted you're here, of course. I think it's been seven years since we laid eyes on each other."

"I'm sure you have that right. You remember everything."

"That was my job."

"There are a lot of things that might kill you, Evelyn. Dementia isn't one of them."

"Fair enough. What's on your mind?"

"The husband I thought I knew, but didn't. The picture that has emerged on this trip disturbs me. I wonder what happened and what it says about the future. I don't plan on being alone the rest of my life. What can I learn about men, about relationships, from what happened?"

"Give me the 25 words or less version of the picture you say has emerged."

"My husband became a mean, abusive bigot who alienated our daughters, neglected me, and almost succumbed to a most vindictive pettiness."

Evelyn shook her head of long, snow-white hair. Blue eyes twinkled behind wire-framed glasses. "I'm sure he always spoke highly of you."

"You need details?" Minnie asked. She suppressed a giggle.

"I do."

Minnie described Bradley's neglectful, inattentive behavior toward her, including the retirement night disaster. She explained how he abandoned Crystal because she ended her track career and detailed his tirade about Sandra's white boyfriend. Finally, she told him of Bradley's aborted disinheritance plan.

Evelyn nibbled on her thumb. "I sense a pattern. The people he hurt were all women."

"You noticed that too?"

"It's significant. While I'm not a psychologist, I know misogyny when I see it. If he were alive I'd say work on his issues with women. But, he's gone, so detailing the why mostly wastes time. You say he wasn't always the way he was at the end?"

"He wasn't."

"What happened?"

"I don't know."

"The traits may have always been there. Something triggered his bad behavior."

Minnie rapidly blinked her eyes. "I hope it wasn't something I did."

"If it was just about you, why go after your daughters over trivial issues? If Crystal was done with track, what difference should it make to him? And, my God, this is 2016. Who gets bent out of shape over interracial romances?"

"Given the election returns, maybe lots of people."

"Point taken. But, still, that was over the top."

"What do I do now?"

A gleam appeared in the older woman's eye. "Trust your feelings. Figure out what you need. Don't worry about what other people think. Identify what you find important and don't settle for less."

Minnie parted her lips. "Meaning?"

"Your friends will start fixing you up soon. They'll have a model for who you should be with – a black man between age X and age Y, a net worth of ABC dollars, who looks this way, but not that way, who weighs less than 200 pounds but more than 150, who's taller than six feet.

"Throw that stuff out. If he meets your need for tenderness, for attentiveness, for how he treats your children, etc., is younger than you, is older, is black, brown, or white, is wealthy or poor, drives a Jag or a jalopy, go for him. Don't worry about what somebody else thinks you should have." Minnie nodded.

The professor stretched her arms. "What you had turned sour, for whatever reason. Next time, make sure you get what you find important."

They finished the evening with wine and catching up on people they'd known and worked with. They told nursing war stories. When they stood and started for the exit, Minnie asked, "Who have you set me up with for golf tomorrow?"

"Dick and Mary Russenburger. He's a retired hospital executive. Ran the for-profit hospital in Lincoln for years. Got filthy rich because the company that bought it gave him a boatload of stock and it split three times. He retired four years ago. He's 66 and Mary's 63. They're nice people. He has a fourth for you, a young woman who works at his old company. She played on the Nebraska women's golf team. You should have a great time."

∞ ∞ ∞

The fourth was Rhonda Boyd. Minnie spent most of the round in awe of her game. She had it all – length off the tee, deadly, precise irons, soft hands around the greens, and a deft putting stroke, supplemented by an innate feel for the game few players not on tour possessed. When the round ended and they walked into the clubhouse, Minnie decided she'd risk offending Boyd by asking her age.

The brown-haired woman grinned. "Take a guess at how old I am, then I'll tell you."

They'd stopped outside the women's locker room. Minnie recalled the structure of Rhonda's game. "You look 37 or 38, but you play like either you're 25 or 50 – 25 because you have the power of youth or 50 because you play with such wisdom. I'll split the difference and say 40."

Rhonda anchored a hand on one hip. "You're a good observer of people. I'm 41. I started playing when I was eight. I played through high school and college and got a year on the LPGA tour. I injured my shoulder in a freak fall that essentially ended my career. Staying on tour meant two years of rehab while I kept practicing and working with an instructor. I didn't have financing for that. I enrolled in graduate school, got my MBA, and moved on with life."

Minnie looked at the scorecard, then said, "You shot five under 67 today on one of the hardest courses I've played. Without bad luck on two putts, it could have been 65. Playing with you was fun and I'm grateful for the chance."

Shifting her stance, Rhonda said, "I could say that about you. I haven't played with many women your age who have your total game. You were even par and could have been three, four strokes better with some breaks."

Had Rhonda left the word "black" out of her description of women Minnie's age? Better not be paranoid, she thought. Accept praise when it comes. This world is hard enough. She left her reply at, "Thank you. I appreciate that."

The Lincoln golf round done, Minnie drove east, then headed south on I-29 for a Thursday of shopping in Kansas City at the Country Club Plaza and barbeque at another Kansas City landmark, Arthur Bryant's restaurant. She played golf Friday at Swope Park, touted as one of the country's best municipal courses. The weather turned nasty and she finished in a cold rain. Except for being her last golf day on the trip and the fact she was three under par at the time, she might have packed it in when the wind came up and the rain started on the 15th hole.

She stopped at a Starbucks, changed out of her wet clothes, and warmed herself with their hottest tea. By seven thirty Friday night, she'd arrived in Norman, Oklahoma, checked into her hotel, and let Jerry know she'd meet him for breakfast Saturday morning.

Her relationship with Jerry mystified Minnie. Being her first born, he held a special place in her heart. They talked easily and he'd do anything for her, as his handling of the funeral arrangements proved. During his bitter divorce, he trusted her with his innermost feelings.

Though Bradley commanded Jerry's loyalty because he remained in the Baptist Church, Minnie provided Jerry a shoulder he could cry on during difficult times. She sensed he walked a tightrope while navigating the discord between his parents. She believed he wanted to express his discomfort with how Bradley treated her, but something held him back.

Jerry's two sons, Robert, nine, and Scott, seven, complicated things. Jerry's ex-wife, Candace, made things difficult. She moved to Minneapolis, taking the boys out of the Donaldson family orbit. She did the bare minimum their court orders required in helping foster a relationship between them and their father. It wasn't lost on Minnie that neither attended Bradley's funeral. Candace probably made sure they weren't there.

∞∞∞∞

Saturday morning, Minnie found Jerry waiting in the lobby of the IHOP they'd agreed on for breakfast. She marveled at how well put together her son remained, four years after his football career ended. Though now a junior high school assistant principal, he still had the sculpted arms, narrow waist, and powerful legs of the linebacker who anchored the Oklahoma Sooner defense and survived four seasons in professional football. He'd avoided even a scratch on his handsome, round face. Except for a nagging ankle sprain his sophomore year, he stayed injury free. If football traumatized his brain, at 29 the signs hadn't appeared yet.

They embraced and asked for a table. Soon, she drank tea while he nursed a cup of coffee.

"Tell me about the trip," he said. "You must have had an adventure."

"I have," she replied, then launched into a highlight reel version of her life since leaving Dallas 25 days before. When she finished, she said, "Now I have something I must ask you."

He leaned toward her. "What?"

"What did I not know about your father that I should have?"

She sensed tension creep into the space between them as they faced each other across a table tucked away in a corner. The buzz of conversations and the clanging of plates and silverware faded as they honed in on each other. "What do you mean? And why do you ask?"

"Your father did and said things that hurt your sisters, things I didn't know about at the time and never would have expected. I now wonder what else I missed."

Jerry sipped his coffee, but said nothing for a few moments. Then he spoke. "I promised Dad I wouldn't talk about one thing I know, but he's dead now, so maybe I should tell you."

His quiet voice and furrowed brow said this was serious. Minnie reached across the table and squeezed her son's hand. "I won't love you less if you decide you can't tell me."

He took another deep breath and one more sip of coffee. He put down the cup. "Dad had a thing for boys."

Minnie stared at Jerry. Her skin tingled. She squeezed her eyes shut, then opened them. She wondered if the room really spun as she sensed. She managed a question. "He had what?"

"Dad had boys give him head."

That afternoon when she saw Bradley with a young man in his car flashed through her mind, as did his nasty comments about Dodge Church and her gay friends. Spreading her fingers across her chest, Minnie asked, "How'd you know?"

"I caught him. He confessed and swore me to secrecy."

Her mouth fell open. "What happened?"

"Three years ago, I went home for a weekend. The downhill slide with Candace had started. I needed time with my Dallas buddies, my high school football crowd."

Minnie rubbed her hands together and frowned. "Go on."

"The guys and I were hanging out at Bachman Lake Park, drinking beer and watching planes land at Love Field. I saw Dad's car turn into a parking lot. He had this young guy – looked 17 or 18 – with him, somebody I didn't know.

"I snuck up behind Dad's car. The guy's head disappeared for about ten minutes. He got out of the car and spat before they left. Dad said he never knew I was there."

That afternoon, when she saw Bradley with what looked like a teenage boy in his car, his direction would have taken him to the same place. "You confronted him?"

"The next day at church Reverend Johnson preached this hellfire and brimstone sermon about the sin of homosexuality. I watched Dad take it in, shouting 'Amen!' I seethed inside at the hypocrisy.

"That afternoon, I told Dad I'd seen him. He denied it at first. Then I showed him the photo of his car at the lake that I took with my phone. You could see the kid in the front seat."

Minnie pressed her knees together. "He owned up to it?"

Jerry nodded. "He denied having full intercourse with these guys. It was just blow jobs, which he paid for."

Minnie's stomach churned. "Did he say how long he'd done that?"

"Said it started in college, though he didn't pay for it then."

Minnie, her expression as intense as in her most competitive golf rounds, leaned across the table and mouthed as quietly as she could, "I gave that man dozens of blow jobs."

"He said it wasn't the same."

She kept leaning over the table. "You asked if he and I did that?"

"I asked if he enjoyed getting oral sex from women. We never mentioned you specifically, but he knew what I meant."

Minnie sat back and dragged her hand across her cheek.

"He swore you to secrecy?"

"I wanted to tell you, but felt I couldn't."

"If the shoe was on the other foot – if I shared a deep, dark secret and said you couldn't tell anybody, I know you'd honor that. I can't fault you for not saying anything."

Rubbing the back of his neck, Jerry asked, "Did he put you at a health risk?"

Minnie shook her head. "Research indicates there's not much chance of a man contracting HIV through receiving oral sex. The hospital made us test regularly. I was always negative."

Jerry rocked back and forth. "That's good."

Their food arrived and they detoured into why Jerry's sons weren't at their grandfather's funeral. "Candace said they couldn't miss school. I found flights that would've meant missing only one day. She said if we'd had the funeral on a weekend, they could've come. Just more of her control freak bullshit."

"I'm sorry," Minnie said. "If you'd told me, I'd have talked with her."

"My relationship with Candace is bad enough. The two of you having a shouting match would only make her more determined about keeping them away from us."

Minnie finished her eggs and pancakes. She put down her fork and said, "Since you've revealed Bradley's secret life, there's something I should tell you. The reason for one part of a plan your father hatched, but didn't – or couldn't – carry out, is now abundantly clear."

"Plan?"

"Before I left Dallas, Chris Maxwell told me Bradley called him a few weeks before he died and said he was thinking about changing his will. Chris told him he should think about it, which he did. There were some legal complications with his plan. He died before he made any changes."

"Which were?"

"I would have inherited only money from insurance policies I was already the beneficiary of and a few dollars out of the kindness of his heart. That's the part he might not have been able to do. Your sisters would have each gotten small sums. That part he could have done. Your portion wouldn't have changed.

"He planned on rewarding you for keeping his secret. I thought it was because you stuck with the Baptist Church when the rest of us left. I now know that wasn't all."

"What about the rest of his money?"

"Rock of Ages would have gotten it."

Jerry tugged at his ear. "What was he upset with Crystal and Sandra about?"

"Crystal wouldn't try one more time for the Olympics. He didn't like the fact Sandra has a white boyfriend and lives with him, something I didn't know either until this trip."

Now, Jerry flinched, as if he'd heard a loud noise. "Does that bother you?"

"No."

He rubbed the back of his neck again. "Well, that's good, because I'm in that boat too now."

"Oh, really?"

Jerry pulled out his phone and punched up a photo of a medium-build, 30-something, dirty blonde woman in a blue, mid-calf length dress. She wore wire framed glasses and a thin smile. A tall, broad-shouldered, brown-haired teen in khakis and a blue polo shirt posed beside her. "This is Rachel Jordan with her son, David. We've been seeing each other since spring. No promises about the future but, for the time being, it's working for us."

Minnie handed Jerry his phone back and grabbed her chin. "How'd you meet?"

"She spoke at our school district career night. I called her a few days later and we started going out."

"Can I meet them?"

Jerry shook his head. "Not this trip. Rachel teaches chemistry at OU. She's at a conference in Chicago. David's father runs a hedge fund in California. The man has more money than sin, so he flew David out there this weekend. I dropped him at the airport last night."

"Are you happy with Rachel?"

"Very much so, Mom. Very much so."

∞∞∞

Jerry and Minnie said their goodbyes in the restaurant parking lot. Minnie headed east on State Highway 9. She drove 85 miles before turning south on the Indian Nation Turnpike for the 40-mile trip to McAlester. She navigated familiar back roads to her family's homestead, 150 acres tucked into a forest west of town.

Barns and the farmhouse she grew up in and now rented out appeared in good shape. She made a mental note that the house might soon need painting.

Windup of the trip had fallen into place. She'd spend tonight at a hotel in Sherman/Denison on the Texas-Oklahoma border. Sunday, she'd drive into Dallas and attend services at Dodge. She wasn't up for doing laundry, reorganizing and culling Bradley's things, and other chores she'd find at home. They could wait until she returned from her Thanksgiving visit with friends in Austin.

She'd stay at a Dallas hotel Sunday, Monday, and Tuesday, using the mornings for meetings with Chris Maxwell about money and the afternoons and evenings for giving friends the blow-by-blow account of the trip many wanted. Cynthia McFadden promised dinner Tuesday night and three nursing buddies – Judy Shields, Dawn Brooks, and Marlene Timmons – arranged a Wednesday lunch.

When she reached U.S. Highway 69/75 and turned south, it was 3:35 p.m. That left two hours to Sherman/ Denison – two hours of solitude during which she could put the last three and a half weeks in context. Her mind clicked through places and people she'd seen – strangers, old friends, and family members. Each category tugged at her as the sun drifted toward the horizon.

She might have dismissed the strangers with whom she'd shared golf rounds, drinks, and meals, but no, she wasn't doing that. The people she'd met promised richness she needed. She'd contact some of them soon.

Most had been more than cordial, all loved her golf game, and many had been impressed with the idea of the trip as grief therapy. They didn't know things she learned on the trip exorcised what little grief she felt about Bradley Donaldson's death. Jerry's revelation and all she'd learned about Bradley's meanness confirmed that the man barely deserved her grief.

From old friends, Minnie took away something that might make a difference in the life that lay ahead. She stopped at a gas station/convenience store and wrote out her list:

From Nancy Hicks and Samantha Kindle in Atlanta – neglect no friends, no matter how far away, how long lost, or how new;

from Johnson Maxwell and Cheryl Gray in Reston – stay in touch with children;

from Connie Wilson and Gretchen Downs in Detroit – keep the political activism pledge;

from Keshia Rice and Joe Curtis in Chicago – remember her service commitment; and

from Evelyn Connors in Lincoln – satisfy her needs in relationships with men and ignore what others think about who she should or shouldn't be with.

As for family, Jerry's story explained the will scheme. He unknowingly protected his inheritance by guarding his father's disgusting, hypocritical secret. The minor transgressions Crystal and Sandra committed didn't justify disinheriting them. Minnie's disdain for Bradley Donaldson grew by the mile.

She also figured out something else. One thing Sandra said nagged at Minnie – her daughter's statement that she hadn't expected either parent would oppose an interracial romance because both had white friends during her childhood. That seemed so true she hadn't replied at the time. Now, she saw the flaw in Sandra's premise. Minnie had white friends, Bradley didn't. Bradley executed transactions with white people, but he didn't have white friends.

She sorted through Bradley's acquaintances and their couple activities. Minnie couldn't think of one relationship he had with a white person, outside of business, which didn't involve her. He attended sporting events, played cards, and went out drinking with black men, not white ones. She instigated their socializing with white and mixed couples. Plays, movies, and dinner dates with such people occurred because of her friendships. Bradley attended banquets and awards programs sponsored by white organizations only if they served a business purpose.

Bradley's tribal reaction to Sandra's involvement with blonde-haired, blue-eyed Ronnie shouldn't have surprised anyone who knew him. And that was the problem, Minnie now understood. She didn't know him.

PART II

Chapter 9

September 2016

T wo days after Minnie's retirement party, 1500 miles from Dallas in Wilmington, Delaware, a 26-year old white man named John Dawson made a decision that changed his life and hers. Neither knew the other existed but that didn't matter. Had he decided his dilemma the other way, life for both would have been much different.

On the Sunday morning Minnie played golf with her friends in Michigan, John finally decided he'd fulfill a commitment he'd made. For weeks he'd wrestled with whether he should go through with starting a job at a Dallas law firm he'd accepted two years before. He debated keeping his promise versus taking one of the different tracks he now had available. Three times he'd picked up the phone and dialed all but one of the digits that would have gotten him out of his pledge. Each time he stopped and told himself he couldn't do that.

Now, as he loaded his new Lexus, checked his family home for forgotten belongings, hugged his parents one last time, and drove the car out of town, John concluded he'd made the right choice. He felt terrible, but knew he'd feel worse if he'd made a different choice. When he reached I-95 and turned toward Baltimore, his mind cleared a little.

Grasping John's dilemma required understanding the complex, rarified world of big law firm recruiting and the scruples with which Marion and Martin Dawson raised their only child. The former provided the opportunities that created the dilemma. The latter made taking the opportunities impossible. The rule John couldn't break was that his word was his bond.

Going back on a promise required a damn good reason.

"I changed my mind" and "Things are different now" didn't qualify. Every reason he thought of for breaking this commitment felt like a mealy-mouthed excuse.

John was Marion and Martin's pride and joy. He'd ranked first in his class in every school he ever attended, including the University of Pennsylvania Law School, which was why this problem existed. John now had so many job options, moving all the way to Dallas seemed foolish.

Four years earlier, he enrolled at Penn Law School, having only a vague idea of what job prospects awaited when he finished. He'd graduated summa cum laude from Brown University, but he didn't know how hiring in the legal world worked. A few days after he started law school, he met Samantha George from Plano, Texas and his awakening began.

She knew everything about how law graduates got hired. Friends of her parents who practiced in big Texas firms educated her. Like John, she'd attended an Ivy League college – in her case, Princeton. They enrolled at Penn on the same September day in 2012. Unlike John, Samantha had a plan.

Lying naked with him in her apartment after they'd made love one night in October, she explained how she'd navigate the law graduate hiring maze. She'd work her butt off the first year, earn top grades, then do a summer clerkship with whatever small firm, corporate legal department, or government agency she could find that hired first years.

Back at school her second year, she'd interview with the best Houston and Dallas firms, firms that wanted students from the top of their class. She'd clerk at two or three of them the following summer, accept an offer from one, then cruise through third year law school. She'd take the Texas bar exam, spend a year clerking for a federal judge, and start her business litigation career in the fall of 2016 at whatever Texas firm she picked.

Samantha assured John their romance would fit with her

plans. She suggested he interview for a clerkship in Texas for the summer after their second year. Everything she could see said he'd do as well in law school as she would, maybe better. They'd have similar opportunities. They could do this together.

It went perfectly until Samantha fell in love with someone else during that summer in Texas. She did five-week clerkships at two firms in Dallas and spent three weeks at one firm in Houston. There she met a University of Texas MBA student interning with a bank. She fell head over heels for him and announced their engagement in late September. She was still headed for Texas, but not with John.

He fell in love too that summer – with the 200 lawyer Dallas firm of Vinnick, Whitford, and Marks. John meshed immediately with its smart associates, aggressive young partners, and old school senior partners impressed with his dedication and ethical compass. VWM craved having in its ranks the number one student in his class at Penn Law School, especially after he knocked out of the park every assignment anyone gave him during his clerkship.

Driving southwest that Sunday morning, John realized timing can mean everything. He accepted VWM's offer almost immediately and assumed Samantha was committed to Dallas as she'd claimed. She said she was doing the short clerkship in Houston only because a college classmate was clerking at the same firm. As far as John knew, Samantha would accept with one of the two Dallas firms that offered, he'd join VWM, and they'd make their home there.

Now, having cleared Washington, D.C. on I-95, John lamented not waiting until he returned to school that fall before deciding about VWM's offer. Law school recruiting rules required that the firm keep the offer open until the first of December. By then, he knew Samantha's plans didn't include Dallas and didn't include him.

Getting over Samantha wasn't hard, but having accepted

the job created a problem. The Marion and Martin Dawson code decreed that was that. It didn't matter that he had many other options in places much closer and less foreign than Dallas.

In the back seat of the car and in the trunk he'd packed what little he owned. He and that stuff would arrive in Dallas Monday night. Tuesday he'd move into the furnished apartment he'd rented relying on brochures and online photos. Wednesday he'd organize things. Thursday he reported for work.

As he pushed toward Nashville, Tennessee, his overnight stop, John began envisioning life in Dallas, however long he remained there. His decision that he'd honor his commitment didn't mean he'd stay at VWM forever. Marion and Martin hadn't taught him he must endure a bad situation indefinitely in the name of keeping a promise. If VWM didn't work out, he'd leave after giving it a fair shot.

That was getting ahead of himself. For the time being he'd live and work in Dallas and make the best of it. He knew he could do the work and do it well. He wondered how the people at VWM would accept him, since he wasn't from Texas. He couldn't predict details of his daily work life until he got there.

His non-firm life, especially his prospects with women, crept into his mind about the time he crossed the Virginia-Tennessee border. What could he do about that? John hadn't had a sustained relationship since the thing with Samantha crashed and burned early in his third year of law school.

It wasn't for lack of trying. He'd dated a lot during that remaining year of law school and the year he clerked at the Delaware Supreme Court. Half the six women he went out with hadn't warmed up to him, so he didn't give his experiences with them much thought. Two of the other three struck him as so immature, so frivolous, he saw no reason for wasting time with them. Neither could maintain a meaningful conversation that concerned anything John even minimally cared about.

He found the third woman, a Yale graduate from a wealthy Virginia family, engaging on things that interested him – economics, climate science, the direction of American society. She, however, made clear she didn't give a rat's ass about sports, commercial fiction of any kind, or music that wasn't classical. John loved sports, inhaled mystery and crime novels, and liked all kinds of music, including Motown, old school rhythm and blues, country, jazz, and classic rock. After two uncomfortable evenings he crossed her off his list.

Was that his fate? Navigating a world made up of snobs on one hand and, on the other, party animals who giggled their way through mindless conversations about trivia? Maybe, in time, he'd find the balance he sought in a relationship with a woman. He could hope, couldn't he?

∞∞∞

A new city usually inflicts some pain. John's early days in Dallas, however, proved less traumatic than he'd feared. By the middle of his second week he had plenty of work assignments from partners and senior associates. Learning the town wasn't difficult. Time flew by, but fences needed mending back home.

"Are you in jail, John?" Marion Dawson asked when she answered the phone on a Thursday night, 11 days after he left Wilmington. His mother seemed annoyed, almost angry with him. "We've been calling since Sunday. We just get voice mail."

John sat at his wooden, wobbly-legged kitchen table, sipping from a water bottle. He looked around the room. New pots and pans he bought at the mall Saturday night still hadn't been cleaned and put away. They sat in unopened boxes on the counter. "I've been busy, Mama. I'm a real lawyer now with clients whose work I'm responsible for. It can take a while."

He sensed defiance in her reply. "I'm sure that's important, but we're important too. Don't let this happen again. We must hear from you."

Looking across the room at the nearly full wastebasket sitting beside the small, old fashioned gas range, John said, "Yes, Mama. I have a direct line in my office. You can call me." He gave her the number. A whiff of that stale garbage reminded him he should take out the trash. "I'm there most nights until around nine o'clock Central time, ten o'clock your time."

"I'm worried about you. Don't let this job become your whole life. Are you getting out and meeting people?"

"Not yet," he replied, wondering when he'd have time for such a thing. "But I will. I promise."

"I certainly hope so."

John never told his parents about his dilemma before he left for Texas. Unlike his law school friends, they wouldn't have seen it as a close call. He said he was going. He was going. Now Marion and Martin needed to understand how important it was that he do well the job he had. "I like what I do. I can get good at it."

"We're sure of that. We're very proud of you. Now, go to bed and get your rest. And make sure you stay in touch. You see yourself as this big time lawyer now. But, to me, you're still my baby."

∞∞∞

So, John settled into a routine at VWM. Each morning, he ran three miles and worked out at a health club, then arrived at the office just after eight o'clock. As he told his mother, he seldom left before 8:30 p.m. He spent nearly all day Saturdays and some Sunday mornings in the office. Sunday afternoons he worked on his golf game and indulged his pro football fixation, though he soon learned he should keep quiet about his beloved Philadelphia Eagles, especially when they played the hometown Dallas Cowboys.

By Christmas, John had integrated himself into the fabric of VWM as well as any new associate could in four months. He had a way about him that made it seem he'd been there forever. He learned the history of the firm and its corporate section and worked at gaining a thorough understanding of the firm's client base. He became the go-to corporate associate in his class of lawyers who started with him in September. He was so good partners piled on tasks, which he turned around like clockwork.

His five corporate section classmates represented the best and brightest. Two attended law school at Harvard, one at the University of Chicago, and two at the University of Texas. Three clerked for federal judges. One of the Texas graduates, Don Young, clerked for a Texas Supreme Court judge.

One day in early February, John stopped by Don's 43rd floor office with a lunch invitation. "La Madeline?"

"Sounds good, except I've heard one bad thing about you, Dawson. It starts with a D."

"D?"

"I heard you're a Democrat. Around here that makes you part of – what was it they called it in law school – a 'discrete insular minority?' I'm not sure I should have lunch with you."

Adjusting his green tie and turning toward Don as they walked to the elevators, John asked, "How'd you hear about that?"

"Maggie Brandt. She's of that persuasion too. I always liked Maggie. I wonder where I went wrong."

John remembered the one political conversation he'd had at VWM. Margaret Brandt was a senior corporate associate. He'd stopped by her office one afternoon for advice on an issue that came up in one of his projects. He noticed a Hillary '16 button pinned on a handbag that sat on her couch. Stepping back as they waited for the elevator, he said to Don, "Oh, come on, you can't be serious? People don't see things that way, do they?"

Inside the elevator, Don replied through a thin smile, "I'm exaggerating only a little. Generally, associates live and let live. I'm not sure about a few partners."

"Like who?"

"I'd better not say, but if I were you, I wouldn't go around bragging about my leanings. Don't end up on Democratic fundraising lists – except the Democratic judges in Dallas County, who are taking over, from what my litigation friends tell me."

At the restaurant, they entertained each other with college basketball talk through a short wait in line. Resisting the pastries, John ordered a chicken salad. Don picked tomato basil soup and a turkey croissant. They sat in the back, near a fireplace with glowing gas logs. There they talked about how they each landed at VWM.

"I grew up in Bedford," Don explained. "That's one of the mid-cities between Dallas and Ft. Worth. I did college at Rice and law school at Texas. I clerked at the Texas Supreme Court – briefing attorneys they called us. I went from that to VWM corporate associate. I'm just a plain vanilla guy from Texas. Nothing like you."

John took a bite of salad. "I am the fish out of water, I suppose. Even the people in our class from out-of-state law schools grew up in Texas and came back. There's nobody else from somewhere like Wilmington, or who clerked for the Delaware Supreme Court."

Pausing his spoon halfway between his mouth and his soup bowl, Don asked, "Why did you take that clerkship? You were number one in your class at Penn. Didn't federal appellate judges, hell even Supreme Court justices, fall all over you?"

"I didn't try for a clerkship with one of the High Nine, but I had offers from judges on the Second, Third, and D.C. Circuits, plus four or five district judges. I went with Judge Koufax in Delaware for two practical reasons."

"Yeah?" Don asked, grimacing as he put down the spoon.

"Reason one – where would I get a better education in corporate law than the Delaware Supreme Court?"

"Point taken. It's the premier corporate law jurisdiction in America. What else?"

"Though they sometimes hear cases at the state capitol in Dover, the court's offices are in Wilmington. I lived with my folks, rode the bus or my bicycle to work, and saved for a car. I never had one in college or law school. Between my savings and the firm signing bonus, I paid cash for my new car."

"And you're a Democrat?"

They both laughed before John asked, "The personal and the political don't always match up, do they?"

∞∞∞

Despite their political differences, John and Don grew close during their first year at VWM. They worked together on big projects, including a massive corporate reorganization for a Dallas-based hotel chain. Both preferred each other's company to that of any other classmate. At some point, Kate Hart, a fifth year corporate associate who sometimes checked their work, noticed how much time they spent together and that they resembled each other. She stared calling them the "Twins."

"We don't look like each other," John said one night over drinks at a popular after-work spot near the office. He went there only occasionally because the place lacked the character of neighborhood bars in the East. It didn't have wooden stools, a brass foot rail, or the smell of salt from food he knew he shouldn't eat. "We are about the same height –"

"Just over six feet."

"I bet we weigh the same."

"About 175, right?"

"I was 173 at my last physical," John said. The booths and tables were crowded that evening. A Thursday night college football game between Southwestern Something State and East Slovania Tech blared from the television set above the bar.

"Brown hair?"

"Brown hair."

"Your face doesn't look like mine. Your nose is bigger."

"That's about all that's different. Two sets of blue eyes, thin lips, high cheek bones. And brother, we are both pale."

"We should live in the sun this summer."

"Not happening with our jobs. I have enough trouble getting into the gym at the crack of dawn or late at night, much less the golf course regularly."

"You got that right," Don replied, lifting his beer glass. Suddenly, piped-in music drowned out the television set and the murmur of conversations and laughter. Couples headed for the dance floor.

John shook his head. "I drink wine; you drink beer. That makes us different, see?"

Raising his voice over the now-pounding beat, Don said, "Yeah, Kate is wrong. We're not twins. We should straighten her out."

∞ ∞ ∞

From time to time during that first year, John's mother called, admonishing him that he shouldn't work too much. Initially, he saw her calls as expressions of concern about his physical and mental wellbeing. In March, however, she revealed that his welfare wasn't her only interest.

As he worked in his office one chilly night, she called and first ragged on him about keeping his apartment clean. Then, Marion Dawson hit her son with her real point. "Are you meeting any girls, John?" she asked.

"Women, Mama? I'm 26 years old. I don't think I should date 'girls.'"

"You know what I mean."

Had the question come from someone else, he'd have answered with a half-truth about imaginary females he'd targeted. Being mendacious with Marion Dawson, however, wasn't in his repertoire, so he said, "No. I'm still getting on my feet at work. It's important I make a good impression on the partners."

"John, how will I ever have grandchildren if you don't work at meeting a nice young lady you can marry and have a family with?"

Was that desperation he heard? His mother had joked about this once or twice, but never come out and said it so directly. "I've got lots of time."

Her voice choked with emotion. "Have you ever thought that maybe I don't?"

Her response startled him. John shifted in his chair. "Come on, Mama. You're still young, if that's what you're worried about."

He heard bitterness in her reply, making him wonder if he'd stumbled onto a long-simmering Marion v. Martin feud. "I'm 64 now. That's not young. This is what I get for waiting until I was 38 to have you. Then I let your father talk me out of having another baby. I'd have a better chance at grandchildren if you had a sibling."

He tried reassuring her. "I get it. But, right now I should focus on work. All things in time."

"You don't understand. I won't have grandchildren if you don't find somebody you can marry. And I don't want you getting a girl pregnant like your cousin Tim did."

John didn't need reminding about that family trauma. He pinched the bridge of his nose and gritted his teeth. "Be patient. It'll work out."

He heard despair in her voice. "You say it will, but how can I be sure?"

"Just trust me. Now, I should go. I have an early morning meeting and I'm not ready."

Chapter 10

The year after Bradley's death sped along for Minnie until it didn't. In time, her life bogged down in boredom and loneliness.

She sold the company and banked 40% of the proceeds in interest-bearing accounts, such as they were. She put 45% into conservative investments like U.S. treasuries, municipal bonds, and blue chip stocks, leaving 15% for aggressive plays in growth stocks and venture capital projects. Some of those paid off and some fizzled. For the year, she came away 10 per cent ahead and started the process over with the part of her fortune she didn't mind risking.

During the spring and summer of 2017 she sorted Bradley's belongings and miscellaneous assets, distributing them to his siblings, the children, charities, and educational institutions. Minnie didn't give Rock of Ages Baptist Church anything.

She found in Bradley's desk likely forgotten Series E savings bonds that hadn't been allocated in the will. She planned on passing the $25,000 to his alma mater, Prairie View A&M University. Always the college development officer, Sandra convinced her mother she should throw in another $75,000 and endow a $100,000 scholarship there in Bradley's name.

Minnie reorganized the house, making what had been the master bedroom a library and the other first floor bedroom she'd used as a retreat into her own space. She bought a new bed and mattresses, updated the closets, and added a bigger television, other media equipment, and bookcases.

She spent two weeks in Louisiana helping Crystal and Michael welcome Sarah Alexis Harris, who arrived May 12, 2017, packing eight pounds, four ounces on a 21-inch frame. Those 14 days in Alexandria left her nostalgic for her own early parenting years. She promised a return in mid-August.

All that and a few other chores got her only to mid-June. As before, her days consisted of golf – playing or practicing or both – reading books, working out, and attending plays and movies with friends. By early July she was, except for golf, bored out of her mind.

Right after the Independence Day holiday, she invited Cynthia McFadden out for lunch. They met at a plush downtown restaurant across the street from a hotel where Cynthia was attending a civic engagement workshop.

"Could I confess something you'll say is really stupid?" Minnie asked as they sipped wine before their food arrived.

"What in the world could you confess that would be, as you say, really stupid?"

Minnie rubbed and twisted her hands and spun the college class ring she wore now that she'd quit wearing her wedding rings. "You'll laugh."

"I promise I won't laugh."

"I may go back to work."

Cynthia shook her head and almost choked on her wine. When she got herself under control, she asked, "You're thinking about what?"

"I said you'd laugh at me."

After clearing her throat, Cynthia asked, "What's this about?"

"I'm bored. Plus, I'm thumbing my nose at the world. You know I'm attending church regularly now? I keep hearing service is part of being a Christian, especially progressive Christians like us at Dodge. Shouldn't I be serving my fellow human beings? Nursing is how I can best serve."

A smirk accompanied Cynthia's response. "Couldn't you just join a few do-gooder organizations? Volunteer? Why put yourself through the nursing grind again?"

"I won't be 55 until the 16th of next month. My health is great. I quit because I was tired, worn out. I wanted a break. I'm rested now."

"You don't miss it, do you?" Minnie couldn't tell if Cynthia was inquiring or admonishing.

A sly grin broke out on Minnie's brown face. "I kinda do."

Cynthia's body stiffened. "You can't miss wiping butts or worshiping at the feet of arrogant 30-year olds who think they hung the moon because they have M.D. behind their names, can you? Not to mention record keeping hassles and the upstairs/downstairs politics?"

Minnie wrapped her hands around her wine glass and leaned toward her friend. "I don't miss those things. But there are things I miss."

Cynthia narrowed her eyes. "Like?"

"I miss sharing the happiness of family members when a loved one leaves the hospital with a good prognosis. I miss picking up a newborn from the nursery and placing that child in a parent's arms for the trip home. I miss helping newbie nurses learn the ropes."

That earned a frown and another head shake. "This is a bad idea. If you went back, how much would you work?"

"Part time."

Cynthia exhaled. "I certainly hope not full time."

"Heavens no! I'd go back only if I could do about 20 hours a week and have some control over my shifts. Nobody gets complete control, but if they want me at Lutheran Memorial, I need some say."

Cynthia kept pressing her opposition. "If you thought I'd endorse this," she said as they stood outside after lunch, "you were dead wrong. You'll regret this if you do it."

∞ ∞ ∞

A few days after the lunch with Cynthia, Carol Robbins called Minnie with a golf invitation. She was playing in Jackson Creek's member/guest tournament and needed a partner. Minnie accepted immediately.

Some Jackson Creek members knew how well Minnie played and didn't appreciate Carol bringing in a "ringer," especially a black one. "I don't care," Carol said on the practice range that early August Wednesday morning. "Just once, I want to win this tournament. Playing with you gives me my best chance. If some members don't like it, they can try kicking me out. My family has been part of this club for 70 years. Good luck with that."

As in the October match the year before, the outcome wasn't decided until the end. Minnie's birdie on the final hole proved the difference. Robbins-Donaldson won the stroke play, best ball tournament by one shot at eight under par 64.

"I owe you," Carol said as they sat in the grill afterwards, munching on nachos and drinking light beer. "You saved me."

"You made as many birdies as I did," Minnie reminded her, looking at their score card. "We each had four."

"You made 14 pars, with no bogeys. That's why we won."

"We both did our part."

Carol turned the conversation from golf. "Tell me how you're doing. We haven't talked much since last fall."

Minnie nodded agreement. "Just that lunch in January."

"And?"

"From outside, everything looks great. I have plenty of money. I've re-made the house like I want. I spend my time working out, playing golf, reading books, watching movies and television shows, and attending plays. I go see my new grandchild whenever I want. Nobody tells me what to do or when to do it. Most people would say I couldn't have a better life."

"That's not the whole story?"

"It's not."

"Want to tell me about it?"

"Let's go to your house, clean up, and hang out in your sitting room. I'll fill you in."

∞ ∞ ∞

Minnie loved Carol's sitting room for two reasons. First, the early American furniture and earth tones – dark rugs and wall coverings and varnished mahogany shelving – gave the space a warm feel anyone could appreciate. Second, the Robbins family's choice of portraits and artifacts symbolized an inclusivity few rich white people embraced.

A few years ago after a golf round, Carol explained how it got that way. Visiting Carol's house for the first time, Minnie gasped when she saw portraits of Frederick Douglass, Martin Luther King, Jr., and Marian Anderson on the walls along with the usual suspects – George Washington, Abraham Lincoln, John Glenn.

Richard, Carol's husband, for years decorated the room with portraits and photos of American heroes and family luminaries. One of his prominently displayed ancestors served in the Union Navy during the Civil War. Carol's grandfather fought as an infantry officer in Patton's Army in the Second World War. Their teenage daughter looked at all that one day and asked, "Why are the only pictures in this room of old white men?"

The daughter's question sparked two years of soul

searching in the Robbins household. Carol changed first, insisting that if the room was to remain a shrine to national and family icons, the honorees must include women. Portraits of Susan B. Anthony, Eleanor Roosevelt, Sally Ride, and Carol's great-grandmother joined the old white men.

But the Robbins women knew something was missing. "We realized," Carol said, "we'd left out much of the country's history. If we really were celebrating America – as we intended – we should include people of color. Richard didn't see that at first, but my daughter and I insisted. Eventually, he came around."

So, Minnie sat on a couch beneath portraits of King, Lincoln, Ride, and Ida B. Wells while she told Carol her troubles. "I'm bored and I'm lonely. That's the bottom line."

"Days like today help, don't they?"

"They do, and I appreciate them. Thank you."

Carol nodded. "But, they aren't enough, right?"

"I can solve the boredom problem by going back to work part time, which I'm thinking about doing. I'm not sure what I do about the loneliness."

"Do you miss Bradley?"

Minnie sighed long and deep. "I do and I don't. You of all people know how we'd grown apart. I was furious with him for neglecting me, for insisting I work for him, even though I'd retired. I hated him for that. I thought about leaving. I probably should have but I didn't have the energy for a fight.

"When he died, I barely felt anything. He was just somebody who wasn't around anymore. Then I found out about his betrayals, his bad acts, including some toward the children. What little grief I had went away. So, I wasn't the bereaved, suffering widow.

"Now, ten months later, I realize there was one thing about being together. I had someone in the space with me. That provided comfort I miss now. I'm not sure which is worse – living with somebody who's a pain or being alone. They both suck."

Carol took two deep breaths. A nervous anticipation settled over the room. Finally, she spoke. "Are you ready to date?"

Minnie said nothing for a moment. She'd suspected the question might come, but wasn't sure how she should respond. She'd thought about it, with decidedly mixed feelings. Eventually, she said, "I might be. I can't really say."

"That sounds like no."

"I didn't mean it that way. I fear the things a woman in my position would about going back out there. The idea of somebody new unsettles me, despite how bad things were at the end with Bradley."

"But?"

"I'm not kidding about the loneliness. I feel that intensely." Minnie squirmed on the couch, wondering if she should reveal all her feelings. She decided she and Carol had developed enough trust she could go all the way. "I need someone who'll hold me at night, who'll kiss me, who'll touch me."

Carol stood up and rubbed the black woman's shoulders. Minnie rose and they embraced. Neither said a word for several moments. Then Carol spoke. "I get it, my friend. I get it."

∞ ∞ ∞

Minnie went about her life the next few weeks, including another Louisiana visit with Crystal, Michael, and Sarah Alexis. Near the end of August, she acted on the working-again idea. She called her old hospital supervisor.

"How soon can you start?" came the reply.

"I only want to work 20 hours a week."

"I asked how soon you can start."

"How about right after Labor Day? I have one more golf tournament that weekend."

"You got a deal. Come see me this week so we can do the paperwork."

Later that day, Carol called. "I know someone you should meet," she said. "Are you up for coffee with him?"

Minnie felt her insides flutter. "Well, in my case, tea. But yes, I'm game."

"I'll have him call you. His name is Mark. Mark Gibson."

"What can you tell me about him?"

"Decide for yourself if he's worth your while. Aside from assuring you he's not an axe murderer, I'm letting you each draw your own conclusions."

In different ways, those two calls that August day set in motion what would unfold between Minnie Donaldson and John Dawson. The first put her back at Lutheran Memorial Hospital where John wound up not long after she resumed her nursing work. The second jump started her dating life. John and Minnie could happen only after that played out.

Chapter 11

A few days after the Labor Day holiday, Ed Ward summoned John to his 42nd floor office. At 55, Ward helped lead VWM's corporate practice. He controlled huge chunks of business from a variety of clients.

Ward arrived at VWM in 1987 from finishing second in his class at the University of Texas Law School. With an aggressive personality and a penchant for glad-handing, it wasn't long before he excelled at reeling in clients. A tall man with a quick smile, the sandy brown hair of his early years was turning gray, but he'd maintained his sleek frame and All American boy good looks. When John arrived in 2016, he thought Ed was in his late 40s.

Ward doled out work to associates like John, Don Young, and Kate Hart. The three of them, in fact, comprised Ward's current "A" team – John and Don, two fast track baby lawyers he trusted more than most first years, and Kate, a seasoned fifth-year associate who helped him watch over their work. While they toiled away, he traveled the country, winning new business nearly everywhere he went.

John sat in Ward's spacious office and waited as the older man finished a phone call. He gazed at the artifacts that decorated the space – framed baseball action photos, souvenir bats and gloves, and autographed balls mixed with paintings of lush rural scenes.

A few minutes of small talk ensued about the approaching MLB playoffs and Ward's new grandchild. He pulled a green file folder from a stack on his desk. "Here's your next assignment from me."

A dark-skinned black man with short hair stuck his head through the office doorway. He looked about 30 and wore khaki slacks, a blue dress shirt, and a green tie, but no coat. The man waved and said, "I'm here."

Ward looked up from his note pad. He returned the wave and smiled. "Thanks, Kevin. Give me a minute."

As he tapped a pen against his desk Ward explained, "That's Kevin Monroe. He owns a lawn service company. He's here about work I need done at several of my rental properties."

The phone rang. After seeing the caller ID, Ward said, "I should take this. Step outside for a second, if you would, and close the door behind you. Thanks."

John stood up and headed for a waiting area outside Ward's office. Monroe, sitting in one of three chairs there, thumbed through a magazine. He dropped it on a small table, rose, and extended his hand. "I'm Kevin. Kevin Monroe."

"John Dawson."

They sat down. "Nice to meet you. You're one of Ed's right-hand men?"

John smiled at that characterization of Ward's minions. "That's an interesting way of putting it, Kevin." John had learned the trick of repeating a name after an introduction as a way of helping remember the person.

"That's what he calls you. He's told me all about the young guys and gals at the law firm who work for him, the best and brightest, I surmise. I haven't had many chances at putting names with faces."

"You're his lawn man?"

"Among other things. He owns mucho real estate. My lawn service company does the landscaping at his 12 rental houses and three apartment buildings. I do many other chores for him."

"I heard he owned a lot of rental property. I wondered how he managed it."

"You're looking at how."

Ward opened his office door. He told John, "Just read the file and call me with questions, if you have any. You'll see what's needed. It's a straightforward question. I bet you can answer it with a couple of hours of work."

"Got it."

Before John could walk away, Kevin offered a business card. "Call me sometime," he said. "I always want to get to know the up and comers. Never can tell when one might put together an empire, like my man Ed here."

∞ ∞ ∞

Labor Day weekend gave Minnie joy and heartburn. Joy resulted from traveling to Shreveport, Louisiana, a 175-mile trip from Dallas, and winning an individual golf tournament. When she arrived at the course, she relished watching players unload bags and sit on their bumpers or tailgates and swap street shoes for golf shoes. A sense of being among her tribe swept over her.

Driving home Monday, toward a magnificent sunset, life felt perfect. She rode with memories of broken tees littering the practice range, freshly mowed grass, sweetly struck shots, and putts that dropped instead of lipping out. She looked over at the first-place trophy sitting in the passenger seat every chance she got.

Facing her first day back at work Wednesday gave her heartburn. That meant putting everything in order Tuesday. Her tasks included organizing her nursing gear, finishing or rescheduling home maintenance and landscaping projects, and letting friends know her diminished availability for lunches, golf rounds, and movies didn't mean she'd been kidnapped.

The chores reminded her that if she hadn't decided on working again she could sleep late Tuesday morning, find a lunch companion, then attend a movie by herself or with friends. She could spend Wednesday at the practice range, working out flaws that surfaced during the tournament.

Why had she decided she'd go back to work? Was this one of those things that just seemed like a good idea at the time? There was nothing wrong with her life. As she'd told Carol Robbins, she had plenty of money, did what she wanted when she wanted, and answered only to herself.

Recalling her conversation with Cynthia McFadden, she wondered if she'd exaggerated nursing's rewards and her boredom. True, she'd experienced a few days when she ran out of things to do, making her think she should get back into the nursing world. Was acting on that feeling necessary? Maybe she should tell the hospital it had all been a mistake and she'd remain retired.

When she hit the outskirts of Dallas, she put aside her ruminations. By the time she parked in the garage, she felt lighter. Fatigue from the tournament and the drive home settled over her. A long, hot bath and tea offered an inviting prospect as she strolled into the kitchen and dropped her keys on the counter. Not worrying tonight about the coming weeks, months, or years eased her mind.

Tuesday morning, Minnie got up and worked methodically. She focused on her tasks one at a time. She assembled her gear – backpack, scrubs, shoes, socks, pens, lotion, scissors. She called her landscaper and postponed two projects. She ran through the list of people she should tell she was returning to work and, except for Cynthia, decided text messages sufficed.

That took an hour before she called Cynthia, expecting a storm.

"I put off calling you until now because I knew how unhappy you'd be," Minnie said. "I start work tomorrow."

"I thought you'd go through with it. When you get disgusted, I'll say I told you so. How was Shreveport?"

"I won the women's division. I shot 70-68-73, so I wasn't always at my best. But I'll take a win. Got a nice trophy and the usual array of golf merchandise."

"Any other good players there?"

"Two young women who played at Louisiana Tech made a run at me Monday before falling back. One knew Crystal. I won by three shots."

Cynthia couldn't stay away from Minnie's nursing decision. "What shift are you working?"

"For now, seven to seven, full shift – 12 hours – Wednesdays and half shifts – six hours – Thursdays and Fridays. After a few weeks I'll work Tuesdays, not Fridays."

"That's 24 hours! This has disaster written all over it. I thought you said 20 hours a week."

"This works for the time being. I'll get to that."

Cynthia let out a heavy sigh. "I'll believe that when I see it."

"I gotta go. I have loose ends that need tying up."

"Yeah, sure. I'll be waiting for the distress call."

∞∞∞∞

Late Tuesday afternoon when Minnie returned from running errands, her cell phone rang. She didn't recognize the number and thought about not answering. Then she remembered that last week she'd given two people at the hospital the number and wondered if the call came from one of them. "This is Minnie." She heard a deep, male voice.

"Hello, Minnie. This is Mark Gibson. I'm a friend of Carol Robbins. I think she told you I'd call."

Minnie stopped, took a deep breath, and looked around her kitchen. A person named Mark Gibson existed and Carol was fixing her up with him. "Oh, yes, Mark. How are you?"

He spoke clearly and deliberately. "I'm fine. I don't know if you're busy and I won't hold you. I just wondered if we might get together sometime soon. Carol has told me so much about you. I'm always interested in meeting someone as fascinating as Carol says you are."

"You're too kind, as is she."

"I doubt that. Carol has a reputation for honesty." Minnie generally avoided trying to tell from a voice if a person was black or white. This time she couldn't help herself. She quickly decided Mark Gibson was black.

"I'd love meeting you, but it'll have to wait a bit. I retired from nursing a year ago, but I've decided I'm going back to it. My first day is tomorrow. I should see how things work before making any commitments. Since I have your number in my phone now, I'll call you after I see how things shake out. How's that?"

A pause ensued on the other end Minnie interpreted as disappointment, maybe even irritation. She visualized a brown-skinned man with a mustache and short hair, speckled with gray. He said, "I'm sure you'll need time for figuring out how your life will unfold now."

"Let's talk in about two weeks."

"Thanks. I look forward to meeting you."

So, Minnie prepared for her first day back at work intrigued by the possibility of a date with Mark Gibson. Did he look the way she'd imagined? What was he like? But first, there was the business of getting back into the nursing routine.

∞∞∞

What Minnie didn't know was that on her first day back at the hospital, John Dawson took another step on the path that led them to each other. What he did didn't seem like much but, as things turned out, it meant everything. He let himself entertain the possibility of meeting a law school classmate in a place two University of Pennsylvania law graduates wouldn't usually connect – East Texas.

At 9:35 a.m., the phone rang in his 41st floor office, interrupting work on a buy-sell agreement between two auto parts dealers. "John Dawson. May I help you?"

A voice John knew, but couldn't quite place, responded.

"I bet you can. This is a blast from your past."

"Say again?"

"It's Bob Sawoski. Bet you didn't think you'd hear from me."

John nodded. Yes, Bob Sawoski was one of the last people he expected he'd hear from today. They'd been friends in law school, but hadn't seen each other in two years. "I sure didn't. How the hell are you?"

"I'm great, John. I hear Texas is treating you well."

The comment represented idle chatter or indicated extraordinary due diligence. "Can't complain. They keep giving me new assignments. I've even started figuring out how I rustle up my own business. That's important around here, and they start teaching you early."

"I heard that," Bob replied, biting hard on the word 'that.' "I'm learning too."

"You still at that firm you started with out of law school?"

"Sure am. Winters and Davis in Philadelphia."

"You're in your third year, right?"

"Right. I didn't clerk after law school. Couldn't afford it."

John doubted the 'couldn't afford it' line. Bob graduated from Cornell and his family owned hardware stores all over New Jersey. Probably, he hadn't had good clerkship offers or just decided he'd get on with practice. "It has its advantages and disadvantages," John offered finally.

"I guess it does."

John felt creeping impatience. What was this call about? He tapped his foot under the desk. He and Bob had been friends in law school, more than mere acquaintances, but not bosom buddies. "What can I do for you?" he asked.

"Oh yeah, the reason I called – I wondered if you could direct me to somebody who can do local counsel work for me. We have a hearing next month in Marshall, Texas, not far from you, I understand."

"About 130 miles."

"The Eastern District of Texas – Marshall Division – has become a hot spot for patent litigation, which is what I do. We need a local lawyer who can sponsor admissions, give us the lay of the land, maybe smooth things with the judge."

"Wouldn't somebody in Marshall be better?"

"We tried that. Everybody we'd consider hiring has a conflict. We decided we'd look in Dallas and Tyler. I know you, so you're the first person I called."

An idea popped into John's head. "Assuming no conflict, Mary McCaskill can help you or will know who can. Young partner in our litigation section. Rice undergraduate, honors Texas Law School grad. Texas Law Review articles editor. Grew up in Carthage, near Marshall. Knows a lot of people over there. Really nice person."

"Sounds perfect," Sawoski uttered softly.

"I heard she's out of town today. Give me your number and I'll have her call you."

They chatted another few minutes about old times. Finally, Sawoski said, "It'd be a shame if I got that close to Dallas and didn't see you. Think we could connect while I'm there? Come over and I'll buy dinner."

John thought about begging off, but saw reasons for leaving his options open. He might enjoy a night out of town. "Maybe not a bad idea. I'll mark the date – October what?"

"October sixth, a Friday."

"When you finalize everything, call me and I'll see what I can do."

Chapter 12

John called Kevin Monroe later the day of his conversation with Bob Sawoski. John didn't know many black people and he'd decided he should remedy that. He could have started with one of VWM's five black lawyers. He would try cultivating friendships with several of them soon. Kevin, however, intrigued him and he wanted some friends who weren't lawyers.

He pulled Kevin's card from the bundle he kept in his desk and dialed. He got voicemail and left a message. Two hours later, his phone rang. "John Dawson. May I help you?"

"I don't know." A deep-voiced chuckle came through the phone. "Can you? This is Kevin Monroe."

"I'll do my best. Thanks for calling me back, Kevin."

"It's my day to talk to Vinnick Whitford lawyers. I just got off the phone with Ed Ward."

"We're everywhere, aren't we?" John got to the point. "I wondered if we could have lunch or a drink sometime. You might be a man I should know."

"I'm okay with a long-term investment lunch. I said when we met, you may build the next VWM empire. Nothing like getting in on the ground floor. I'm free Friday. How's that?"

John picked up a friendly, but no-nonsense tone on the other end of the line. He looked at his paper and electronic calendars. "I'm good. Where should we meet?"

"I'm seeing Ed at 10:45 a.m. Friday. Short meeting, I think. Let's hook up in the elevator lobby on 42 at eleven o'clock? We'll figure it out then."

On the way home that night, John thought through his entree to Kevin Monroe. The more he saw and read, the more he viewed his racially isolated existence as a liability. He saw negative practice implications. Personal reservations bothered him as well. The world was changing, the outcome of the 2016 election notwithstanding.

John didn't comprehend Donald Trump's victory. He'd never considered voting for him and didn't understand a lot of the people who had. He'd seen plenty of evidence, in the 2016 campaign and since, that the man was a racist. If politics had been his thing, as it was for Maggie Brandt and some of his undergraduate classmates, he'd already have started working on beating Trump in 2020.

From John's perspective, Trump couldn't stop one trend he saw every day in his practice. Black and Latino lawyers made up more and more of the junior staff in corporate legal departments. Those young lawyers would advance into senior positions as he moved toward and into partnership. They'd hand out business five, 10, 15 years from now. John realized if he couldn't relate to them, his career might stall.

Should the reason for seeking relationships with black people be just economics? That didn't seem right, he thought, as he sat at the last downtown stop light before he hit Central Expressway. His parents hadn't known many black or brown people. Beyond a stray comment about something in the news, they didn't discuss race. Their moral code, however, seemed inconsistent with using black people just for what they could do for him financially.

Maybe not knowing any black people made for a personal void. He remembered a white college friend who hung around a lot with blacks. The guy knew much more about popular culture than John and many of his other white friends. He seemed at ease with all kinds of people.

Didn't Chris marry a black woman? He sure dated a lot of black women. John made a mental note to see if he could track him down and find out how his life had unfolded. Wasn't he in Chicago, working as a park planner? Somebody in their undergraduate crowd knows where to find him or knows what happened to him, John thought as he navigated the expressway.

By the time he got home, John had worked out in his mind why he should pursue a friendship with Kevin Monroe and with other black people. Now, he wondered, how would Kevin, and others he approached respond.

Minnie felt out of place when she arrived at the hospital at 6:30 a.m. Wednesday. She checked in at her fourth floor duty station. For the first weeks, she'd agreed with the staff supervisor she'd work on general patient floors. She'd volunteered for spot, emergency duty in intensive care. The hospital badly needed ICU nurses. Someone with Minnie's experience could pinch hit, at least in shortage situations.

"You must be Minnie," said a young black woman nurse, extending her hand. "We've heard so much about you. You're practically a legend in this hospital."

"I thought I was just old, spelled with a capital O," Minnie replied, shaking the woman's hand. Her ID badge read Brittany Evans. She looked under thirty, had medium-brown skin, a slim figure, and a thin, pleasant, lightly made up face dominated by big brown eyes. She wore green scrubs, gray running shoes, and a necklace with a Christian cross. Minnie wore neither jewelry, except a watch, nor makeup while on duty. In intense pressure situations, either might get in the way.

"We're glad you're here. Things have been busy and we're short staffed," Brittany said.

"Then I should get to work," Minnie told her, picking up a clipboard. "Are these my patients?"

"Yes," said the nurse behind the desk. "I'm glad you're back, Minnie."

"Jackie, it's good being back." Jackie Davis, a chubby white woman in her late 40s Minnie had known for years, had worked all over Lutheran Memorial. Minnie regarded her as one of the "good guys" on the nursing staff. "I don't know everybody, like I did before, but I'll catch up."

"Everybody who was here when you were here knows you," Brittany said. "New people like me know who you are."

Minnie scanned her patient list and said out loud, "Thomas needs medication. I should check IVs on Saxton and Collins. Cotton needs assessing. And that doesn't count patients I should go by and introduce myself to so I can see what they need." She smiled. For a moment, today seemed like old times. Exhaustion, she knew, would set in by the end of the shift. For the moment Minnie felt in her element and happy about being there.

Minnie got through her first day back in the nursing world with only ordinary patient crises. Soon, however, the glow of those early hours faded. By two o'clock the next afternoon, four hours into Thursday's six-hour shift, she felt frazzled from balancing record keeping – input directly into the hospital computer system – and patient needs. Saxton, Collins, and Thomas weren't responding to medication. Cotton kept complaining about the positioning of her bed.

She rallied, however, after Jackie Davis intervened. "You look like, well, shit. I can't say it any different," Jackie said when Minnie lingered at the desk between patient stops.

"I feel like it. I'm tired," she replied, touching a temple while closing her eyes.

"It's in your head."

"Of course, it is. I know that. I'm in great physical shape, as good as any nurse here, including the ones under 30. But I'm worn out mentally. I forgot how hard this is." She leaned on the desk.

Jackie sat up and crossed her arms over her chest.

"Why'd you come back?"

"I was bored. Plus, I felt I should do something useful."
"Really?" came the reply, along with a skeptical stare.

Minnie rocked back and forth before she stuck her head over the desk and whispered, "That's how I felt. It's not how I feel now."

Jackie's expression and tone lightened. "Your heart's in the right place. Adjusting will take time. You knew that, didn't you?"

"Maybe I didn't."

Now, Jackie's blue eyes zeroed in on Minnie. "It's okay. You're still good at this. I see that in how you take charge with the newbies, how you stay on top of things. The patients love you, even a few doctors, too. You know what you're doing."

Minnie glanced down and bit her lip. "I'm glad you're sure, because I'm not."

A patient's call bell rang. Jackie turned off the red light and spoke into a microphone, "Can we help you?"

A scratchy, weak female voice replied. "Can someone come? My head hurts."

"I'll tell your nurse. Someone will be there soon." When Jackie closed the mic, she looked up at Minnie. "That's Saxton in 410C. She's one of yours."

"I should get back to work."

"That's how you get through this. Take care of your patients."

Minnie nodded and turned in the direction of Saxton's room. "You're right."

∞ ∞ ∞

Friday, Minnie's third day back at work, her old friend, Judy Shields, heard the news of Minnie's return and stopped by the breakroom where Minnie ate lunch with three other nurses. Even though she worked only a partial shift that day, Minnie brought a light lunch – a half-sandwich and an apple – as much as an excuse for sitting with the others as for really needing lunch.

Judy, who was currently working in ICU, was a year older than Minnie but couldn't think about retiring for a while. Her family needed her paycheck. She started at Lutheran Memorial a year before Minnie arrived and befriended her when many of the other white nurses remained cool. The staff included only a handful of black nurses in those days. Initially, few close friendships developed between black and white nurses.

Minnie and Judy, however, hit it off. They supported each other through the births of five children – Minnie's three and Judy's two – the deaths of parents and siblings, minor tragedies like car accidents, and a few triumphs, like graduations and grandchildren.

Two years ago Judy's husband, Dick, developed a heart condition, meaning he could no longer do the backbreaking construction work he'd done most of his life. He'd always made good money, but they now lived on his disability benefits and her nursing salary. They were far from destitute, but Dick's illness quashed Judy's plans for retiring about the time Minnie did in 2016.

$$\infty \infty \infty$$

John's lunch with Kevin Monroe went as he'd hoped. John found him fascinating and much more than met the eye. Yes, he was a yard man and property manager who made a living working for the Ed Wards of the world. His interests, however, extended far beyond his company's services.

Between bites of salad, he told John, "I spend much of my leisure time reading classic literature – prose and poetry."

"Yeah? What do you like?"

"George Eliot, the 19th century English novelist, is one of my favorites. Wrote a lot about social outsiders, which is one reason I like her work so much."

John's hand flew to his chest. "Oh, yeah. She was a woman who wrote under a man's name, right?"

"For a time. She eventually used her real name, but she wrote her best-known works – *Silas Marner, Middlemarch, The Mill on the Floss* – as George Eliot."

"What was her real name?"

"Mary Anne Evans."

"And you like poetry too?"

"John Milton, the 17th century English poet, is probably my favorite. He wrote a great deal about religion and saw himself as a voice of England. He even signed some of his work, 'John Milton, Englishman.'"

"Any interest in contemporary literature?"

"I read people like Margaret Atwood, Zadie Smith, and John Updike."

Though an avid reader, John favored commercial fiction genres, so his list included few such luminaries. "What's the Kevin Monroe story?" he asked with a grin.

"I grew up in Magnolia, Arkansas. I finished first in my high school class, won a Stanford scholarship, and majored in English. I met my wife in California. She was a Ph.D. student in Spanish at Cal-Berkley. Pat planned on working for the U.S. State Department in Latin America, but both her parents, who lived in Dallas, fell ill a few months before she graduated."

"So, what happened?"

"She's an only child and was close to both of them," Kevin said. "We moved here."

"What kind of work did the two of you find in Dallas?"

"Not hard for her. She took a job at SMU as a Spanish professor. Can you imagine how they fell all over themselves when this black woman Berkley Ph.D. showed up on their doorstep without being recruited?"

Having heard how desperate some universities were for black Ph.Ds, John chuckled at the idea. But what about Kevin? As a kid, he'd made much more than pocket change tending lawns in Magnolia and nearby towns. He decided he'd start his own landscaping and lawn service business. "The property management thing followed with some research and a couple of on-line courses."

When John mentioned he enjoyed TV drama, Kevin launched into a comparison of British and American television. "I regard nearly everything on American television except sports as a waste of time. Newton Minow had it right about the 'vast wasteland' and all that business."

John nodded, hoping Kevin would assume he knew who Newton Minow was. In fact, John learned about Minow only after going on-line and researching him back at the office.   When he discovered Minow chaired the Federal Communications Commission in the 1960s he said to himself, "I'll have to stay on my toes with this Monroe guy. He may be out of my league."

Chapter 13

B ob Sawoski called John during the last week of September and said his hearing now would begin Thursday, October fifth. "We have so many motions on the list the judge scheduled an extra day. We won't finish until Friday afternoon."

"I plan on driving down there so I can see you," John said. "How does the new schedule affect your travel plans?"

"Mary McCaskill found us a local lawyer in Tyler who knows the judge well. We'll headquarter in his office. We're going in there Wednesday afternoon. Tyler has a big enough airport for a corporate jet. It's only 50 miles from Marshall, so it's an easy drive.

"Our client's general counsel has a college friend who lives in Tyler. They're having dinner Friday night. We won't leave until Saturday morning."

"You and I could have dinner Friday night?"

"Yes."

"Where're you staying?"

"Residence Inn. Their suites make good workspaces."

"I'll book myself there."

∞∞∞

The day of John's Tyler trip, he came in early since he planned on leaving early – at four thirty – and he had three projects he wanted done before getting away. Finishing them would let him spend his weekend work time on the new matter Ed Ward had asked him to handle, drafting a partnership agreement for investors in a convenience store chain.

When he walked into the building, John noticed Kate Hart standing at the lobby coffee bar beside an attractive woman who looked about 30. She was medium height, had short blonde hair, and wore dark slacks topped by a creamcolored blouse. As John strolled toward the elevator bank, Kate leaned over and kissed the woman on the lips. They lingered a few moments, Kate holding the blonde's hand. The woman slipped an arm around Kate's waist and kissed her back. The two finally parted, reluctantly John thought.

Riding the elevator, John realized what he'd seen. He felt a hole open in his stomach. Another one bites the dust, he told himself. Kate Hart is gay!

John excelled at putting things out of his mind and focusing on tasks at hand. That quality fueled his stellar record in school and now helped power his legal career. When he sat down that morning and turned on his computer, nothing mattered except the e-mails he exchanged with clients and colleagues, the documents he ground out, and the calls he took and made that concerned his projects. What he'd seen in the lobby would come back but, during the day, nothing mattered except work.

In the car that afternoon, rolling east on I-20 toward Tyler, John let his mind wander back to the morning. He'd never told anyone of his crush on Kate Hart, partly because he knew the perils of getting involved with a colleague and partly because she'd never done anything that encouraged an advance. For several months he'd contemplated the ethics and practicality of making a move.

He'd never considered the possibility she was gay. Looking

back, he understood why he hadn't, though it all sat out in plain sight. First, Kate never showed up at formal or informal firm functions – happy hour, recruiting dinners, banquets, client entertainment – with a male companion. She always appeared alone.

Second, she never talked about men. Some of the firm's female lawyers, modern career women though they may have been, still commented on this or that "cute guy" or "hunk" they'd seen in the building lobby or at a recruiting event. Not Kate.

Finally, she never invited people from the firm for parties, drinks, or dinners at her house. Doing so, John realized, could mean revealing details of her private life – who she lived with, who stayed over, who helped her organize social events.

Now, John wondered, why had he seen what he saw that morning? Did Kate and her partner get careless with their public display of affection or was she just coming out? He'd ask Don Young, who knew everything about everybody in their section.

Whatever the story of her love life, Friday morning crushed John's crush on Kate. The two people he saw had romantic feelings for each other. Their relationship involved more than casual touching. John believed sexual orientation was a born-in trait, wired at birth. Kate Hart was lesbian and had been all her life, no matter when she realized it.

∞∞∞

Saturday morning, John made an impulsive decision that seemed like a good idea at the time. Rather than travel U.S. 69's eight miles of divided highway back north to I-20 from downtown Tyler, he decided he'd check out the kind of Texas countryside he hadn't seen much of since his 2016 arrival in the Lone Star State. He'd drive the 35 miles of State Highway 64 between the western edge of Tyler and Canton where he'd pick up I-20 for the remaining 50 miles to Dallas.

After filling his gas tank at 7:35 a.m., he took 64 West out of town, past dingy one- and two-story buildings that looked as if they once housed thriving businesses. They now seemed old and reminiscent of better times.

Driving through the deserted streets of Tyler that morning, John reflected on the previous evening. It had been the diversion from work he'd craved. After the think time on the drive over, a steak dinner, and catching up with his classmate, John experienced a different end of a day than he had in a while. He didn't know how much of a recharge this excursion would ultimately provide, but he wasn't complaining. At least he'd spent a night out of his apartment.

Though he relished his work and felt optimistic about the future at VWM, the sameness of his days sometimes wore on him. Friday's revelation that Kate Hart was off limits hadn't helped, no matter how much of a pipe dream a relationship with her might have been.

On the drive Friday, John contemplated his lack of social life. He tried not feeling sorry for himself. Nothing required that he bill more hours than every other associate in his class. He'd chosen that, not someone else. After over more than a year and change in Dallas, perhaps he could lighten up and make time for other things.

That balance idea grabbed him as he wondered about finding a female – maybe more than one female – who could talk about serious issues yet had a fun side. That wasn't too much to ask. Was it?

Intermittent fog interrupted John's musings. There hadn't been fog at the hotel or the gas station, just an overcast sky. Now a dense covering sporadically obscured the roadway. John switched on his headlights. Then, as quickly as he'd run into the fog, he ran out of it. Bright sunshine illuminated signs for Tyler airport.

He wondered whether Bob and his crew had left town. They had planned an early departure. John turned off the highway and swung down a road toward the executive terminal. There, he noticed a sleek, white jet – maybe a 10 passenger model – sitting on the tarmac. A tall, lean man in the tell-tale pilot's uniform of white shirt, thin dark tie, and black pants walked around the plane, doing an inspection. Was this Bob's plane? John scanned the sky over the airport. If they hadn't departed, fog wouldn't hold them up now.

John turned left out of the airport back onto Highway 64. Two miles west, the divided highway ended in favor of a two-lane road through heavy woods. He noticed a lush green area – a horse or cattle ranch, he thought – and that the fog had returned.

This patch didn't disappear. John drove another two miles and crossed the Neches River into Van Zandt County from Smith County. Perhaps this country road idea hadn't been so hot. It was really foggy. He could barely see.

Soon – maybe a mile – after the river, John felt himself going downhill. He could see, really, nothing. Well, he could see the dashboard. Maybe he should pull over. He slowed the car. He remembered a 70 mile-per-hour speed limit sign from just before the river bridge. Fat chance of that, he thought. He wondered how long the fog would last.

Suddenly, John felt a rise in the road. It seemed almost like an airplane takeoff. How fast was he going? A second later, he saw a light that was very near. *My God, that's an on-coming car, isn't it? The driver doesn't see me! He's in my lane!*

The light, now a blur, barreled toward him in the fog. John swerved. How much shoulder did he have over there? He hadn't looked before the heavy fog hit.

John felt the car skid off the road and start downwards, into a ditch. He heard a loud bang. *Must have been the front end hitting the ground or a big rock in the bottom of the ditch. Would the car flip over?* For an instant he felt as if it would. Out of the corner of his eye, he thought he saw a house.

Just as quickly as he'd veered downward into the ditch, he felt himself rising. Up an embankment, maybe? Again, he wondered if the car would flip over. He was leaning left, wasn't he? Toward the driver's side door? Back toward the road?

The car righted itself. Things stopped. Did he hit the brakes? Were those trees he could barely make out in front of him? Had he run into them?

At that instant, the pain hit. He felt stabs in both legs. Had a bone snapped? Something plowed into his chest, followed by another sharp pain in his shoulder. Finally, he got hit in the head. A thought of an air bag floated by him. Everything went black.

For days, John didn't remember any of this. Even when it started coming back, details, like exactly what he saw and the precise movements of the car, eluded him. Five miles west of the Tyler airport on Texas State Highway 64, at 7:55 a.m. on Saturday, October 7, 2017, John Dawson was out of it.

∞∞∞

Minnie hadn't planned on being on duty at Lutheran Memorial on the Saturday of John's accident. She thought the day held only a golf round and a relaxing afternoon and evening of reading, watching British TV drama on DVD, and perhaps catching a college football game. She'd fit in a workout sometime.

Friday her supervisor called and pleaded that she work the Saturday 3:00 p.m. to 11:00 p.m. ICU shift. Judy Shields had a family emergency that required an unexpected out-of-town trip. The nurse who'd ordinarily cover for her caught a bad cold two days before.

Minnie still played the Saturday golf round. She started early and finished at 10:50 a.m. A shower, an hour and a half nap, and a light snack let her arrive at the hospital fresh and ready for the car wreck casualties, gunshot victims, and people who did stupid things that landed them in hospitals on weekends.

"Wonder what nonsense we'll see tonight?" she asked Martha Henley, the more experienced intensive care nurse on duty that day. Martha started work at 7:30 a.m., so she could brief Minnie on patients who'd come in earlier in the day.

"Already seen a little," Martha answered as they stood at the nursing station. "Two emergency surgeries this morning. One man, one woman. Both car wrecks. The woman suffered internal injuries. She'll make it, but she's in a lot of pain. The man just has a bunch of stuff broken."

Minnie looked at the charts. "I'll check on the guy first. He should wake up soon, based on time of surgery. John Dawson, right? Know what happened to him?"

"Bad one-car accident near Tyler. Flown in on the bird. Broke one leg, tore up the knee on the other. Broken collarbone, separated shoulder, concussion. That's the big stuff. Lots of cuts, bruises, and abrasions. He'll keep you busy."

John Dawson's chart showed a 27-year old man who'd undergone surgery that morning for the multiple injuries Martha described. His nearest relatives were out of state and had been notified. Minnie wondered why he'd been flown in from 80 miles away. Had the nearby hospitals been full?

Whatever lay behind that, they'd have Dawson around a while. Minnie had seen hospital stays of four weeks with his kind of injuries.

She looked into his room. He wasn't awake, but he was

stirring. He worked at shifting his torso. He turned his head from side to side a few times, then yawned and swiped his tongue over his lips.

Beyond the bandages and bruises on his face, Minnie saw a handsome young man who probably didn't lack for female admirers. She wondered if he'd wake up freaked out about how this accident would affect his looks. She'd consoled many patients more distraught about their appearance than surviving.

After the once over, she started out of the room. As she reached the door, the patient mumbled something she couldn't understand. Minnie turned around and moved beside the bed. "Mr. Dawson," she asked, "are you awake?"

Lying on his back, his eyes open and blinking, just above a whisper he spoke. "I could ask where I am, but that seems obvious, doesn't it? I'm in a hospital, right?"

"You are, Mr. Dawson. Lutheran Memorial in Dallas."

"Who're you?"

"I'm Minnie, your nurse today."

"What happened? Lots of things hurt." He closed his eyes. The burst of energy that accompanied his awakening faded.

"You were in an accident, a bad one from the look of your chart."

"How come I'm in Dallas? I was somewhere else. I can't remember where."

"Your chart says you were flown in from Tyler."

"I don't remember that."

"You suffered a concussion. You may not remember much for a while."

He moved his head and opened his mouth, but nothing came out.

"Look," she said, "don't talk right now. I'll take your vitals and let you rest. We can talk later, okay? The doctor who did your surgery will come by in about three hours."

She checked his temperature and recorded the blood pressure and pulse readings from the monitor to which he was attached. His numbers weren't great, but none created a cause for alarm. They were what she expected for a man who'd endured a traumatic accident and undergone three hours of surgery on multiple parts of his body. She finished her work and left.

At the nursing station, Martha handed Minnie a phone message slip. "That's a number for Dawson's mother. She called while you were in with him. She asked for his doctor or his nurse."

"Not much I can say, but somebody should call her back."

Martha took a deep breath, then released it before she spoke. "HIPPA sucks, doesn't it? He can't yet say who we can talk to and who we can't. But, here he is in a hospital a zillion miles from home and nobody can tell his mother what's really going on."

Minnie took the message slip and dialed on her cell phone. A woman answered on the first ring. "Is this the hospital?"

"Mrs. Dawson, this is Minnie Donaldson at Lutheran Memorial. I'm your son's nurse today. How can I help you?"

"Oh, thank God! Somebody I can talk to. How is John? How's my son? What happened to him? They just said accident when they called. Can you tell me anything?"

"Calm down, Mrs. Dawson. I can't tell you much until he gives us permission and he can't do that right now. I just checked on him. He's okay. He suffered some serious injuries, but he's okay."

In the woman's voice Minnie heard momentary relief, then apprehension. "Oh, thank you, Miss, did you say Donaldson? Is that your name?"

"Yes. Minnie Donaldson."

"Tell me what happened."

As she paced around the area near the desk, Minnie said, "Here at the hospital, we often don't get many accident details. All I can tell you is that he suffered multiple injuries in an automobile accident some distance from Dallas. He was flown in by helicopter and had surgery."

Minnie could feel Marion Dawson's growing exasperation. "What's wrong with him? What do you mean 'multiple injuries?'"

Minnie sighed and shrugged her shoulders. "I can't get into that. Are you coming to the hospital tonight? I understand you're out-of-state."

"His father and I are on our way. We're at the airport now. We'll be there in a few hours."

"You're coming from?"

"Wilmington, Delaware."

"When you get here, I imagine he'll be awake and can give us permission to tell you about his injuries and his condition."

Now Marion Dawson sounded angry. "I certainly hope so," she snapped.

"We'll take good care of him until you get here. Now I should go, Mrs. Dawson. Have a good flight."

Chapter 14

M artin and Marion Dawson remained in Dallas for 12 days
of John's hospital stay. Until his release from ICU
eight days after the accident, they got little time with him,
something which annoyed Marion and Martin took in stride.
Once John moved to a private room on a general floor,
his mother stayed with him almost continuously. Martin,
however, roamed the halls, watched game shows on television
in the visitor's lounge, and, in the cafeteria, read the Dallas
Morning News front to back.

In John's room, his mother soon wore out her welcome. On
his second day out of ICU, his 10th in the hospital, John told
Marion, "Mama, you and Dad should head home. I'm fine. The
doctors say this just takes time. There's no reason you should
stay."

"Nonsense, John," his mother replied, her chin held high.
"You need us here, especially me. And what about when you
get home? You'll really need me then, since you don't have a
wife or girlfriend who can take care of you."

John squashed the scream he almost unleashed in response
to the sexism in his mother's words. He said only, "I'll be here
two and a half more weeks. There's no reason you should stay
that long."

Standing by his bed, hands on hips, Marion asked, "Who
says?"

"Minnie, my nurse."

"She's not your nurse. She just works here. They have plenty
of other nurses. Is that what they say?"

"None of them say anything." His face no longer hurt as
much. Some bandages had been removed and others replaced

by smaller ones.

"You sure pay a lot of attention to her. What's the deal?"

"There's no deal. Minnie's just nice to me. She tells me what's going on. The other nurses – and the doctors – could care less if I know what's happening or what's going to happen."

Marion dragged her hand through her hair and said, "I still say you pay too much attention to her."

John ignored his mother's attempt at pulling Minnie into their drama. "Mama, please think about going home. If I need you when I get out of the hospital, we'll talk about your coming back."

"I don't understand. I just want to help you get well."

"If you do, you'll let me get some rest. Please, think about when you and Dad can go home."

He drifted off to sleep. The next day, John told his father he thought it time he and Marion headed home. Martin concurred. "Kicking and screaming" as Martin put it, John's mother acquiesced a day later.

$$\infty\infty\infty$$

Before the machinations with his mother, John started remembering what happened, including that the accident occurred as he returned from the Tyler trip and his visit with Bob Sawoski. While still in ICU he called Don Young and asked that he get the accident report and read him the official account. Don had it by the next day.

When they spoke by phone, John asked, through the pain in his chest, shoulder, and face, "How'd you get that so fast?"

"Connie Thyne, a young litigation partner, represents a TV station. One of their reporters got it for her."

"And it says?"

"You were going too fast, skidded off the road, careened into a ditch, ran up an embankment, and hit some trees."

"I wasn't going too fast," John said in a wavering voice. Bruises under his chin made talking hurt. "I was creeping along because of the damn fog. Does it even mention that?"

"Just says intermittent fog in the area."

John's nostrils flared. Talking might have been painful, but he had a point to make. "Intermittent, my ass. I couldn't see at all. Plus, there was a car coming at me in my lane. That's why I ran off the road, not because I was going too fast. Anything about another car in there?"

"No. Report admits the investigation is incomplete and that they haven't talked with you because of your injuries."

John's body tensed. He looked down at the cast on his broken left leg. "They damned sure haven't."

"No witnesses, no other evidence, but based on how hard it appeared you hit the ditch and the trees at the top of the embankment, the investigating officer concluded you were going too fast."

John felt his heart speed up. "That's bullshit!" His face hurt from the effort he put into the expletive.

"Settle down. Nothing will come of it. Nobody else got hurt. No charges out of this."

Don's calm didn't mollify the patient. "You know what that report could do to my insurance rates?" John asked.

"One of the firm's litigators can work on that. Quit worrying about it, okay? You have plenty of other things you can worry about."

"What about the car?"

"Totaled, it appears. I'm talking to your insurance company."

John cleared his throat. "Who found me?"

"A guy who lives up the hill from where you ran off the road. Name is Robert Easter. Said he heard something."

Despite the pain when he talked, John couldn't resist explaining, "I thought I saw a house out of the corner of my eye when I lost control of the car. Maybe it was his house. I should call and thank him. Anything in there about why they flew me over here?"

"No, but I called the Van Zandt County Sheriff's Office. They said the hospital in Tyler was full up on emergency patients. The paramedics felt you weren't in immediate danger and they saw on your ID that you live in Dallas. So, they took you by ambulance back to the Tyler airport and...."

"I wasn't more than five miles past there."

"They put you on a helicopter that was on site and ready to go."

"I get that. There was no fog at the airport." John breathed a sigh of relief. "Lucky me, I guess."

"Actually, you were. Your surgery took three hours."

"So Minnie told me."

"She's the nurse I talked with about you on the phone Saturday night, right?"

Mention of Minnie invigorated John and he spoke up, ignoring his pain. "Yeah, that's her. Middle-aged black woman. Real nice. Real nice. About the nicest one here, in fact. And the one who most seems like she knows what she's doing."

∞∞∞

Minnie didn't see John again until the Thursday of his first week in the hospital, one day after Don gave him the accident report details. She opened his door at 9:45 a.m. Her shift on the fourth floor started fifteen minutes later. She made a detour so she could check on her first ICU patient since her return to nursing work.

"How're you doing, Mr. Dawson?" she asked. She couldn't help looking at the monitors that displayed some of his vitals.

He looked up at her. His face, chest, and shoulder still hurt, though less than the last time he saw her. "I'm okay. Can I ask a favor?"

"Sure. What?"

Since he didn't feel as much pain, talking was now easier. Still, he mainly made his request of her with pleading eyes. "Please don't call me Mr. Dawson. The only Mr. Dawson I know is my father and he's 71 years old. I don't need that."

Minnie broke out a smile, then turned serious. "It's just a sign of respect, how I was raised. With people I don't know well or that I serve as a nurse, I use an honorific." "Makes me feel old," he managed to say.

"I'll call you by your first name." She paused and lightly touched his hand. "I'm not your nurse today, since I'm not working in ICU. Your blood pressure is down, now 130 over 68, which isn't bad. No fever, which you had a little of on the weekend. I'd say you're better, John."

∞∞∞

After eight days in the ICU, and Friday's surgery that repaired the torn anterior cruciate ligament in his right knee, doctors decided John could move to a regular patient floor. He wound up on four, where Minnie often worked.

"I was afraid I wouldn't see you anymore," John said, remembering the day she came by during that first week while he remained in ICU. Memories of Minnie's light touch warmed his insides. "I missed talking with you."

"Saying that is nice of you, John. I'm glad to see you again." She took his arm and checked his pulse.

"I guess I'll be here a while, right?" he asked, again feeling comforted by her presence and her touch.

"I'd say two and a half weeks, since you've been here a week and a half and you've been released from ICU."

"That long?" He closed his eyes and hung his head. She nodded. "I've seen these injuries many times."

John heard experience and authority in her voice. He looked up. "How long have you been a nurse?"

"Since finishing college, with a few years off for having children." Suddenly, a big grin appeared on Minnie's face. She asked him, "Is that a back door way of asking how old I am? A gentleman ought not ask a lady her age."

Smiles remained hard for John because of the cuts and bruises on his face, but he could now return a little of her grin. "That's something my mother – and my dad – would say. They're old school, through and through."

"I met your parents briefly that first Saturday night you were here. Lovely people. They're proud of you."

"I bet Mama bragged on every report card I ever got."

Minnie finished the pulse check and put down his arm. Standing with hands on hips, she said, "Not quite, but she told me you graduated summa cum laude from Brown University and number one in your class at Penn Law School."

"That just means I have the capacity for being anal."

"Perhaps. Could mean you're real smart."

"Maybe."

"Anyway, it's 33 years, so 55 answers your real question."

When Minnie walked into her kitchen Thursday, her last work day of the week, her cell phone rang. Mark Gibson, the caller ID said.

"Hello, Mark. I was just thinking about you today. You beat me to the punch." 'Today' was a little white lie, though she had put calling him on the list of things she should do soon.

"Great minds think alike, and all that, I suppose. How are you, Minnie?"

"Really good, Mark. How've you been?"

"Pretty good. Might we get together soon?"

His directness put her off. Couldn't he have asked how her return to work was going? He knew about that, of course, since she'd given him that reason for delaying a meeting when he called the first time. Couldn't he have asked what had happened in her life since they last talked? "I suppose we could," she said, barely disguising her disappointment with his approach.

"I'm free tomorrow, Friday. Let's meet for a drink at five o'clock."

Again, she found his directness annoying. He didn't ask what her schedule looked like for, say, the next week or so. "I can't before next week. I worked on the past weekend, as well as my regular Tuesday, Wednesday, and Thursday shifts. I need recuperation."

She sensed irritation in his response. "That's unfortunate. But, it is what it is. What day next week works for you?"

"How about next Friday, the 27th? I should be in good shape by then."

"We'll meet at Darby's on Central Expressway."

His reply sounded like a command, not an invitation. Still, she said, "That's fine. I'll meet you there. Next Friday."

Unlike the anticipation that swept through her after their

first conversation, Minnie now felt uninspired by the prospect of seeing Mark Gibson. His pushiness about the date and place of their meeting dampened her enthusiasm. Couldn't he have asked her what places she liked?

Minnie reminded herself today was about arrangements. If anything came of this, they'd develop a rhythm regarding such things. This October Thursday marked a milestone. After a year of celibate widowhood, Minnie Donaldson had a date.

PART III

Chapter 15

October 2017

A few days after John's parents headed home, Kate Hart visited him. Initially, her presence made him uncomfortable. It revived his disappointment that a relationship with her couldn't happen. Still, he appreciated the gesture.

"I'm getting punchy in here," he said after she sat in the chair beside his bed. "Seeing a familiar face is nice." It was almost six thirty on a Friday afternoon. She'd come dressed in work clothes – dark slacks, a light top, and a bright blue scarf tied at her neck. She was tall and thin with soft facial features and active blue eyes. He still found her maddeningly attractive but put out of his mind thoughts of ever kissing her lips or stroking her body.

"I can't imagine what being in here is like," she said. "Resembles prison, I guess. Don Young told me you might have another week or two."

John looked her over. He'd never made much of her short haircut. Now, though he wouldn't call it butch, it reminded him she was gay. "That's the story I get. I start rehab soon, which will give me something I can do besides wishing I was somewhere else."

Her eyes darted around the room. "How're they treating you here? Do you feel taken care of?"

He frowned. "It's a mixed bag. My doctors are okay. They're doctors. Some nurses I can take or leave." Then his eyes brightened. "There is one real nice nurse, Minnie, who takes my mind off how isolated I feel. We've had long, involved talks. She even came by at the end of her shift last night so we could finish a conversation we started but broke off while she saw other patients. That was nice."

"What do you talk about with her?"

"The world. Life. Stuff."

"Anybody else from the office been here?"

"Don, of course. Ed Ward called today and said he'd come by tomorrow, which is Saturday, right?"

"Yes, it is. You'll see more people soon. We now know you're out of ICU and can have visitors. Maggie Brandt said she'd call next week about stopping by."

John gave a thumbs up. "She and I can talk politics."

Kate nodded. "That's Maggie's thing, isn't it? She's freaked out about Trump. I don't care much for him either, but Maggie is obsessed."

"What's going on in the section?"

For 20 minutes, Kate covered the work VWM corporate lawyers had been doing and who was handling projects John normally would have been assigned. She wound up by saying, "I hope you're not worried that we don't need you. We're getting by, but everybody – senior partners, junior partners, associates, your classmates – wants you back as soon as possible. We're stretched thin."

He smiled carefully. A few small bandages remained on his face, but most of the pain there had gone away. "I've been worried about that. You know, out of sight, out of mind."

She shook her head. "Don't spend any time thinking about that."

He rolled his eyes upward. "That's good news."

Kate stood up and moved around the room. She said nothing for a few moments. He looked at her playfully. "What?"

She dug her hands into the pockets of her slacks and rocked back and forth on the balls of her feet. "I'll tell you one other thing while I'm here."

"And that is?"

"There's someone I'd like you to meet once you get back in, shall we say, circulation."

His eyes widened and he sucked in a breath. "Oh? You're fixing me up?"

Her eyes glowing, she stepped nearer the bed and leaned toward him. "You could call it that."

John realized he should say that he knew about her. "Taking pity on a straight guy who has nobody he can date?"

She flopped back into the chair. John read that action and her expression as relief that the issue had come out in the open. "So you know?"

"I saw you at the coffee bar in the building lobby the day before my accident," he explained. "I could tell you have something going."

"Her name is Mary Ellis. She made me come out as I hadn't before. She said she'd leave me if I tried hiding our relationship. I decided I preferred letting the world see who I am to ending things with her."

John slightly parted his lips. "Who in the firm knows?"

"Now, a lot of people. For a long time, only Maggie Brandt."

"Why her?"

"I knew she wouldn't judge."

He wrinkled his nose. "How are people taking it?"

"Maggie and a few others are supportive. There's a silent group. I can't tell who doesn't care and who thinks I'll burn in hell but won't say so."

"Worried about the partners?"

She twisted her neck and fiddled with a ring on her right hand. "A little. It's a very conservative place, but I'd hope they're not so stupid they'd deny me partnership over this."

"Would you sue them?"

Kate laughed loudly. "Heavens no. There are a lot better ways of making their lives miserable than that. Think about it, John. You were number one in your class at Penn. Figure it out."

A topic for after she leaves, John told himself. He changed the subject. "Tell me about the person you want me to meet."

Kate shifted to explanation mode, making John believe she appreciated putting aside the topic of her sexual orientation. "Her name is Jody Lawrence. She's an intellectual property lawyer at Morgan & Williams. Harvard Law School. University of Georgia undergraduate. From a little town near Knoxville, Tennessee. Very nice person."

His instincts said he should sit up and show her he was listening, but his shoulder pain and leg casts still limited his movements. "How do you know her?"

"We're in a business women's group together – a networking thing."

John saw Kate's offer as a hopeful development, but he remained wary. "What makes you believe she'd have any interest in me?"

"She's lonely as hell. We go out for drinks regularly. She finds most men she meets superficial and only concerned with getting into her pants."

John felt his skin tingle. "She said that?"

"In more graphic terms, yes. She's a serious person who can still have fun. She strikes me as your type – and you as hers."

He looked around at the yellow walls. For some reason, he noticed for the first time most of the monitoring equipment he'd had in his ICU room wasn't in this room. "Does she know I'm laid up for another few weeks, then who knows how much rehab before I'm a normal human being again?"

"No, but she will."

"You'll tell her?"

"I will. Once you're on your feet, she'll check you out."

John bit his lip. Inside, calm settled over him. "You have my blessing, Kate. I need all the help I can get right now."

She smiled at him again. "I have your back. By the way, I'm aware of your crush on me."

John gasped. "You couldn't be. I never said anything."

By now Kate stood near the door, her wallet and keys in hand. "I took three interpersonal communication classes in college. Every one included something about non-verbal behavior. I saw it written all over you. Now that you know I'm gay, I'm sure the crush goes away. You're very rational. You won't fixate indefinitely on something that can't happen. You'll move on. You should meet Jody and see what happens with her." She walked out of the room.

∞∞∞

Over the next week, John reveled in a steady stream of visitors. Ed Ward, as promised, showed up at ten o'clock the morning after Kate's visit. He appeared with Kevin Monroe in tow.

"We were working at one of Ed's apartment buildings," Kevin explained. "He asked if I wanted to tag along. I said of course. It's good to see you, man."

"Thanks for coming, Kevin," John said, squeezing his eyes shut. "This is a nice surprise."

"I knew you guys had been getting to know each other," Ward said and pointed at Monroe, then John. "It seemed a shame that I'd come here without him."

The three men chatted for 10 minutes about John's accident, his hospital experience, and the prognosis. Kevin excused himself for a call. Ward used the private time for putting John's mind at ease about his status at the law firm. "I hope you're not lying here moping about billable hours, your bonus, or anything else about your job."

"You must have talked with Kate."

"She called this morning and warned me you were freaking out, as she put it, about such things."

John swallowed a couple of times. "I confess. I did that, a little."

In a quiet, firm voice, and with his shoulders thrown back, Ward said, "Take it from me, you're good. All the corporate partners want you well, so you come back better than ever. Don't rush and don't worry. Your spot is secure and you'll have plenty of work when you return."

Ignoring his shoulder pain for a moment, John waved his right hand through the air. "It might be another two weeks before I get out of here, then rehab."

"So Don Young told me. That doesn't change anything I said."

"I doubt I can come back immediately after I get out of the hospital."

The older man's tone turned matter-of-fact. "I wouldn't think you could."

"The doctors tell me very little. I have one nurse who's been at this for thirty years and has seen injuries like mine a zillion times. She says it's almost always four weeks."

Ward held up both hands, palms out. "Don't worry. I have plenty of say about this kind of thing. Anybody who plans on screwing you, goes through me. Okay?"

John nodded, just at the moment Kevin returned. For a half hour they talked baseball, football, and golf, which Kevin had taken up recently. Ward and Monroe left with John cheered up by the conversation and feeling better about his situation at the firm. As he settled down with *An Unquenchable Thirst*, the memoir of a former nun in Mother Teresa's order, the thought of an introduction to Kate Hart's friend scampered across his mind. To his surprise, it didn't make him giddy.

∞ ∞ ∞

All week before her Friday date with Mark Gibson, Minnie subbed on the third floor for a nurse on vacation, leaving her fatigued and out of sorts. To make matters worse, she did her all day shift – 12 hours – on Thursday, not Wednesday. Nevertheless, when the workday ended at seven o'clock she stopped by John's fourth floor room. Ostensibly, she wanted to ask about a medication he'd start soon. Maybe, she just wanted to see him.

John had a visitor who was leaving when Minnie arrived. "A girlfriend?" she inquired after the woman's exit. On the way home, Minnie wondered what made her ask that. She tried, with little success, forgetting how an affirmative answer would have bothered her.

"Oh, no," he said. "A colleague, Maggie Brandt, a lawyer who's several years ahead of me at the firm. I go see her for two reasons – when I have a shareholder equity question and so I can commiserate with another Democrat amidst all the Republicans in the firm."

Minnie and John had briefly discussed politics a few days before, so his statement didn't surprise her. She responded in kind. "I need that here sometimes, too. The nurses are about evenly split, but nearly all the doctors and administrators live on the dark side."

He blinked his eyes. "You aren't on duty, are you? You usually finish up about this time."

"I came by so I could see if you got started on the

medication you told me they plan on giving you. I'm making sure you take it because I know it helps heal multiple injuries like you've had."

"My nurse today said I'll start it tomorrow."

Hands on hips, Minnie asked, "Who was that?"

"Brittany Evans, I think."

Minnie motioned toward the door. "I saw her when I came in, so she's still here. I'll ask her about it on my way out."

He pressed a forefinger against his lips. "Thank you. I really appreciate how you check on things for me."

"Part of being a good nurse."

"Are you done for the week? I usually don't see you except on Tuesday, Wednesday, and Thursday."

What did it mean that he'd memorized her schedule? "Yes, done for the week. I'm back Tuesday morning. I should be on this floor."

"Got a big weekend planned?"

She pondered for weeks why she responded as she did. Instead of politely telling him she couldn't talk about her personal plans, she offered an evasive, incomplete answer. "I'm going out, for a change."

"Oh?"

"It's a long story. Maybe I'll tell you about it someday. I just hope I can have some decent conversation." Then she added, "You know, the way you and I do."

Looking at him from the end of the bed, Minnie saw John's lips press together. She sensed his injured shoulders droop as he said, "That would be nice."

Minnie left John's room with two questions. Hadn't she seen and heard disappointment in his final words and body language? Why did she say the things that must have provoked those reactions, especially the 'the way you and I do' comment about their conversations? Though she thought frequently about both questions during the next five days, she walled off her mind and heart from the answers she saw lurking in the shadows.

Chapter 16

D arby's sat amidst a cluster of restaurants, retail shops, and convenience stores just east of Central Expressway, a mile south of I-635, the LBJ Freeway. Since Minnie hadn't worked that Friday and was coming from home, she had only a 20-minute drive, even in afternoon traffic.

She found herself annoyed as she parked in front of a gray building trimmed in red. She remained peeved that Mark Gibson hadn't asked her preferences on place or time for their first meeting. She was as displeased with herself she hadn't expressed her feelings.

Because of social media and his company's website, Minnie now knew what Mark Gibson looked like. Photos suggested his medium brown skin matched hers. He's lighter than Crystal but darker than Sandra, Minnie thought when she saw the pictures. He was average height and medium build. His features seemed modest – an ordinary sized nose as black men went, lips on the thinner side, brown eyes covered by long, thick lashes, but modest eyebrows. From photos, he qualified as a handsome man.

She didn't find much personal background information. He earned a business degree from North Texas State in 1987, likely making him 52 or 53. He hadn't been in the military as far as she could find. He'd spent much of his professional life in commercial real estate, but now was Senior Vice President for Business Development and Community Relations for an auto leasing company. She hadn't found marital or other family history.

From her table beside a window overlooking the parking lot, she saw a brown-skinned man with short hair, dressed in a khaki suit, white shirt, and a brown tie get out of a late model

American car and stride into the restaurant. She was confident she was looking at Mark Gibson.

Minnie had left her name with the hostess, who now directed toward her table the man she saw get out of that car. She rose and extended her hand. "Mark, I'm Minnie Donaldson."

"Minnie Donaldson! It's so good to meet you!" he exclaimed loudly as he shook her hand. "Carol didn't lie! You're a very attractive woman!"

Minnie looked around. A few people at other tables glanced up, but mostly they paid the scene no mind. I hope it stays that way, she thought. He lays it on thick.

They sat across the table from each other. Minnie wished she'd taken the booth she'd been offered, putting him farther away from her and hiding him from other patrons. "Have you been here long?" he asked. He looked at his watch. "Yes, it's half past five. That's what we said, wasn't it?"

"That was in your text yesterday," Minnie said, reminding him he'd set the time, not her. "I've been here five minutes." She tapped her fingers on the white table cloth. "You're fine."

He rubbed his hands together and looked around for a waitperson. "Have you ordered? Let me get us somebody." He lifted an arm, snapped his fingers, and waved at a woman across the room. "Can we get some service over here? Miss? Some service, please." Minnie grimaced and dropped her head. She rubbed the back of her neck.

A server hurried over and took drink orders – white wine for Minnie, Scotch and soda for him.

"It's so nice I can finally put a face with the name. Minnie Donaldson. Minnie Donaldson. Carol talks about you all the time. I just couldn't wait to meet you. Tell me how you've been."

"I've been fine, Mark. As you know, I'm just getting back to work and – "

"Oh, yes. You did tell me about that, right? I wondered about that. You know, if I could retire early, I'd never think about working again. You must be really dedicated to your profession."

"I hope it wasn't just about the money. Based on where you live, I know you must be doing well, or somebody was. Your husband died, didn't he? I guess he took care of you, right?"

Minnie's eyes went cold. Inside her comfortable flats, her toes curled. She was not hearing what she thought she was hearing. "Yes, Mark, my husband is deceased. I work by choice and I enjoy it."

"That's great. Nursing is really important, a great profession. I have an aunt who's a nurse in Cleveland. Don't know her well. My dad's younger sister. I think she's nearing retirement. She's not much older than you, I'd think. I've met her only once."

The pale, middle-aged, red-headed server arrived with the drinks. Her annoyed expression screamed how much she dreaded waiting on this table. "Do you want to run a tab?" she asked.

"I'm here only long enough for one," Minnie said, as much sending Mark a message as answering the question. "I'll pay for mine now," she said, digging a $20 bill out of her wallet.

"Oh, we'll be here long enough for more than one," Mark almost yelled. "I've got it. Let me give you a credit card."

"I have a big golf day tomorrow," Minnie told him, pointedly leaving the $20 on the table. "I can't stay out long tonight."

"Oh, you can have a couple," he replied through a loud laugh.

"I'm getting ready for a tournament, and I have a playing lesson with my pro tomorrow. So, no, I won't be staying out late tonight. I never drink much before a tournament or taking a playing lesson."

A pained expression took over Gibson's face. "Carol told me you're really into golf. Never could see much in that sport myself. Chasing a little white ball around seems kind of, well, I don't know, pointless. To each his own, I suppose."

Minnie bit her lip and didn't comment, but asked, "So, what do you do for fun? Is there a sport you're into?"

He shook his head while taking a swallow from his drink. "Not much on sports – playing or watching. Played a little basketball in high school. I gave that up a long time ago. I play cards."

"Oh?" A thought flickered in Minnie's mind that perhaps the man wasn't hopeless. "You wouldn't play bridge would you?"

"Naw. White folks game. Not my thing." He stopped when he saw her stare. In a weakened voice, he said, "I guess you play or you wouldn't have asked, right?"

He's at least capable of seeing that he stepped in it, Minnie thought. "I play. I have many black friends who play. We rather enjoy it."

He lowered his head and raised open palms. "Didn't mean any offense. Just hasn't been part of my life."

She didn't respond, but asked herself what she ever did that made Carol think she'd go for this man. Did she believe she could send her any man as long as he had black skin? She tried another tack. "So, you must tell me about yourself, what you've been doing all these years."

"I'm glad to. But only if you promise you'll do the same. I really want to hear the Minnie Donaldson story."

Mendacity, Minnie thought, comes in many forms. She couldn't imagine a more untrue statement than the one Mark Gibson just made. She knew hearing about somebody else's life was the last thing that would interest this man.

On her way home, after that one glass of wine and sitting through Mark's boring, long-winded, and uninspiring exposé on himself, Minnie debated whether she should tell Carol how bad an evening she had. Did Carol have so little understanding of her needs she'd think she'd have any interest in spending time with such a boorish man? Minnie's leg muscles quivered and she ground her teeth.

She reached home and calmed down. After several deep breaths, she decided Carol might not have seen Mark's selfcentered, overbearing side. They became acquainted while serving together on a charity board. Minnie figured Mark held his seat because his company, probably one of the charity's major donors, put him there.

She bet he handled tasks the firm's top executives didn't want, like sitting on charity boards. Perhaps that's one thing the Senior Vice President for Business Development and Community Relations did. Minnie realized Carol's knowledge of Mark Gibson may have come only from attending board meetings with him.

That reminded Minnie that despite how disappointed she was, she hadn't shut the door on seeing him again. *Maybe I owe Carol giving him more than one shot*, she thought when he said he'd call next week and she didn't tell him he shouldn't bother. I can't blow him off after one drink on a Friday afternoon when I have so many things on my mind. He's a physically attractive man. Maybe he'll act differently next time.

∞ ∞ ∞

John's last week in the hospital before his first rehab stint began Saturday, October 29, the weekend Minnie told him she was going 'out.' He had no idea what she meant and he kept telling himself it didn't matter. She was just his nurse. Still, he fretted until he saw her Tuesday morning, November 1.

"Hey! You're on my floor," he said when she entered his room. "This is my lucky day."

"You should stop that," she said through a playful grin. "People will think things. Then they'll say things. We can't have that, can we?" His facial pain gone, he matched her smile.

She got to business. "Let's check your vitals." She grabbed his wrist and felt his pulse.

For the first time he noticed the sleek, muscular tone of her arms. This woman had spent serious time in a gym. "I'm just glad I can see you. I'm bored. I can read only so many books."

After putting down his arm, she looked at the stacks on the stands beside the bed. "What do you have there?"

"I just finished Mary Johnson's *An Unquenchable Thirst.* I'm starting *Balance of Power,* a novel by Richard North Patterson."

She recorded the reading from the blood pressure monitor. His numbers now reflected what she'd expect in a healthy, 27-year-old man. "The book you just finished – what's it about?"

He reached over and held up his copy of *Thirst.* "A nun who spent 20 years in Mother Teresa's order, the Missionaries of Charity, then quit."

"Interesting. So it's nonfiction?"

"Yeah, a memoir. It was good." He opened the book, then closed it quickly. "Could have been 150 pages shorter and no worse for the wear."

Those words provoked a bemused smile. "I notice something about you, John. I wonder if anybody else has ever said what I'm gonna say."

"What's that?"

Minnie raised her eyebrows. "You speak like a person much older than you are."

"What do you mean?"

"Well, like what you just said about the book being no worse for the wear if it had been shorter. That's something people my age – people in their fifties – say. My parents might have said that."

With a wavering smile, he responded, "I don't know. I spent a lot of time with older people when I was growing up."

She nodded slowly. "What was that about?"

He shifted in the bed, as if trying to shrug his still injured shoulders. "I gravitated to older people – adults and more mature teenagers. Kids my age did stupid things. Most didn't say anything worthwhile."

"When did you become aware you preferred older people?"

"In high school. By my sophomore year many of the guys, and some of the women, I knew best had left for college or the military. They were as much as five years older. After that, I started hanging out with guys in their 30s and 40s who worked at the bowling alley or at this garage not far from school."

She looked at her watch. "I have to get on with the day. I'll come back and we'll talk about your stacks of books. I'm intrigued. I pick next for my book club. I may find an idea or two in there."

∞∞∞∞

As promised, Minnie stopped in John's room when her shift ended at three o'clock. He immediately asked about her book club.

"It's no big deal," she replied. "Nine women who meet once

a quarter, drink wine, have dinner, and talk about a book we've all read. We rotate selections, so each person picks a book once every two years or so."

"How long has the group been in existence?"

Standing beside John's bed, she said, "Sixteen years. I started it along with my friend Christine Boyd, partly as a way of encouraging interaction between black women and white women."

He raised his eyebrows. "She's white?"

"She is. We met through a professional women's group. She knew almost no black women and thought she should change that. So, we formed the book club. It's now five white women and four black women. That's been stable for ten years."

"No men?"

"Christine and I wanted a women's group. We're proud of how it's worked out." A pained expression appeared on Minnie's face. "I tried getting my husband into a couples book club I'd been invited to join. He wouldn't hear of it."

John scratched his jaw and stared at Minnie. "Why the hell not?"

"That's a long story, John, which I'll tell you when we have way more time than we do now. Let me see what you're reading, but then I should get home."

"I have a dozen books here, brought in or sent by friends and family," he said, licking his lips and smiling. "What's your pleasure? Fiction? Nonfiction? Mystery? Crime stories? Politics? Memoir? It seems I have some of everything."

He handed her four books and she shuffled through them. She said, "You told me about this one – Mary Johnson's *An Unquenchable Thirst*. Oh, and here's something by Richard North Patterson. I've read things by him. He's good. This title doesn't sound like what you mentioned this morning."

John shook his head. "It's not. This is *Exile*, a novel about the Arab-Israeli conflict. The book I mentioned is *Balance of Power*, which I started today."

She held up another book. "I should've read this a long time ago but, believe it or not, I haven't."

"Ralph Ellison's *Invisible Man*." He grinned. "I read at it in college. This time I'm paying attention."

She tapped her chest. "I should consider it for the book club. I hear it's something blacks and whites should read."

"I'm half through it and I'd say that's right."

"Sounds like you read more than one book at a time."

"I'm afraid so. Sometimes I just can't resist starting something that's intriguing, even if I'm not done with what I've already started."

She shuffled her feet. "I've been guilty of that."

He tilted his head away from her. "What's the last book you picked for the group?"

Now she stood still, silent for a moment. "It was two years ago. Oh, how could I forget? I know. *The Winds of War* by Herman Wouk. When I assigned it, people whined about the length, 885 pages or so. Afterwards, most said they found it absorbing and appreciated how much they learned about the lead up to World War II."

"How about the sequel?"

"*War and Remembrance*? I finally finished it last year. It's great too. I saw the TV movie years ago. As usual, the book was better."

They continued going through the books. She called a halt when she said, "I must get home. My landscaper arrives at four thirty and I can't be late."

"Get any ideas?"

Minnie smoothed the top of her green scrubs and said slowly, "I did. What I liked was talking with someone – a man even – who reads. That's a treat."

Chapter 17

"**I** know someone you should meet," Dawn Brooks told Minnie as they walked together out the hospital door five days after Minnie's unsatisfying date with Mark Gibson.

"A man, I presume?" Minnie asked, looking into the brown eyes of the dark-skinned nurse she'd known for 20 of the years she'd worked at Lutheran Memorial. Dawn was five years younger, but they weighed the same and each stood five feet, ten-inches tall. When they weren't wearing nursing garb, Dawn bragged on her larger breasts by showing more cleavage than Minnie ever would.

Dawn always wanted the best for her friends. That goal undoubtedly lay behind her fix up Minnie effort. She constantly asked Minnie how she was doing after Bradley's death. Minnie never told her how much she'd soured on her late husband or the things she learned about him after he died.

Dawn had survived a lot herself – a bad marriage, the death of a beloved spouse, and raising three children without much help. Minnie thought of her as being as good a friend as she had and especially valued her honesty, sincerity, and compassion for people.

"Yes, a man," Dawn confirmed, while they matched strides across the parking lot in the gathering darkness of a pleasant fall evening. "I know you have a lot of gay friends, but you don't really believe I'd try setting you up with a woman, do you?"

Minnie frowned as they neared her car. She said calmly, "I didn't think that. Who is he?"

"Clifford Nguyen."

"Asian guy?"

"Vietnamese-American. So, yes, an Asian guy. Vietnamese mother. His father was a black U.S. serviceman."

"Why do you think I'd be interested in him?" As the words left her mouth, Minnie wished she could reach out and pull them back.

Dawn gasped. "That's a little harsh isn't it?"

Minnie dropped her chin before she looked up and said, "I didn't mean that the way it sounded. I'm asking what he's about, not dissing his heritage."

"So you'd be interested in meeting him?"

"I didn't say that. Just tell me who he is. A doctor? Does he work at the hospital? I don't know some people here since taking a year off. How old is he? How do you know him? Stuff like that."

They reached Minnie's car. "Hold on," Dawn said. "I'll tell you about him if you'll keep quiet for a few moments."

Minnie looked at her watch. She'd planned a night of golf practice at the driving range. This Wednesday had been her long work day. Young, arrogant doctors tried her patience. At the moment, taking out her frustration on a bucket of balls held a lot of appeal. "I have five minutes. Give me the short version. If I'm intrigued, we can talk more later. How's that?"

Dawn moved her head side to side. "It'll have to do."

Minnie ignored her friend's irritation. "I'm listening."

Returning home from the range that night, Minnie reflected on what Dawn told her about Clifford Nguyen. After a year alone, could she suddenly have two suitors? Clifford sounded good, but Mark Gibson had sounded good.

According to Dawn, Clifford was 50 years old, having been

born in 1967 in Vietnam. She wasn't sure when or how he got to the United States. He was a civil engineer now who supervised big construction projects, often overseas. He'd been married to a Vietnamese woman, but divorced her 10 or 15 years ago. Dawn thought he had one or two children. He moved to Dallas six months ago because his company, based in Houston, opened an office in the mid-cities. She described him as intelligent, well spoken, and kind. They sang together in a community choir.

Lots of gaps in there, Minnie thought as she pulled into her garage. She had part of a résumé, but little else. She liked what she found about Mark Gibson through her sleuthing, but she didn't discover his boorishness.

Her experience so far with Mark made her fear another disappointment. She stopped. Wait! That wasn't fair. She hadn't met Clifford. *Don't pass judgment without information*, she told herself.

Inside the house, she sat down at her computer and sent Dawn an e-mail that said she'd welcome hearing more about Clifford Nguyen. She wrote that she certainly didn't see meeting him as "out of the question."

Without waiting for a reply, she shut down the computer and started for the shower. As she did so, she wondered what she should do about Mark Gibson. She hadn't told him she wouldn't see him again. Maybe she should take the initiative. He'd redeem himself or she'd ditch him.

Back at the computer, Minnie sent Mark an e-mail asking if he'd accompany her to an art exhibit Saturday afternoon. She suspected art exhibits weren't his thing. He might decline, confirming her suspicion this wasn't going anywhere. If he accepted, she took consolation that the exhibit ran only two hours. Bailing if he acted out wouldn't pose much of a problem. She pointedly didn't make dinner a part of the invitation. If he behaved, she could add that. If not, she'd spend her evening doing something else, without him.

∞∞∞

Mark Gibson arrived at Minnie's house at 1:43 p.m. Saturday. She'd planned a one thirty departure for the exhibit, a showing of pieces by two young women Carol Robbins befriended several years ago while they studied art at the University of Texas. Both graduated and now held full-time jobs, but painted in their spare time.

Carol promised she'd help them get their art careers off the ground. She used her network of social and business contacts in assuring that today they'd have a sizeable audience. She secured the location, a community museum ordinarily out of the two young women's price range.

The Carol connection helped Minnie see the exhibit as an ideal second date with Mark Gibson. Minnie could let her know she was seeing him while she paid her respects to the young artists. She'd have her checkbook close at hand. What Minnie didn't know was how incensed at Mark Gibson, she'd find herself by the time she saw Carol that afternoon.

Minnie controlled her irritation with his tardiness. Thirteen minutes late wasn't a mortal sin, just a sign of disorganization and insensitivity. He hadn't called and warned her he was running late.

"I'm sorry," he said when she answered the door. Above gray slacks he wore a dark blue blazer and an open-collar white shirt. "I underestimated how long getting here would take."

Minnie forced a smile. "The world won't end if we don't get there exactly when it starts."

"I'm glad you see it that way. Shit happens."

Dressed in a beige top, dark slacks, and comfortable flats, Minnie ignored the expletive for the moment. She had no moral scruples about profanity and wasn't beyond using a little of it herself. But she saw four-letter words as appropriate only at particular times, like during and in connection with sex, while playing golf, or in the company of people with whom she'd informally established ground rules for what was okay and what wasn't. Right now, terms like 'shit happens' didn't fit her sputtering acquaintance with Mark Gibson.

"Let's take my car," Minnie said, standing in her front doorway. "I know where we're going."

"Good with me," he replied. "Can you get out?"

"Sure. You parked behind the car I don't use much. I kept my husband's car as a backup. I'm on the other side. I'll get my keys. Meet me at the garage."

After retrieving her keys and handbag from the kitchen counter, Minnie opened the inner garage door, then pressed the button that raised the outside overhead door. Uncertainty nagged at her. She'd missed something. Mark walked into the garage, opened the car door, and settled into the passenger seat.

Minnie slipped into the driver's seat, buckled her seat belt, and started the engine, bringing to life the air conditioning and the radio. Then she remembered what she'd missed. "Oops! I forgot the tickets. They're on the kitchen table. I'll be right back." Minnie opened the car door and left it that way while she collected the tickets. She heard Johnny Lee's *Looking for Love* coming from the radio.

Back in less than a minute, Minnie closed the car door, again buckled her seat belt, backed out the driveway, and started down the street.

"What in the world are you listening to?" Mark asked, as *Goodhearted Woman* by Willie Nelson and Waylon Jennings now blared from the radio.

She held her chin high. "That is KJKK-FM 100.3, Dallas Ft.

Worth's country oldies station. They call it "Classic Country."

Minnie felt Mark go still in the seat beside her. She sensed his eyes boring in on her. She didn't look at him, but felt his contempt. It filled the car. When he spoke, his tone turned scathing. "You listen to that country shit? You didn't just accidentally leave the radio tuned there?"

"I listen all the time. It's what I usually have on in the car."

He said nothing for a moment as the tension built. Finally, he spat out, "I never met a sister who liked that shit."

Only intense self-discipline kept Minnie from stopping, turning around, and depositing Mark Gibson back where he'd parked his car. Having no interest in looking at him, she kept her eyes fixed on the road.

She finally said, "I assume you're suggesting you don't know black women who listen to and enjoy country music. I find that insulting and condescending, as well as inaccurate. I'm good friends with several black women who enjoy country music. Even if I didn't know them, I'd listen and enjoy it myself, no matter what other black women do."

His voice rose as he said, "I'm sorry you're offended, but I'm blown away. Country is for rednecks and hillbillies. Black people don't need that shit. It's like you're sleeping with the enemy."

Minnie took several deep breaths. With cold resolve she said, "I'm not discussing this further with you, Mark. I enjoy many kinds of music, including, no, especially, country music. That is my choice. I don't appreciate being told that my musical tastes have some racial identity implication. For the rest of our time together today, let's focus on other things."

Minnie largely ignored him during the exhibit. She brushed off his attempts at engaging her. When she saw Carol, the artists and potential buyers surrounded her friend. From a distance, Minnie held up her checkbook, signaling that she'd bought something. She waved and mouthed, "Thanks for the invite. I'll give you a call."

"I'm glad you brought Mark," Carol shouted over the din.

"We'll talk," Minnie replied loudly, sliding toward the door. She wondered if from as far apart as they were, Carol could sense the chill Minnie felt at being near Mark Gibson.

At home, she stopped at the end of the driveway, unlocked the car doors, and announced she had places to go and things to do. To Mark's plea that they "go somewhere, have a drink, and talk things out" she said only, "I have nothing to discuss with you. Please let me get on with my errands." He got out of the car and she drove away.

Chapter 18

It was just after midnight when Minnie opened John's hospital room door and found him awake, reading a book titled What's the Matter with Kansas? "What in the world is that about?" she asked. "And why are you still awake? You should rest."

John laid the book across his middle. "I could ask what you're doing here at this hour," he said, looking up at her. "I thought you work during the daytime."

"Normally, that's right. My supervisor begged me to take this one graveyard shift. She has nurses out sick and several who have other problems that make people miss work."

"I like seeing you, day or night."

"That's kind of you. Let's check your pulse," she said, taking his wrist. She looked again at the book. "That's a strange title. What's it about?"

"The subtitle – How Conservatives Won the Heart of America — really explains it. It's about how Republicans get poor and middle class white people to vote for them, against their economic interests."

"And how do they do that?"

"By riling them up about social issues like guns and abortion and stoking their prejudices against black and brown people. I'm only half through, but that's the gist so far."

Minnie pulled a pocket-sized spiral-bound notebook from her scrubs and wrote down the title. "I should read that. Once again, John, it looks like you've given me a great book suggestion."

He released a short burst of laughter. "So you're reading other things I told you about?"

"I assigned our book club *Invisible Man*. I ordered *Exile*, the Richard North Patterson novel about the Middle East you mentioned."

He shook his head. "You should give me suggestions. I bet you've read interesting things I've never thought of."

After scratching her left ear, then holding up an index finger, she said, "I have one for you, a novel by Ann Patchett. She's a New York *Times* bestselling author. *Bel Canto* is based on a true story. I found it compelling."

"*Bel Canto?*"

"It's about a hostage taking in South America. I won't spoil it for you, but I sense you like stories about different kinds of people. That's some of the appeal of that book." She wrote out the title and author on another page from the notebook, tore it out, and handed it to him.

She sensed him looking intently at her as she stood at the middle of his bed. She wore gray scrubs with her medium length hair pulled back and tied behind her head. As usual, she'd left off the makeup. "How've you been?" he asked. "And how did you get hooked into working at this dastardly hour?"

"I learned a long time ago that on a hospital staff you will need favors. That means you'd better do some for other people. Not much different than life in general, I suppose. My supervisor needed somebody who'd cover this shift. I said I'd do it. We both know it's a favor I'll need returned sometime."

He took another shot at his first question. "And how have you been? Anything big going on?"

"I've been fine, and no, nothing big has been going on." That, of course, wasn't true. Mark Gibson had happened the previous Saturday. She wanted to tell him that tale, but she thought it something she shouldn't discuss with a patient, even one with whom she'd developed the easy rapport that now existed between them. Maybe, when she wasn't his nurse and he wasn't her patient, she could tell him that story. Would such a day come? For reasons she didn't understand, she hoped so.

"I heard I may get out of here next week," John said, apparently satisfied with her dodge about what had been going on in her life.

"Sounds right."

"Dr. McCall said next Thursday or Friday."

"How's rehab going?"

He pinched his lips together in frustration. "I don't know. I'm not sure it's doing me any good. They're still teaching me the exercises. With two bad legs, I can't do all the stuff they want."

She formed a steeple by touching her fingertips together. "That will get better. I know it will. When's the cast coming off the leg you broke?"

"Monday or Tuesday of next week, a few days before the doctor says I might go home. He said I'd get a walking cast."

"What about the other leg, the one with the knee you tore up?"

"I have a light cast that should come off about the same time as the other one. I think I get a boot for that one."

She gave him two thumbs up. "Sounds like you're on track. I'll tell you what I tell everybody who goes through this. Do the rehab, no matter how much it hurts. It will make your life a year from now so much better, and it will help prevent you from walking with a permanent limp."

He frowned. "Have you seen that happen?"

"I sure have. I know one woman – now deceased from cancer – who had a knee operation in her 40s, wouldn't do the rehab, and limped the last ten years of her life."

Nodding his head, he said, "I got it." He paused. "So, what

do you do on this shift? You can't be as busy as you are during the day. Aren't the patients asleep, unlike me?"

Minnie shifted her weight and looked at her watch. "It's 12:23 a.m. now. I'll keep checking on patients for the next hour. I have some patient care chores for a time after that. Then, I'll catch up on paperwork. Around four o'clock I'll start getting ready for morning rounds with the doctors."

"What time does that start?"

"With some, 6:15 a.m."

"What time do you get off?"

"Seven."

He looked up with a gleam in his eye. "Let me guess. You're going straight to the golf practice range after you get off, right?"

Her face brightened. "How'd you know that?"

"Pure and simple deduction. You once told me you enjoy golf practice early in the day. You said that if you work all night, you can't sleep right away. I put two and two together and figured you might go and do your golf practice right after you get out of here. You're not going home and sleep. It would make sense that you'd either do that or head for the gym. I can look at you and tell you must work out a lot."

"Guilty as charged on all counts," Minnie said. Then she added, "Your mother was right about you. You're a smart man. A really smart man."

∞∞∞∞

Once she finished talking with John, Minnie focused on gritty tasks the night shift demanded. First, her 71-year-old male patient needed an enema. He was to have surgery in the next two days, but until his bowels came unstuck it wasn't happening. He had been in the hospital three days and stool softeners and muscle relaxers hadn't produced the desired results.

Minnie asked two colleagues, Linda Baldwin and Joan Hanks, to meet her outside the patient's room at 1:35 a.m. She gathered the enema supplies and put them on her medical cart. For a moment, Minnie stood outside the patient's room waiting for Linda and Joan. She reminded herself Cynthia had warned her about returning to nursing because she'd have to resume doing this kind of thing. The process was so ingrained into Minnie's world that the prospect barely phased her. When Linda and Joan arrived, the three women walked into the patient's room, Minnie put on her smile, and asked, "Mr. Jones, are you ready to get flushed? Can you turn over, or do we need to help you?"

"I can turn over," he said in a weak voice. "I'm ready."

Minnie handed the supplies to Joan and pulled open the man's gown. "It's showtime girls," she said when she inserted the enema instrument. Joan and Linda grabbed gloves from boxes taped to the walls. The familiar sound of plastic covering hands reinforced Minnie's comfort level.

∞ ∞ ∞

After Minnie left John's room, he closed his eyes, but didn't sleep. He reflected on his time with her. It amazed him how easily their conversation flowed, how at peace he felt as they talked. And it wasn't just tonight. It had been that way all through his hospital stay, including the early days when much of the conversation concerned his pulse rate and blood pressure.

Was this supposed to happen between patient and nurse? If it was, why hadn't it happened with any of the other nurses who'd attended him? Faces of some of those nurses flashed through his mind. Did age decide who he connected with? Several had been young – just on either side of his age – but he hadn't developed the same rapport with them he had with Minnie. Did race matter? Several had been white, but that hadn't made any difference. Several had been young and white. Not one made much of an impression.

He tried remembering names. Betty? He couldn't recall her last name. Jan Johnson? Yeah, that was one of them. But was she a young black one or an older white one? In contrast, the details of every conversation, every moment, with Minnie seemed locked in his mind.

For a second, the vision he'd had of Minnie as she'd just appeared in his room, took over his consciousness. In semi-darkness she looked more vibrant than in harsh daylight. Her face, uncomplicated by makeup, seemed pure, with a raw appeal he hadn't seen in a woman before. Did it matter that the face was 55 years old? That it was black?

Her trim, fit body captivated him, though her loose fitting scrubs meant he could only imagine details. Tonight, he'd focused on those arms, obviously toned by years of weight training and swinging golf clubs. He let himself wonder what being held in them felt like.

Finally, he opened his eyes and turned out his reading light. Whatever was going on, he acknowledged he didn't understand. He told himself his attraction to her would fade once he got out of the hospital and no longer relied on the care she gave him. That would solve it, wouldn't it?

Then he thought of something else. Once out of the hospital, how would he stay in touch with her? Before falling asleep, he admitted he craved contact with her as much as he craved getting the casts off his legs and regaining normal mobility. That was a hell of a note, wasn't it?

Chapter 19

Because John spent more than a month, including two weeks on a rehab floor, at Lutheran Memorial, tradition dictated that the staff on his floor give him a going away party – a "celebration" they called it. Minnie wasn't there that Friday, which made the event bittersweet for him. He still didn't know how he could contact her, other than calling the hospital. How would she react if he did? While he obsessed about that problem, he smiled his way through cupcakes and apple juice and thanked those who were there.

After the party and the paperwork, a nurse and another attendant wheeled John out front where Don Young and Kate Hart picked him up and drove him home. A wheelchair got him to the car, but he needed crutches at his building. A discharge nurse had instructed him on using the crutches. They came in handy as he navigated the sidewalk from the parking lot and the breezeway that led to his apartment. Having no stairs in the equation made him appreciate that request he made in 2016 for a first-floor unit.

Don coordinated a group of five VWM lawyers and other friends who took turns staying over during John's first few nights at home. They slept on a small sofa bed Don picked up at a discount furniture store and that they fitted into the corner of the living room.

On Sunday after the Friday release, Don arrived at 6:35 p.m. for his turn at staying over. As he walked in, John was winding up a heated phone conversation while sitting at the kitchen table. Don hung his jacket on a door knob and asked, "What was that? You were practically shouting at whoever was on the other end of the line."

In a loud voice, John said, "My mother doesn't know when she should let some things go."

"What won't she let go?"

John shook his head. "This woman thing. She was ragging me about asking nurses from the hospital to come over and help out now that I'm home. I told her you organized a group of my guy friends who're staying with me until I get more mobile. She said I should ask nurses to do it because one might get interested in me."

"Yeah?" Don scratched his cheek and frowned. "Why would any of them come over and do that?'

"They wouldn't. That's just how my mother thinks. She asks me all the time how I'm doing on finding the love of my life. Here I am hobbling around, two days removed from a long hospital and rehab stay, having my friends help me with life's most basic functions, and she's worried about that."

"What did you tell her?"

"I told her she should back off. What I should have said was Mama, shut the fuck up. I still have trouble telling my mother where to get off. If I don't learn, she'll drive me nuts."

Now sitting at the table, Don crossed his arms and wrinkled his nose. "What's this about? I can't imagine it came out of the blue."

"I know what it's about. My mother thinks that if she doesn't stay on me day and night about finding a girlfriend, I'll never meet anyone I can marry and she'll never have grandchildren. One of the perils of being an only child, I suppose."

Don leaned back in his chair and chuckled, "My mother has no need for nagging me about that. My older sister has three children, my younger sister two, and my brother one, with another on the way."

"Seems like you're exempt on that score." John yawned and tapped his shoulders with his hands. "Anyway, that's what the call was about. At least it ended up being about that. I was happy when she and Dad called. At first, they just asked how I'm doing and about my prognosis. Dad said about 25 words and went back to doing whatever he'd been doing. It turned nasty when Mama went off on me."

The doorbell rang. Pizza that Don ordered had arrived. They spent the rest of the evening eating it and watching Sunday Night Football.

In the weeks after John got out of the hospital, Minnie found herself depressed on work days. At first, she resisted admitting that what Tuesdays, Wednesdays, and Thursdays lacked was John. Soon enough she realized what was wrong and pretending it was something else didn't help. How in the world had this happened? On the Tuesday morning after Thanksgiving, as she drove toward the hospital, the questions closed in on her.

Minnie inventoried friends and family in whom she might confide. Cynthia McFadden? Dawn Brooks? Judy Shields? Carol Robbins? Evelyn Connors? Her son Jerry? She found something wrong with each as the recipient and guardian of such news. Cynthia especially, and perhaps Dawn, would likely harp on the race disparity and the age gap. Dawn wouldn't keep it quiet and Cynthia might not. Carol might push the Mark Gibson idea, meaning Minnie would have to tell her what a boor he was.

Revelation of Minnie's infatuation with a 27-year old white

man would set off a battle inside Judy Shields between her own compassionate, live-and-let-live nature and her risk-averse, take-no-chances conservatism. Minnie could predict Jerry's reaction. He'd profess understanding and express the hope his mother would balance her emotions with practicality. That was all well and good, but wasn't the right prescription for the moment.

Then there was Evelyn Connors. If Minnie had put Evelyn's number in her phone, she'd have called her old professor right there on the road. Evelyn's words from the year before rang in her ears. "Don't worry about what somebody else thinks you should have," she'd said. Didn't that give Minnie a green light?

In some ways it did, but now wasn't the time she should call Evelyn. She remembered what else Evelyn said about men that night at dinner in Lincoln. "If he meets your need for tenderness, for attentiveness, for how he treats your children, etc., is younger than you, is older than you, is black, brown, or white, is wealthy or poor, drives a Jag or a jalopy, go for him."

Minnie knew John's color and age. She couldn't say whether he otherwise qualified under Evelyn's criteria. Was he all the things that would merit telling her friends where they could take their objections? When she found out, if she found out, she'd talk with Evelyn.

Driving along, she had a revelation. There was no wise man or wise woman who could advise her about this, at least not now. She was on her own for the time being. Either she discovered what she could have with John – what they could have with each other – or she should forget it. She knew, at that instant, she wouldn't – couldn't – forget it.

On her way home that same afternoon, she faced a basic fact about a possible relationship with John Dawson. No matter how much they had in common – books, conversation, politics, who knew what else – two differences would define them in the eyes of any world she could think of. Those differences were race and age. Or were they age and race?

Minnie knew well ethnically mixed couples who lived good lives together. They reported occasional nasty glances. Whispered disapprovals, from both sides of the racial divide, reached their ears from time to time. The couples she knew thumbed their noses at the haters and went about the business of living. It wasn't stress free, but they all said things other than race occupied their attention. Being an interracial couple still meant navigating being a couple.

During the last five years, two close black women friends divorced their black husbands and were now happily married to white men. Minnie was more than casual friends with three white women blissfully entangled with black husbands or long-term boyfriends. That included Brenda and Mark Henderson whose daughter, Jo Lynn, ushered her around the Clemson University campus during her fall 2016 trip. She also had developed a friendship with a black woman joyfully married to a Korean-American man. That couple raised two smart, caring daughters, both of whom showed up at Bradley's funeral.

Then Minnie realized something else. Two of her children had now dived into interracial romances, with the same delights and problems as her friends. She expected Sandra and Ronnie would marry within a year or two. Their major concern wasn't who didn't like that they were together, but figuring out where coaching basketball would or wouldn't take Ronnie and how Sandra's life and career fit with that.

In March, Jerry brought Rachel Jordan with him when he stopped in Dallas en route home from spring break on the Gulf coast. They seemed set in Norman since she had tenure in the OU chemistry department and he was content with working his way up the public school administration ladder. Jerry and Rachel, however, faced the task of blending a family in which each had children with a distant ex-spouse who wasn't always cooperative.

What about children of their own? Could they solidify their situation before Rachel's biological clock struck midnight? She wasn't that far from 40. Whatever the color difference meant, they had many other things they could worry about.

When Minnie shined a light on the racial difference between her and John, she couldn't say it didn't matter, but it mattered most because of age. Cynthia would ask, "You're seeing a *27- year old* white man?" Had John been a *57 year - old* white man, Minnie thought Cynthia might complain about her lover's lack of pedigree in black society but grudgingly go along. With John, being 27, the howling might never stop. Age would become a multiplier that made race more than it was by itself.

Chapter 20

B ack at VWM, John initially found he could work at most six hours a day before mental and physical fatigue overtook him. He didn't need crutches, but he walked stiffly and slowly and tired easily. His secretary, colleagues, and staff retrieved documents, files, and library materials for him.

Don, Maggie, Kate, and other lawyers in the corporate section took turns bringing him lunch and water. During his first few weeks back, even partners accommodated his mobility limitations by trekking to his office so they could give him assignments, rather than insisting he meet them in their offices as the partner-associate relationship usually required. When he went anywhere, it most often was the men's room.

Gradually, his stamina increased, and his mobility improved. By mid-January, he could get around the office sort of normally.

Despite progress that made work easier, John felt his rehabilitation wasn't going well. On Tuesday, January 16, the day after the Martin Luther King, Jr. holiday, he decided he'd do something about it. He called Lutheran Memorial and asked for the fourth-floor nursing station.

"Who're you trying to reach?" the operator asked.

"Minnie Donaldson. She usually works on that floor," John replied, hiding his irritation with being interrogated.

"I'll take a message for Ms. Donaldson," the operator said.

Now he was upset. "You can't just put me through?"

"Ms. Donaldson is on the nursing staff. We take messages for them and ask that they return the call. Could I have your number, please?"

John felt like screaming, but played along. He gave her his

mobile and office numbers and asked, "You'll make sure she gets the message? It's important."

He heard only a minimal commitment in the response. "I'll give her the message."

The operator's assurance notwithstanding, John didn't hear from Minnie all week. He plotted his next move, determined he'd get around the gate keepers. He even thought about camping out in the hospital parking lot so he could intercept her when she arrived for work or departed for the day.

On second thought, he decided against that. Appearing desperate didn't serve his ends. Seeing and talking with her had become essential, both because he wanted her advice about rehab and because he wanted to see her. He feared she might regard an in-person approach as rude and inappropriate. If at all possible, contact between them should result from a call that followed a phone message.

Finally, on the Saturday morning after his Tuesday call, as he struggled through the final stages of his daily walk, John's phone rang. But for the fragile condition of his legs, at the sight of her name on caller ID he might have leapt off the sidewalk. In a quiet voice, however, he managed a simple, "Hi, Minnie."

With a heavy sigh, she said, "I am so sorry calling you back has taken this long. Somebody at the nursing station lost your message."

"I'm just glad I hear your voice now."

Though he didn't ask for it, she gave him more explanation. "Your message got buried under stuff on the desk. One of my colleagues found it last night as I was leaving. I worked until eleven o'clock, so I didn't get home until midnight."

"Calling then would have been okay. You know me. I was awake at midnight – reading."

"Oh?"

"Finishing up *Balance of Power*, the Richard North Patterson novel I started in the hospital but got side tracked from. It's really good. I hope you'll read it, so we can talk about it sometime."

"I'd love that. But first, tell me how you're doing."

John took her inquiry as a positive. Maybe she enjoyed their conversations as much as he did. He'd have been disappointed if she'd just asked what he called about. As it was, she'd given him the perfect opening for telling her what he wanted, yet created an opportunity for real conversation. "I'm back at the firm. I can now work a whole day. For a while I could barely do six hours. In a firm like ours, that's not sustainable. We're too busy.

"I'm bouncing back, so I can't say there's been no progress. But I don't think this rehab deal is going that well, which is some of why I called you."

Her breathing accelerated. "Can you move around without pain?"

"Going up and down stairs hurts. I feel good on level ground."

"How about your upper body? You had lots of shoulder and collarbone damage as I remember."

"You remember right. I'm okay on that. Chilly weather isn't good, though."

"Not surprising. You'll have stiffness and discomfort in cold, damp weather, maybe for a year or two."

He let out a long exhale. "Can't go home, except during the summer, I suppose. Wilmington gets cold, a lot colder than Dallas."

She took two quick breaths. "Let me hear about the issues you're having with rehab, but not now. I'm playing golf this morning –"

"Of course."

"And I'm late. I am free Sunday after church – say one o'clock? Where do you live?"

"Richardson."

"Let's meet at the Starbucks on Northwest Highway, just west of Central Expressway."

"I know where it is. I'll see you there at one o'clock tomorrow."

"It'll be good to see you again, John. Really good."

∞∞∞

The Starbucks where John and Minnie met buzzed with people and the whir of machines spitting out expensive coffee drinks. He arrived first and found a two-person table tucked away in a back corner. Minnie showed up five minutes later. John watched her navigate the service line, spot him sitting in the back, and wave enthusiastically as she made her way through the crowd.

John realized he'd never before seen her out of hospital scrubs. She wore a light blue top over a plain yellow skirt that stopped just below her knees. As he had in the hospital, he noticed her toned arms. Today, he realized those arms were darker than her brown face. He assumed that resulted from playing golf in the sun in short sleeve shirts while wearing a hat.

He glimpsed, for the first time, her bare legs, also toned in the gym and on the golf course and, similarly, darker than her face. Muscular calves supported her aggressive gait. Her looks and movements conveyed strength and confidence.

"I was afraid you wouldn't recognize me without a hospital gown," he said as they sat down after he stood and greeted her with a handshake. "Seeing you out of your scrubs seems weird, but you look nice."

Minnie smiled at John across the table. "Thanks. This is new for us, isn't it? When I first see a patient out of the hospital, I always feel strange."

John thought he should shift the topic. "I can't thank you enough for coming and seeing me about this rehab problem. I really appreciate it."

"Before we talk about that – which we will – tell me more about being back at work."

"It was hard at first. I'd get there and have a burst of energy, which faded fast. More than once, I wanted out after two or three hours. I was that tired."

"After you got out of the hospital, how long before you went back?"

"I went home November 17th, got my casts off November 30th, and started work December seventh, so about three weeks. That was a Thursday. I'm glad I did that, rather than start on a Monday. Working only two days, then having a weekend helped a lot."

"People who've been in a hospital as long as you were make a big mistake when they go back on a Monday and work a whole week before a break."

He lowered his voice. "I missed you at my going away party at the hospital."

Minnie hesitated, then smiled. "Your celebration?" she asked as he nodded. "I had a prior commitment that day. It was Friday, when I usually don't work. I had something I'd agreed I'd do that day."

John pondered her vagueness. What kind of 'prior commitment' kept her away? "No big deal," he said finally. "I wish you could have been there, but things happen sometimes. You're here today."

She propped her elbows on the table and balled up her fists before resting her chin on them. "Tell me about your rehab.

You look like you're coming along. I got the impression on the phone yesterday you're making some progress."

He shrugged. "I'm not myself and it doesn't feel like I'm getting close to being myself. I confess, I took time off from it during the holidays. I just don't feel I'm getting back to normal."

"Do you feel stronger?"

"A little. It's true, I can work longer, but I just don't feel right."

She blinked her eyes and slightly parted her lips. "What are they having you do?"

He suppressed a smirk. "I go three times a week – Saturday, Tuesday, and Thursday. I spend an hour with the therapist, mostly stretching. Then he sends me to the weight room. He showed me things at the beginning, but now he seldom goes in there with me. I've not had a lot of direction on weights. As we discussed on the phone, I'm stiff and sore a lot of the time."

Minnie wrinkled her nose. "Where do you feel that?"

"All over. It's worse in my upper body, though I don't have a lot of pain there. I have more pain in my legs."

She leaned forward and held up her hands, palms out. A confident grin spread across her face. "This sounds fixable. I have ideas for you."

He took a notebook and pen from the pocket of his blue plaid shirt. "Fire away."

She rattled off a series of weight room and stretching suggestions and finished by saying, "Before we leave, make sure you give me your e-mail address. I'll send you some exercises you should try – yoga-type things that'll strengthen your core and help relieve the soreness and stiffness. Especially spend more of your weight-room time doing leg lifts. That will build up that quad muscle, the one above the knee you tore up and needed the ACL repair."

"Okay," he said, handing her a business card.

"The other thing I suggest is frequent massage, maybe two or three times a week for a while." She reached down and pulled a card from her handbag that sat on the floor. "Call this woman and tell her I sent you. She's the best massage therapist I know. She's expensive, but you can afford her. Your health insurance will cover most of it."

John put the card in the shirt pocket, along with the notebook. He'd written down every one of Minnie's ideas. "Thank you. This is great. I'll do these things."

She tapped his hand. "Let's get together in two weeks and see what progress you've made."

For the rest of the two and a half hours they spent together that afternoon they talked of books, his law school experience, and their families. He probed – gently – for information about her marriage and her children. She talked eagerly about the kids, but would say of Bradley only, "We were married a long time. Some of it was good, some of it wasn't."

She asked about his parents. She seemed surprised when he admitted his mother could be a pain.

Minnie licked her lips and took a sip of tea. "I wonder if any of my children say that about me."

"I bet you don't regularly hassle them about whether they've found the love of their life."

She bit her lip. He wondered if the topic made her uncomfortable. "Well, all of them kind of have," she said, "but I didn't bug them about it before they did. What does your mother say?"

"That I must find somebody today who'll give her grandchildren tomorrow."

John thought that took Minnie aback, but she only asked, "Is that a big deal for you?"

"Heavens no! I never think about it until Mama brings it up.

I figure if it happens, it happens. I have lots of other things I can worry about these days without putting that on the list."

A smile spread across Minnie's face. "Seems a good way of dealing with it. One day at a time, right?"

"Absolutely."

∞∞∞

On her way home, Minnie replayed the afternoon and regretted some things. She could have been more forthcoming with John about why she hadn't been at his hospital celebration. She didn't lie. She just left out something big. That day she had another commitment, but she could have skipped it or shifted it around.

The real problem was her fear she'd fall apart when he left the hospital, unsure as she was about how they'd see each other going forward. She'd decided she wouldn't risk her coworkers seeing her lose it over a young male patient – and a white one at that.

She also didn't tell him how revelation of his mother's grandchildren fixation unnerved her. Here she was plotting how she might have a relationship with Marion Dawson's son when she couldn't make Marion a grandmother. Marion's desire for grandchildren shouldn't have bothered her in the least, but it did.

She was encouraged by John's declaration that his mother's obsession didn't affect him much. She'd read somewhere that mothers of men involved with older women often got in the way. Maybe he could handle any opposition from her.

As a whole, the conversation just increased her inner conflict about John. An afternoon with him spurred her interest. Talking with him had been a delight. It was the high point of her day, probably of her week. Still, she couldn't ignore the red flag whipping in the late January breeze.

Maybe the obstacles were just too great. She remembered her ruminations of a few days before about friends and their likely objections. Discussing with John the lives of her children reminded her they too might have problems with the idea of their 55-year old mother's involvement with a 27-year old white man.

This had disaster written all over it. Despite how appealing she found John and how alive being with him made her feel, she realized she must explore other options. It was time she called Dawn Brooks about Clifford Nguyen.

∞∞∞

M innie wasted no time making her call. Dawn said she'd see Clifford at Tuesday evening's choir practice. "He'll call soon, I'd think. I told him all about you. He's eager to meet you."

"I hope you didn't oversell me," Minnie said. "I'm just a nurse whose husband died." She still hadn't told Dawn how bad things had gotten between her and Bradley at the end.

"Huh!" Dawn grunted. "You're rich, a scratch golfer, and look 15 years younger than you are. Don't tell me you're not a catch."

∞∞∞

Arranging a date took Clifford and Minnie one brief phone conversation. He had a Saturday afternoon business meeting at the Lowes Anatole Hotel near downtown that ended at four thirty. That location was 15 to 20 minutes from Minnie's house. They agreed they'd meet in the bar at five o'clock. Both said they'd seen enough internet and social media photos that they knew what each other looked like.

She spotted him almost as soon as she arrived. He appeared comfortable and at ease in a yellow dress shirt sans tie, blue blazer, and gray slacks. He waved her toward him.

"I'm sure Dawn told a giant pack of lies about me," Clifford said with a mostly Americanized accent after they greeted each other at a table near the back of the wellappointed bar. Gleaming stainless-steel tables and chairs, subdued lighting, and a polished wood bar with a bank of televisions above tuned to sporting events provided a modern vibe. "I hope you won't hold against me the impossibility I could meet the expectations she set."

Minnie's mind absorbed the physical features that defined his biracial heritage – flatter nose, thicker lips, and broader shoulders than many Asian people, lighter skin, narrower eyes, and straighter hair than many African people. He wasn't short, but he didn't seem tall either. It was as if he split the difference between his ancestries. She tried imagining the unease his features created in the communities that could claim or reject him. She shuddered at the thought of what the rest of the world made of him.

She smoothed down her dark blue skirt and checked the buttons on her crisp white shirt. "Probably the same pack of lies she told about me," Minnie said. "I warned her about making me Wonder Woman."

"She offered high praise. I can confirm that," he said.

"Actually, I give Dawn credit for looking out for me. Nine months after my husband died, she started scouting. Few weeks went by when she didn't say something about this man or that man I should meet, each perfect for me."

He scratched his nose. "Since I'm here, and they're not, I suppose the pressure is on. Where do we start?"

She leaned away a little and placed her left hand just under her neck. "I assume most people you meet ask first about Vietnam and how you got here."

His expression turned hard. "That's true. I can't deny that happens, but I don't let it define me. I'll give you the short version and we can move on."

Hearing his defensiveness and having read about mistreatment of Vietnamese Amerasians, especially black ones, she said, "Actually, you can skip it. I'm more interested in what you do now. Dawn said you spend half your work time out of the country."

His reaction suggested her shift surprised and pleased him. It seemed he relished the possibility a black American woman actually could resist the half-breed refugee story. His face softened. He became animated, using his hands as he responded. "I don't know if it's 50 percent, but I'm not short on frequent flyer miles. I've learned languages because of this job. I had no choice. I suppose that's a good thing."

"Those are?" she asked.

"French and Spanish, plus English which I learned so I could function in this country. Vietnamese is my native language. I know a little Japanese – enough to be dangerous."

"Amazing. I've never known anyone so versatile. Did you seek out a firm with an international focus or did it just happen that way?"

"Just happened. My first job out of college was with a firm in California that did only local projects – water systems, small hospitals, light industrial buildings, things of that sort. They seldom left L.A. County. Then I got recruited – headhunted you might say – by the firm I'm with now. Our focus is international. Here I am." "You went to college at....?"

"San Diego State. I didn't enroll until I was 27 years old, which relates to the story of how I got here. Yes, it includes growing up on the streets of what was once Saigon, refugee camps, and being an outcast. I guess you'll get that story after all."

She leaned back, giving him space. "We were talking about your job history."

"I started that first job when I was 31. I stayed five years. Then I hooked up with the firm I'm with now."

She nodded. "How long have you been with them?"

"Fourteen years. I made partner eight years ago."

"Nice," she said, happy she could revel in his achievements. He possessed what struck her as an easy-going sincerity. His soft voice soothed, especially when contrasted with the loud, overbearing Mark Gibson.

Before she could ask about the mechanics of being an engineer on big construction projects, he switched gears. "It's time I heard about you. Who is Minnie Donaldson?"

She frowned, for a second uncertain of her tack. Finally, she said, "I have hobbies, but I'm like many women my age. My life has been about family. Even though my marriage wasn't great at times – no, it wasn't great at the end just before my husband died – I'm satisfied with having been a wife and the mother of three children."

"Your husband had a heart attack?"

"He did. I guess Dawn told you."

Clifford nodded. "I am sorry for your loss. You were saying?"

She held up the index finger on her right hand, shook her head slowly, and pursed her lips. "Many people assume a woman's career must conflict with family. I didn't."

He seemed startled by the idea. "Really?"

"In the early years of my marriage, I worked because I had to. We were getting our family started. My husband was building a business. We needed my salary. I'd been trained as a nurse, so I worked as a nurse while he did that. We raised the children together, at least in the early years. I'll credit him that and I'll always be grateful for it.

"After a while, I didn't have to work, at least not because we needed the money. We didn't. I put away most of what I made. By then, nursing was as much a part of me as mothering the kids and being a wife. I defined myself as both.

"It's true I retired early, but I was just tired. I went back when I realized it's what I do. I made my peace with that basic truth. They'll take me out of the hospital in a box because I can't see myself leaving for any other reason."

He shook his head and lifted his eyelids. "Not many women have said something like that to me."

"What have women said to you?"

"'I hate my job' or 'I'm glad I didn't have kids because I love my job so much.' Are you saying you had it all?"

She held up her hands, extended both index fingers this time, and shook her head side to side. "I am not. I liked and needed both. I worked at being happy in whatever space I found myself at a given time. When I worked, I worked, so I loved work. When I did kid and family stuff, I did that and loved it. I never saw it as about having it all. It was about my formula for being happy."

He clenched his teeth. "How'd you learn that?"

"Golf."

"Golf?"

Because she'd long since worked through this issue, she spoke quickly, no gathering of thoughts needed. "If you have ambitions of being good at golf, you must accept where you are and like it. If you're honest with yourself and honest with the game, you play the course as you find it and live in every moment you're out there – and only that moment. The second you wander off somewhere else, the game exacts its revenge."

He frowned again and looked around, as if he wondered what other people in the bar might think of what she'd said. "I never, ever thought of that. I tried golf, but I didn't work at being good. I haven't played in five years. Maybe I wasn't cut out for that focus you describe."

"That's possible. I won't say one way or the other because I barely know you. I know what works for me."

His mobile phone vibrated. He pulled it from his pocket. A loud gasp escaped his lips. "I wonder where she is. Is she here?" He turned to Minnie, held up one hand, and said, "I should take this."

"I'll run to the rest room," she said, standing up and grabbing her handbag. He nodded and waved as she left.

When she returned 10 minutes later, two young women sat at the table with him. One was white and gestured excitedly as she talked. The other, who sat quietly, resembled Clifford except that her skin was lighter and she had a smaller nose and thinner lips. When Clifford saw Minnie, he rose, as did the woman Minnie assumed was a relative.

"Meet my daughter, Sarah, and her friend Ann," he said. "I didn't expect them this weekend, but parents get surprises sometimes."

"How are you, Sarah? I'm Minnie Donaldson. Meeting you is a pleasure."

"Thank you. This is Ann Jefferson," she said, pointing at her still-seated friend. "We didn't mean to horn in on you and Dad's time together. I just wanted to make sure I saw him for a minute or two. His office told us he was here at the hotel."

As they sat back down, Clifford explained, "Sarah and Ann are in town for an engagement party for one of their friends. They attend college at Texas Tech. They drove in for the party tonight in Fort Worth."

A few moments of awkward silence followed. Finally, Minnie broke the tension. "Would you join us for a drink?"

Ann spoke up. "Oh, no. We can't. The party starts soon. Thanks anyway."

"That's too bad," Minnie said. She reached for her handbag and gave each young woman a business card. "Sarah, Ann, if you're in town again and have free time, look me up. My work, home, and cell numbers are on the card, as is my e-mail address. Perhaps we can visit about school in Lubbock and your plans after graduation."

"Thanks very much," Sarah said, as both she and Ann got up and edged toward the door. "I'll do that. I'd enjoy seeing you when we can talk. We should get going for the party."

"Here," Clifford said, pointing toward the exit sign. "Let me walk you out. Ann, it was nice to meet you. I hope you have a great time tonight." He paused and looked down at Minnie. "I'll be right back."

Minnie sat quietly and finished her wine. Clifford returned moments later and ordered another round. He said, "That was nice – giving them your card. Even if they never call you, it was a gracious gesture. As Sarah's father, I appreciate your doing that. I didn't expect they'd show up here tonight. Sarah never mentioned being in town this weekend."

"No explanation needed."

"While you were gone, she said it was a spur of the moment thing that came together at the last minute. They decided this morning they'd drive down here. Nobody was more shocked than I was when she called and said they were in the lobby."

"Perfectly fine, Clifford. Kids do things like that sometimes. I'm glad I met your daughter. You sure can't disclaim her. She looks just like you. She seems very poised."

"Thank you. Let me tell you about her." Clifford's description of Sarah's history turned the conversation to their experiences with raising children. They gently touched on their failed marriages but glossed over the goriest details.

They talked until a quarter after seven o'clock, whe n Clifford asked if she'd have dinner with him. Despite being tempted, Minnie replied, "I promised one of my bridge buddies I'd be a fourth tonight. I'm not part of her Saturday night group, but I sub in from time to time when a regular can't make it. I told her I'd get there by eight o'clock. They're delaying 30 minutes on my account. Not showing up would be bad form. I do hope we can have dinner sometime. I've enjoyed our time together this evening."

He smiled and licked his lips. "Are you free next weekend?"

Minnie didn't return the smile, but checked the calendar on her phone. "I'm open Friday. I avoid eating late, so how about half past six?"

"That's fine. I know a special place we can go."

"Oh? Where?"

"Tell me where you live. I'll surprise you."

That did provoke a smile. She gave him her address. He punched it into his phone.

"I'll pick you up at six o'clock," he said. "The place I have in mind isn't far from you. Half an hour gives us plenty of time."

Minnie had seen enough of Clifford Nguyen that she didn't worry about his being late. She didn't know what this was or could be, but it wasn't Mark Gibson. She was sure of that.

Chapter 22

Minnie spent the Monday after her evening with Clifford Nguyen engaged in the contradictory exercise of relishing how pleasant she'd found her time with him while unsuccessfully seeing whether she could cleanse her thoughts of John Dawson.

Saturday showed she liked Clifford. He struck her as a man she could get comfortable with. He seemed easy going, thoughtful, and kind. She still knew little about him, but that should change if she kept seeing him. None of that, however, made her stop thinking about John.

A smile broke out on her face as she considered how much better Dawn Brooks seemed at matchmaking than Carol Robbins. Still, Minnie knew Dawn might fail as badly. Though it didn't appear likely based on the first meeting, and would probably happen for different reasons, Clifford Nguyen might strike out like Mark Gibson had. Time would tell and time wasn't up yet.

She wondered what kind of lover Clifford would make. Saturday provided no hint at all on that. He kept a respectful distance. Other than the greeting and parting handshakes, they never touched. That would likely change on the Friday dinner date.

Would the evening end in bed? Probably not, she thought. She couldn't imagine herself being ready after one night of drinks and one dinner, no matter how charming she found him. She hadn't made a strict 'sex-only-after-x-number-of-dates' rule, but she doubted x=2.

While she entertained those thoughts about what might happen between her and Clifford, John lurked nearby. She'd been confident of the conclusion she reached that she should pursue something with Clifford because a relationship with John made so little sense. Then she realized what had happened. After an afternoon of being enchanted with John, while they talked about everything except their growing interest in each other, she thought getting something going with Clifford would flush her fantasies about John. It had not.

As she puttered around her house that afternoon, doing laundry, organizing the kitchen, and planning spring yard work, thoughts of John flooded her mind and body. She couldn't put behind her the easy flow of their talk or the flutters inside that the sound of his voice generated. Clifford Nguyen might be the right man for her or he might not. No matter what he was, meeting him hadn't erased her dreams of John.

Then her phone rang. The caller ID said "Clifford."

"Hello, Clifford. I didn't expect I'd hear from you today. This is a nice surprise."

He seemed regretful. "I didn't think I'd be calling today, especially for the reason I'm calling."

Little voices whispered, "This might not be good." She said only, "Oh? What's up?"

Now she heard an apologetic tone. "I'm afraid we must postpone our dinner date Friday, maybe for several months. It's something that can't be helped."

"Have you had an emergency of some kind?"

"Pretty much," he sighed. "Actually, one of my partners has and it means I take over his project in Indonesia. I leave tomorrow."

"What happened?" she asked.

"We're building a hospital in Jakarta. Millions of dollars involved. The teenage son of our team leader has been diagnosed with a life-threating heart condition. The son needs surgery, which they're doing Friday in California. My partner must get to San Francisco Thursday night. I'll arrive in

197

Indonesia Wednesday so he can brief me."

"You're taking over the project?" She decided flattery might represent the best course under the circumstances. "It sounds like your partners have great confidence in you since they've asked you to take over such a big project on such short notice."

"It's nice you would say that. I hope that's the case."

Minnie stared at her feet as she stood in her kitchen. After a few seconds, she lifted her eyes and looked out at the still-brown grass in the backyard. "I'm sorry we can't have dinner Friday. I was really anticipating it. I expected it would be the highlight of my week."

"Yes, and I suspect of mine too." He sighed again and paused. "I won't hold you. As you can imagine, I have all kinds of things I must get done between now and tomorrow when my plane leaves."

"How long does getting there take?"

"Houston is an hour, then 26 to Jakarta, one stop."

"I trust you'll sleep on the way. Please send me a text that lets me know you got there safely."

"I'll do that. That's very nice of you. Take care and I hope I can call you when I return, whenever that is."

"You may and I will look forward to it."

Tuesday morning when Minnie arrived at the hospital, she encountered Dawn Brooks in the parking lot. "Are we working together today?" Minnie asked. "I'm on the fourth floor. Where are you?"

"Fifth floor." They went through the revolving doors into the lobby. Dawn stopped and asked, "Did you meet Clifford? I thought you said you were getting together for a drink Saturday."

Minnie stood a few feet away and replied, "We did. I had a nice time."

Dawn pushed up her glasses and slightly parted her lips. "Will you see him again?"

"I hope so, but apparently it won't happen for a while. Maybe a couple of months."

"Why so long? He's not sick or something?"

"He called yesterday and told me his firm is sending him to Indonesia on a big project. The guy who was leading their team there had a family medical emergency, so Clifford takes over."

Dawn ran her hands through her hair. "That's a bummer."

"He leaves today. We were going out Friday night."

Dawn bounced on her toes as she spoke. "So, what did you think?"

Minnie glanced at her watch. "I liked him. Hard to tell much in two and a half hours. I liked the idea of going out with him again. But, I didn't fall in love with him, Dawn, if that's what you're asking."

Dawn put her hands on her hips. "I was not. I just wanted to know how it went."

"It went fine."

"Well, okay. I just wanted to know," she replied, sucking in her cheeks.

∞ ∞ ∞

During the following weeks John and Minnie met three more times, each for the stated purpose of discussing his rehab. Every time they spent 15 minutes covering rehab and three hours or more on other things – books, movies, television shows, politics, the dynamics of life.

Minnie always came away more perplexed than before. She'd thought through the reasons a relationship with John was a bad idea. But, what should she do about feeling as close to him as she did, desiring a deep dive into his soul so she could root around until she discovered everything there? They could meet for a bit longer on the pretext of talking about his rehab, but that couldn't last indefinitely. Soon, they'd have to acknowledge why they kept meeting or stop meeting. The idea of stopping left a bad taste in her mouth.

Increasingly, Minnie believed John was in the same place she was. For one thing, he smiled the whole time they were together. For another, his animated demeanor screamed how much he enjoyed being with her. Finally, he was always eager for the next meeting. Several times she considered directly probing his feelings about their time together. She decided she'd leave well enough alone and enjoy what they had.

One more thing brought home how important seeing John had become in her life. Despite two or three text messages from Jakarta, she spent no time thinking about Clifford Nguyen.

∞∞∞

During February and early March, the time of their "rehab meetings," John wasn't at all perplexed about where things between him and Minnie should go. He even cleared the decks for what he wanted.

He told Kate Hart she need not introduce him to her friend Jody Lawrence, though his rehab was about done. Kate asked if there was someone else. John replied, "The timing isn't right." He left it at that, despite Kate's determined push for a clearer answer.

During those weeks, John focused on two things – getting as much time with Minnie as he could and figuring out how and when he could ask her for a real date. The rehab façade couldn't last forever. Their meetings under that pretext would end. He didn't think at all about the idea of not seeing her once that time came. He just needed a way of getting her acknowledgment that she was where he was.

∞∞∞

On Tuesday, March 13, Minnie got a phone call that set in motion the next phase of her story with John. Things were unusually slow at the hospital. She found herself sitting around because so few patients clamored for attention. It was a welcome lull from the last few weeks when her floor bulged at the seams with people suffering some kind of illness or who'd been in accidents. When an intriguing message showed up at the nursing desk right after lunch, she rode the elevator down to the first floor and stepped outside into unseasonably warm sunshine so she could return a call from Sarah Nguyen.

"This is Minnie Donaldson. You called?"

She sensed hurt and distress in the young woman's voice. "Thank you so much for calling back. I have bad news and I need a favor."

"What happened?"

Minnie heard subdued weeping through the phone. "My father was killed in a plane crash last week in Indonesia. He –"

"What?" Minnie exclaimed before covering her mouth with her left hand. She almost dropped the phone from her right.

The weeping became sobbing. "He'd gone from Jakarta, where he'd been working, to one of the Java Islands--"

"Before he left Dallas, he told me about taking over a hospital project in Indonesia. I've gotten a couple of texts from him since he's been there."

Sarah's sobbing continued. "He had a friend who lives on one of those islands, someone he knew from their time together in a refugee camp in the Philippines. Dad told me a couple of weeks ago he'd set up a visit with this man. He took that trip last weekend and was returning to Jakarta. His plane crashed on takeoff."

"I am so sorry. This must be a terrible blow. You're his only child, aren't you?"

Now Minnie heard sniffles. The young woman blew her nose. "I'm his only family. He had no idea where his brother and sister – his mother's other children – are. His father's family disowned him. Dad and my mother didn't get along."

"The night I met him – and you – we talked about some of that."

With her crying coming under control, Sarah said, "I feel lost without him. Keeping up in school is hard, with this having happened."

In a soft voice, Minnie asked, "Are you in Lubbock?"

"Yes. This week is spring break, which helps some. I'm driving to Dallas tomorrow so I can clean out his apartment. His secretary said she'll help. I'm glad he didn't buy a house in Dallas. I know he planned on it. He sold the house in Houston before he moved up there. One less problem I have."

"Do you have a lawyer who can handle probating his estate?"

"No. I asked a friend who's in law school if she'll help me find someone."

"You have my e-mail address, right?"

"And your phone numbers, of course."

"Send me an e-mail and I'll put you in touch with a man named Christopher Maxwell. He's represented my family for years and handled my husband's estate. I'll contact him and tell him you'll call."

Sarah sighed heavily. "That's such a relief. A weight off my shoulders. Thank you so much."

"You said you need a favor. What can I do?"

Sarah's voice turned cold and hard, with noisy breathing. Anger seeped through the phone. "I discovered day before yesterday there's a problem with getting my father's body back to the United States. His firm will pay for transportation between Jakarta and Houston, which is where we'll have his memorial service. They won't pay for getting the body to Jakarta from the island where the crash happened."

A pained expression took over Minnie's face as she stood on the sidewalk outside the hospital. "Why not? That seems cruel."

"They say he was on his own – an excursion they called it. They claim they're not responsible for that."

"Excursion? That's a strange word under the circumstances."

Now Minnie just heard sadness in Sarah's voice. "I'm raising money so I can bring him home. I can't access his bank accounts until I can get the estate probated. I'm calling people who knew him – friends, acquaintances, work colleagues. I've set up a GoFundMe page."

"How much does getting him to Jakarta cost?"

Minnie heard Sarah's anger flare again. "About as much as from Jakarta to the U.S. – $12,000. I've raised $4,000 so far."

Minnie set her jaw. "E-mail me the GoFundMe information. I'll send you something tonight. You shouldn't have to worry about that."

They talked for another few minutes before Minnie decided she should get back to her duty station. She told Sarah she could call anytime and that they'd touch base at the end of the week.

After work, Minnie drove home and headed straight for her computer. She e-mailed Christopher Maxwell details of Sarah's situation and sent her a message with his contact information. She also found Sarah's e-mail about the GoFundMe page, looked it up, and transferred $8,000 into that account.

PART IV

Chapter 23

March 2018

"Let's check the range of motion in your legs, John," Minnie said on a Sunday afternoon as they worked out together in the fitness facility at North Central Country Club. That was the private club she joined in July 2017, not long before she resumed her nursing work at Lutheran Memorial. Only 20 minutes from home, it was the one Bradley wouldn't join.

John wore a Penn Law School t-shirt and running shorts. Minnie supervised in gray warm ups that said "Louisiana Tech Track" across the front. Crystal gave them to her for Christmas seven or eight years ago.

She directed him onto a floor mat and said, "Extend your right leg. Raise it as high as you can." As he lay on the floor, she rotated the leg side to side, then in a circular motion. Finally, she stretched it over his head. "Now change legs," she ordered. "Let's see how the one you broke is coming along."

John raised his left leg and she rotated it as she'd done with the right. She told him, "I see you can't get this one as high."

Between grimaces he said, "I can't, but I can go way higher than I could two weeks ago."

"Now, lie flat, bend one leg, grab your knee, and bring it to your chest." He complied. "Does that hurt?" she asked.

As he changed legs, he replied, "It feels good. I couldn't do that a month and a half ago."

She grinned. "You mean before you and I started talking?"

"Before you gave me the supplemental exercises."

Now she flashed a cocky smile. "I thought they'd help."

"The exercises and massage made a real difference."

Minnie clapped her hands three times. "I knew massage would help too."

She asked John to perform the exercises she'd suggested and some of those the rehab therapist gave him. Occasionally, she showed him a way he might get more benefit from a particular exercise. After 45 minutes she said, "One more thing. I'll do this with you. Let's see who's king – or queen – of the leg lifts."

They entered the North Central weight room, an expansive area beyond a set of double doors adjacent to the mat room where they'd stretched. John's eyes widened when he surveyed the machines, free weights, and specialized stations. "I see why you joined this club. This looks like the weight room for a big time college football team."

"It is nice," Minnie said. "I live in here when I'm not out on the golf course. If you can't get in shape in this place, just give it up."

At one of the leg lift machines she asked, "How much weight do you use with the leg on which you had the ACL surgery?"

"I'm lifting 60 pounds and doing 20 rep sets."

"That's good. Do three sets."

He tugged at his shorts and rubbed the back of his neck. "Three? I usually do just two."

Minnie shifted her weight as she looked at him. "Let's give you an incentive. I'll do three sets and I'll go first. You can keep up with me, can't you? After all, I'm an old woman on her last leg, you might say, right?"

She set the proper weight on the machine, sat down, and placed her foot in the lifting position. She raised the 60 pounds 20 times, rested two minutes, then did 20 more. Each lift required raising the weight until her leg was straight, parallel with the floor. She rested three minutes and did a third set of 20.

As John moved into position for his turn, she playfully rubbed his shoulders. Did the tightness she felt signal fear he couldn't do three sets of 20? Or was it about how close this brought the two of them?

John handled the first set easily, but by the 14th repetition of the second set she could see him struggling. He reached 20 reps, but the last three taxed him severely.

After a three-minute rest, which Minnie timed, she barked out, "Come on, big guy. One more set."

John started again. By rep 13, he looked fried. She kept pushing him. "You can do it. I'm not letting you quit. Finish! Finish!"

He managed three more lifts. She stood in front of him, hands on hips. She'd peeled off the warmups, leaving a t-shirt and shorts that showcased her fit, toned body. "Keep going John! Four more!" He did two more. Sweat poured from his brow.

Her expression grew fierce. Her nostrils flared. She gritted her teeth. "You have to do this," she implored him. "You have to do it!"

From somewhere, John summoned a burst of energy that pushed him through his 19th rep. "One more!" she cried. "Just one. Last one!"

With a grunt that must have come from deep inside, he lifted his rebuilt knee one final time. The weight rose. She saw the quiver in his thigh, the one he was building up by doing this. A stronger quad muscle would better support his repaired knee. Somehow, he straightened the leg. He'd done three sets of 20. A loud clang echoed through the room when he released the weight.

She moved toward him and wrapped her arms around his shoulders as he slumped in the seat of the machine. In her embrace, his breathing gradually slowed. She wiped sweat from his face with the bottom of her t-shirt, exposing her black sports bra. He looked up at her. She looked down at him. In that moment, something passed between them. Whatever it was, she hadn't seen or felt it in a long, long time.

∞∞∞

"Nice job," Minnie told John as they sat in the club juice bar after the workout. She'd put her warmups back on and he'd changed into white long-sleeved t-shirt and black sweatpants. His hair remained damp from his shower. They both sipped from water bottles. "I'm satisfied you've been rehabilitated," she continued. "As far as I'm concerned, you're good to go. You can ditch the therapist and just workout on your own."

"Should I keep doing the massage?"

"Yes, but once a week is enough. Keep that up for three months, then go only when you feel you need it."

He tapped a loose fist on his chest. "I can't tell you how much I appreciate your help on this rehab deal. I was stuck. I was getting nowhere."

"It was my pleasure," she said softly.

John tilted his head to the side and gave her a sly smile. "Now that you're done with helping me, how will you stay occupied?"

She stared at him several seconds before saying, "I assume you're trying to be funny. You know how busy I stay since I went back to work." She paused. "I do have one thing next weekend – Saturday, March 31st – I'm dreading."

"Oh?"

Minnie wrapped her arms around her chest. "A funeral, well a memorial service, in Houston late Saturday afternoon."

"Long time friend? Relative?"

"Hardly. Somebody I met once."

He furrowed his eyebrows before releasing them. "How'd that happen?"

"It's a long story."

Through a little smirk he said, "I have time."

She leaned back and looked away. "I've told you about my friend Dawn Brooks, who's also a nurse at Lutheran Memorial?"

"You mentioned her name, but I've never met her. I don't think she was ever one of my nurses."

"Dawn is always trying to fix me up. Early this year, she introduced me to a man named Clifford Nguyen, an engineer with an international construction firm. I met him for drinks one Saturday night in late January or early February. A few days later, his firm sent him to take over a major project in Indonesia.

"While there, he visited a friend who lives on a nearby island. Clifford died in a plane crash on his way back to Jakarta. His daughter, whom I met the night he and I went out, invited me to the memorial service."

John lowered his head. "I'm sorry to hear about that. It's tragic."

She folded her hands in her lap. "I barely knew him. I could just not go, of course, but I've become fond of the daughter. I'd like to support her. She's his only family. She's handling the things that go with his death mostly alone. A few of his friends and work colleagues are helping, but it still has messed up her college graduation plans. She dropped some classes so she can take care of things, meaning she won't finish until fall."

"She goes where?"

"Texas Tech."

"That's in Lubbock, right?"

"It is. I don't know anybody who'll be at the service Saturday. Sarah – the daughter – will be consumed with being the bereaved child. I asked a couple of my friends if they'd go with me. They all found something better they could do."

John threw back his shoulders and looked into Minnie's eyes. "I'll go. I'll gladly spend that time with you. You're driving, right?"

Minnie gave him an incredulous stare. "Would you really do that, John? And yes, I'm driving."

"I would. What's the timing again? How about coming back?"

"The service is Saturday afternoon at five thirty. I'll come back Sunday."

"So, we'd leave around noon Saturday?"

"That sounds right. I made a hotel reservation. I can get another room."

"I'll have work this weekend. I always do. I can work some Saturday morning. If we get back by two or three o'clock Sunday afternoon I can finish."

She opened her palms. "I can accommodate that. It's great you'd do this."

"Pick me up in front of my building downtown, Always Tower, at a quarter of twelve Saturday morning. I'll be ready."

"This is so thoughtful, John. So thoughtful."

∞ ∞ ∞

As the week of the Houston trip crawled along, Minnie and John turned over in their heads what a Saturday evening and seven hours in a car together could mean. They looked at it differently, but ended up in the same place.

John couldn't have been more eager. Titillated by the workout, he salivated at the prospect of being as close to her as the trip would bring them. True, they'd spend a lot of time talking, which he was all for. But as much as he relished the possibilities of the talk, the prospect of proximity motivated him more.

During the meetings about his rehab, he became increasingly enchanted with her physical presence, including her hyper-fit body. So what if she was much older than other women he might pursue? So what if she had dark, not white, skin? John couldn't see a downside in spending three and a half hours with her on the road, an evening, and three and a half hours driving home.

Minnie also liked the idea of physical closeness, but that wasn't what intrigued her about the trip. She could keep probing John's personality and inner soul. The time they spent using his rehab as a pretext for getting together permitted long, involved conversations they couldn't have before.

In the hospital, she watched the clock and worried that if she overstayed the time a nurse usually spent with one patient, someone would call her out. Night shifts, few and far between though they'd been, worked better. At night, she worried less about someone's interrupting them or filing a complaint about her fraternizing with a patient.

A car trip posed a different issue. Given the intensity of feelings she'd started having about John, and how she sensed he felt about her, didn't this trip create an opportunity for mischief? She could book separate hotel rooms, but slipping down the hall for a middle-of-the-night tryst wasn't that difficult, was it?

Yes, she'd concluded two dates probably wouldn't suffice for crawling into bed with Clifford Nguyen. She never had the hots for Clifford Nguyen. She did have fantasies of jumping John Dawson's bones, and she wasn't sure she wouldn't act on them.

After these ruminations, however, Minnie knew the best thing she could do about her John Dawson fixation was learn more about him. If this nutty idea was going anywhere, with all the problems she already foresaw, they must know and understand each other as well as possible. That meant talking. What should happen this weekend? Talk, that's what.

For his part, John wasn't worried about whether he slept with Minnie Donaldson during the coming weekend or not. He played a long game. It would happen sooner or later. John remembered the observation one of his undergraduate professors made about people in organizations, indeed in many other aspects of life. "Show me," the man said, "someone who is patient, and I'll show you someone who has everything they want."

Chapter 24

S aturday dawned clear and cool. Minnie packed Friday night, leaving the morning free for golf practice and a workout at North Central Country Club. She followed two hours of hitting balls, chipping, and putting with an hour of stretching and weight lifting. She showered and changed into green slacks and a light yellow, long-sleeved top. At 11:15 a.m. she headed downtown.

She arrived at Always Tower 25 minutes later. John stood out front with a briefcase in his left hand and a suit bag slung over his right shoulder. He wore jeans, a red plaid shirt, and a light jacket. After she unlocked the car doors, he threw his bags in the back and slipped into the front passenger seat.

"I can drive," he offered before buckling his seat belt.

"I'm fine," she replied. "You can drive home tomorrow."

They chatted about the weather until he noticed she hadn't taken I-45, the standard route between Dallas and Houston. "I'm going the back way," she told him. "We're headed for the Cypress-Fairbanks area in northwest Houston where they're having the service and where we have our hotel reservations. I'm going I-35 to Waco, then State Highway 6 through Bryan-College Station and Hempstead to U.S. 290. We can avoid cross-town traffic in Houston."

"Any difference in drive time?"

"Only a few minutes longer according to GPS."

Once they passed the Dallas city limits, she looked over at him and asked, "Why did you volunteer for going with me today? I am grateful, but I'm certain you could have found other things worth doing this weekend."

He didn't answer for several moments. She thought

perhaps he hadn't expected the question. He said, finally, "No need for hiding it, Minnie. I wanted to spend today and tomorrow with you."

She covered her mouth, hoping he didn't hear her gasp. "You mean that?"

"Of course, I mean it. We click. You know that. I know it. We shouldn't pretend, as we did with the meetings about my rehab."

She felt her heart pounding. Could he hear it? "You got a lot out of that."

"I did. But we both know we used my rehab as an excuse for getting together. We talked about rehab for 15 minutes and for hours about everything else."

She couldn't help but laugh. "We did that, didn't we?"

"We sure as hell did."

"That's over now. What happens next?"

Instead of answering that question, he turned the tables. "Why did you let me come today?"

She wrinkled her nose and looked over at him. "I had two reasons. First, I meant what I said about preferring that I not do this alone. You should know I have no qualms about long drives by myself. I took a cross-country trip a year and half ago right after my husband died. I drove every mile alone.

"But, with this it's about what's at the end of the journey. I don't know a soul who'll be at the service this evening except Sarah. I need a companion. Everyone else who might have filled that role opted out."

She stretched her arms and gripped the steering wheel harder. She looked out the driver's side window. They'd reached the gently rolling hills of central Texas, a place winter seldom takes a heavy toll. Green grass and wildflowers already sprouted along the road.

Minnie turned toward John. "You were honest with me. I'll

be honest with you. The second reason was the same as yours. I was intrigued by the idea of spending parts of two days and an evening with you."

He drummed his feet against the floor. In a loud voice he said, "So we're even. I wasn't wrong. I sensed it."

"So you did. Again, I ask, what happens next?"

Her question quieted the car for 10 minutes. Signs announcing the mileage to towns they'd pass appeared and faded into the distance. When one of them spoke again it was a suggestion they eat in Waco. They had plenty of tasks after they arrived in Houston – finding and checking into the hotel, changing clothes, locating and getting to the civic center where the service was being held. Eating in Waco made better sense. Meanwhile, Minnie's question remained, just hanging there in the car.

They found a Tex-Mex restaurant just before their turn off the interstate. Before biting into a taco there, John asked, "Did you really meet this Clifford Nguyen guy just once?"

"Just once," Minnie replied, lifting a forkful from her plate of enchiladas. "We met for drinks on a Saturday night at the bar in the Lowes Anatole. After two hours or so I left for a bridge game with friends. We'd agreed on dinner that coming Friday, but he called Monday and said he'd been assigned to take over a big hospital project in Jakarta. Our dinner date was off. He was leaving the next day."

"Hardly seems enough that you'd feel compelled to go to his service."

"That Saturday evening his college-age daughter showed up at the bar while we were talking and having drinks. She'd driven in from Lubbock with a friend for an engagement party that night in Fort Worth. I gave her my card and told her she should call me when she was in town. I was just being nice.

"After the plane crash she called. I talked with her several times. I gave her a shoulder she could cry on. She also needed help in raising money for getting his body home."

John looked dazed. "His firm wouldn't pay for that?"

"They said he was on what they called an excursion when the crash occurred. They'd pay for the part between Jakarta and the U.S. Getting him to Jakarta from that island where he'd visited his friend wasn't their problem."

John laughed and his jaw dropped. "Frolic and Detour."

"What?"

"The old legal concept of Frolic and Detour. Suppose a plumber fixes a leak at your house. Instead of returning to the shop, he drives across town, stops in a bar, has a few drinks, then runs over somebody. The plumbing company may deny responsibility on the theory of Frolic and Detour."

Now, she laughed. "I learn something new every time I'm around you."

∞∞∞

Back on the road, the conversation turned to their old standby – books they'd each read recently. She told him she'd just finished *The Last Picture Show*, a 1966 novel by Larry McMurtry about 1950s life in a small Texas town.

John exclaimed, "I saw that movie on television a few years ago! It was in black and white, wasn't it?"

"It was," she replied. She wondered if he'd connect two characters in the story – a teenage boy engaged in an affair with a woman in her forties – and them.

If he had, he didn't acknowledge it. Instead, he asked, "What made you read that now?"

She didn't tell him that reason – seeing how McMurtry depicted the May/December relationship. Instead, she gave him a truthful, if incomplete, answer. "A good friend recommended another of McMurtry's novels – *Terms of Endearment.* I liked that so much I wanted more of his work."

"He's a really good writer. I've read other things he wrote, like *Lonesome Dove*, which was made into a great TV miniseries."

She nodded and continued. "When *Picture Show* came out in 1971, I wanted to see it. I was nine, so I couldn't go. My mother said she'd heard there were naked people in it. While I was in college, I finally saw it, as you did, on television – edited carefully, of course. I later saw the unedited version on DVD. A few weeks ago, I decided I'd see how the book compared with the movie while I got another taste of McMurtry's work."

"I get it," he said. "Read anything else worthwhile lately?"

"I finished Hillary Clinton's 2016 campaign memoir."

"What Happened ? I read it too," he told her.

"What'd you think?"

John scratched his head. "I'm conflicted. She was honest about some things, but not others. She could have taken more blame for things she skirted over. Your view?"

After running a hand across her throat, Minnie said, "I'm with you. I'd agree she glossed over some things. I feel bad about not having given her more help in the campaign. I could have contributed a lot more money, for example."

"Ever think about campaigning for her in some of those close states? No chance of making a difference in Texas, but maybe more volunteers in Wisconsin and Michigan would have changed things there.

"If I'd thought about it, I could have delayed for two months coming down here for my start at the law firm. I would have tried helping in Pennsylvania, which I know a lot better than Michigan and Wisconsin. That idea crossed my mind after the election."

Minnie put her head down for a moment, then looked up at the road again. "It crossed mine too, but my life was in disarray in the fall of 2016. First, I retired from nursing in September because I was exhausted and bummed out. I wanted nothing but sitting on my butt except the time I could play golf or see plays and movies with my girlfriends.

"Then Bradley died a few weeks before the election. I organized the funeral, which meant fighting with people inside and outside my family about stupid stuff. I hit the road on my trip. I discovered bad things my husband had done or planned on doing. It was a tough time."

They passed Bryan-College Station and Hempstead. Soon they reached the northwest Houston suburbs. "Let's find the hotel, first," she said, looking at her watch. "It's almost four o'clock. We should have just enough time before the service."

∞∞∞

At 7:45 p.m. Minnie and John slipped into a booth in the restaurant of a Marriott Hotel 15 minutes from where they'd attended Clifford Nguyen's memorial service. John had loosened his blue paisley tie, but otherwise looked the same as he'd looked at the service – starched white button-down shirt, gray suit, black dress shoes, and dark socks. She wore a black dress, black shoes with moderate heels, dark hose, and two items of jewelry other than her watch – a gold pendant on the dress and earrings that matched the pendant.

"It was a secular service," John said as he looked over the menu. "I guess you could call that a homily his minister friend delivered. I think I heard the word God twice."

Minnie chuckled. "I didn't have any idea about Clifford's religion, so I didn't know what I should expect."

"He was born in Vietnam?"

"Son of a barmaid at some air base and a black U.S. Air Force enlisted man from Georgia."

"Are his parents still alive?"

"Sarah told me his father, who owned up to him after he arrived in the U.S., even if the man's family didn't, died five years ago. He had no idea whether his mother is dead or alive."

John fingered a napkin on the table. "You dreaded this a little. How do you feel now about having come?"

Minnie put down her wine glass and threw open her palms. "I was glad I could support Sarah. She's alone in the world now. I asked her at the reception if she'd work at staying in touch with me. Through tears, she said she would."

John's eyes glowed as he said, "I've never seen anybody so happy to see someone as she seemed when we arrived at the reception."

"I hope that's genuine, but I could be cynical and say the $8,000 contribution I made for helping her get the body home might have affected her reaction."

He jerked his head back. "That's what it cost?"

"It was $12,000 from the island to Jakarta. She'd raised $4,000 when she called me. I gave her the rest. I think the company paid $13,500 for the Jakarta-U.S. part."

"I'd bet anything government officials on that island get major league kickbacks. No way that should cost so much. I looked up the island. It's only a few hundred miles from Jakarta."

"I hadn't thought of that. As I said, John, I learn something new every time I'm with you."

He held up his wine glass. "Just means we should spend more time together."

Something of a moment of truth arrived after dinner. They had rooms down the hall from each other. Minnie thought about, at least for a fleeting moment, inviting him for a drink and more late night conversation. She knew all bets were off if they ended up together in her room.

He made things easy by telling her he planned on hanging out in the bar, watching an NCAA Basketball Tournament game with two people he'd met at the reception. Having started the day with a golf practice and a workout, endured the three-and-a-half-hour drive, and experienced the service, bed by herself seemed an appealing proposition. They agreed they'd meet for breakfast Sunday at 8:15 and leave for Dallas by half past nine.

∞ ∞ ∞

John drove Sunday. They again talked books. She probed him about his friends. "What kind of people does John Dawson hang out with?" she asked as they passed Hempstead and headed north toward Bryan-College Station.

"A bunch of lawyers." He described his friendship with Don Young, calling him a "Republican guy I often wonder why I like as much as I do. He has backward attitudes, but is the most loyal friend anyone could have. When I was in the hospital he ran errands for me, called people with news of how I was doing, and took care of things I couldn't do for myself.

"When I got home, he organized the group that stayed with me those first days when I could barely get around. It was amazing. I owe him a lot. Yet, I can't stand his politics. I don't understand how someone so kind and compassionate toward individuals can be so hard-hearted otherwise – about poor people, about people in general."

"I remember him from when you were in the hospital," she said. "He was incredibly nice to me."

"He probably opposes every public policy you or I could

name that would make life better for black people in America. But I imagine he'd say you're the greatest thing since sliced bread."

"Why do you think he treated me so well?"

"I told him you were the only person at the hospital, doctor or nurse, I trusted. That was good enough for him."

She brought up a sensitive topic, especially in light of the unanswered question of what was next for them. "You've told me you don't have a girlfriend – something I totally don't get. Are there women around you've at least been attracted to?"

John sighed deeply. "I'll tell you this, but you can't talk about it. I hope you'll meet this person at some future time. I had a crush on the lesbian in our section."

Minnie didn't flinch as she sat in the passenger seat. "Did you ever make a move?"

"No. She and I talked about it, after I found out she was gay. I didn't know she was gay until the day before my accident. I saw her all over her girlfriend in the lobby of our building. I had assumed she was straight, though after I thought about it, I realized she was hiding it in plain sight."

"What did you finally tell her?"

"She figured it out. I just admitted it when she said something."

"How did you feel about it after all that?"

He shook his head slowly. "Embarrassed. I asked myself how I could have missed it.'"

"Don't feel bad. My gay friends – and I have a lot of them – say they fend off advances from straight people all the time. Are you still friends with her?"

"She was another of those who helped so much when I was in the hospital and as I was getting back into the swing of things at work."

Just after they turned on to I-35 in Waco he gazed out the driver's side window and took a deep breath. Looking over at her, he said, "Let me ask you about something you said yesterday when we were talking about Hillary Clinton's book.

"You found out a lot of bad things about your husband after he died. Maybe you can't or won't talk about that with me, but I was touched when you said you'd dealt with such a thing. Losing a spouse seems bad enough. Then you find out that person wasn't who you thought. I'd find that pretty tough."

She said nothing at first, then gathered herself. She had asked that he disclose his inner thoughts about people around him. She felt she should at least try responding in kind. "I'll give you the short version. I haven't figured out the why of some of this myself. The bottom line is my husband neglected me, was cruel to two of our children, and was a hypocrite.

"I was invisible to him, unless I became a profit center. Things our daughters did that offended him were trivial, but he considered disinheriting them because of those things.

"As for his hypocrisy, he hid his true self from me for the entire time we were married. I wouldn't have stayed with a closet homosexual for thirty years had I known. I'm lucky his behavior wasn't the kind that got me killed by a disease. I'll leave it at that."

∞ ∞ ∞

They rolled into Dallas at 1:35 p.m. John drove up outside Always Tower, but didn't park in front. Instead, he circled the block and pulled into an empty parking lot across the street. He said, "There are things that need saying before we part." He killed the engine and turned to her.

"Things came up while we were driving that I deliberately said nothing about at the time. I wanted our undivided attention focused on each other when I said what I plan on saying."

She marveled at his lack of obvious nervousness. He appeared totally confident and at ease. "Okay, John. Tell me."

"I know why you read *The Last Picture Show* recently. You read it for the same reason I read it during the last few weeks. You wanted to see what you could understand about the affair in the story between Ruth Popper and Sonny Crawford. You wanted to see how McMurtry developed a relationship between a woman perhaps 23 years older than her lover. Like me, I believe you wondered what you could learn about us.

"I don't know what conclusion you drew, but I'll tell you the one I did. The only mistake either of them made was that Sonny didn't realize what a good thing he had, in fact, they had. He let himself get distracted by what he thought was a prettier face in Jacy Farrow. I won't get distracted by pretty faces. If things don't work out between us, that won't be the reason."

Her mouth dropped open. She started to say something, but he held up his hand and asked that she, "Wait until I'm through." She sank back in the seat, but kept looking at him, still astounded he was saying the things he said, yet appeared so calm and under control.

"The other thing I left alone was the question you asked yesterday after we'd been on the road about 45 minutes – 'What happens next?' I'll tell you what I want next.

"This becomes a dating relationship, that's what. So, I'm asking you out to dinner Friday night. I want to take you to a really nice restaurant I know. This isn't for talking about my rehab or anything else we could make up as a pretext for seeing each other. This is a man asking a woman out on a date, nothing more, nothing less.

"One last thing and I'll shut up. I know how old you are and I know how old I am. I know what color you are and I know what color I am. Neither matters to me at all. I hope neither matters to you. The one thing I can assure you of is that I don't care if either matters to anyone else."

She stared at him. Long seconds passed. Finally, she opened her mouth. "There is so much in there, John. We could talk for days about everything you said. Knowing us, we will. Right now, the only thing I'll say is yes, I'll have dinner with you Friday night."

He leaned over and kissed her on the lips, then got out of the car and retrieved his bags from the back seat. She got out and they embraced. As he crossed the street and went into his building, she got back into the car and headed home.

Chapter 25

S utton's Steakhouse sat tucked away in a warehouse area in northwest Dallas, a few blocks off I-35E. The non-descript building gave few hints of how high the restaurant ranked among the city's upscale eateries. John told Minnie, "Black tie isn't required, but I wouldn't be out of place if I showed up in a tux."

"Then I'll wear a cocktail dress and get my hair done," she said when they talked by phone Wednesday before their first official date on Friday.

He settled for a blue business suit, white shirt, and red tie. She wore a rose gold dress that ended just below her knees. She added black pumps with four-inch heels, carried a matching handbag, and wore gold earrings.

They arrived at 6:20 p.m., waited 15 minutes in a tastefully lit lounge, then were escorted through a dining room with a high ceiling and multiple chandeliers. Plush, leather-bound, high-backed chairs accompanied tables of various sizes with ivory-colored tablecloths. Servers in white dinner jackets and black pants or skirts scurried about, pouring drinks, taking orders, and serving food.

Minnie noticed the absence of black diners in the room. She'd been in such circumstances before, of course, especially in private clubs. Her date on those occasions hadn't been a young white man. That was new.

Because she'd been in so many top end restaurants, the dining experience wasn't unfamiliar. John had hyped the service and the food and neither disappointed. She didn't eat steak often, but he convinced her she should try Sutton's small ribeye. Afterwards, she confessed it was as good as she'd ever tasted.

Their conversation unfolded as she'd hoped. Before dinner ended they laughed and shared stories about childhoods, her work, his accident, and, of course, books. By the time they split cheesecake for dessert, she'd forgotten she was a 55-year old black woman on a date with a 27-year old white man.

The end of the evening reminded her. The meal done, John asked her if she needed anything.

"I should freshen up before we leave," she said.

"I'll take care of the bill while you do that. I'll meet you in the lobby."

She picked up her handbag and headed for the restroom. Afterwards she stepped into the lobby and waited for him. Two white men – both her age or older, she concluded – stood talking nearby, their backs to her. Neither saw her as far as she could tell.

"Did you see that old colored woman with that young guy a few tables over from us?" one asked.

"I did," said the other, a taller man with thinning hair. Minnie couldn't see either man's face. "That looked so strange. Perhaps she was a maid or caretaker of some kind who'd worked for his family and he was treating her."

The shorter man shook his head. "I don't think so. Did you see how their hands touched and they giggled, like they knew each other, and not casually? It seemed different from what you're suggesting."

"You don't think they're together in some way do you?"

"They acted like it."

"If that's true, it's the most disgusting thing I've ever seen."

At that moment, two women emerged from the restroom and joined the two men. Minnie turned around and looked for John. He came out of the dining room with a huge smile on his face. Her grim expression stopped him in his tracks.

To John's queries about what was wrong, as they waited at valet parking, Minnie would say only, "I'll tell you in the car." After they pulled into traffic, she shook her head and said, "I never imagined it would be like that."

"What being like what?" he asked and looked over at her from the driver's seat. "I thought you had a nice time. Well, it seemed you did until the restroom trip."

"I did until I got out of the restroom. That's when things changed."

"What are you talking about?"

She reconstructed the conversation between the men in the lobby. She finished by saying, "The worst thing was their assumption I'm a maid or caretaker for your family."

John said nothing for a few moments. He turned toward her and asked, "Would you like to go somewhere – maybe our usual Starbucks – and have some tea so we can talk about this?"

"I'll give you credit, John, for already knowing me pretty well. Yes, I'd like some tea, a cuppa as our British TV friends say." She managed a smile as he turned the car toward their destination.

At Starbucks they joked about being overdressed. They found their usual table in the back and sipped hot tea from paper cups.

"I get it that you're upset," John said. "I'm annoyed too. We should explore why what you heard bothers you so much and what it means for us going forward. This may have been our first date, but I hadn't planned on its being our last. In fact, I have something I want you to do with me Sunday. But answer my question first. Why did this bother you?"

"It all did – the talk about my being a servant, the idea of us together as disgusting."

He frowned. "That's not why, Minnie. That's what you didn't like. Tell me why this bothered you."

She shook her head and muttered, "Okay, Mr. Big Firm Lawyer, Mr. Ivy League honors graduate, what's the difference? You're playing mind games with me."

"I am not. 'What' is the language that upset you. 'Why' is what's inside that makes you feel hurt or upset or whatever else you feel. Knowing that may help us figure out how we respond in the best way for us."

She shrugged her shoulders. "I'll play along. I still think you're showing off how smart you are. I already know that. Your mother made sure I understood it when you were in the hospital."

He held up his hands in a "T" formation. "Time out. I'm not the enemy. Could you just answer my question? Why did what you overheard from two old farts in the lobby of a restaurant so trouble you, especially after we had a great meal and so much fun being with each other under no pretenses?"

She sighed deeply and crossed her arms. "I'm worried everyone thinks that way. Any time we go out, somebody may look at us and say what they said – that our being together is disgusting. John, I'm not disgusting, no matter who I'm with."

He reached over and lifted her hand from her tea cup. He held it for a few moments. Warmth spread from her to him. "No, you're not. You're so far from disgusting, anybody who can't see that is a damn fool.

"But, think of it like this. There are plenty of people who won't see it that way. Besides, we shouldn't worry about what anybody else – friend or foe – thinks. We should focus on what we think and feel. We should talk about this evening in those terms, not what two bozos in a restaurant lobby said about us."

She dropped her head and squeezed back on the hand he still held. "Tonight drove home how hard this might get. And we're just beginning. This was our first real date."

He let go of her hand and touched his lips with his right

index finger. "Let's give ourselves the first chance at screwing this up before we offer somebody else that opportunity.

"That brings me to the next thing I suggest we do together. Would you go with me Sunday afternoon to the prehistoric era exhibit at the Perot Museum of Nature and Science? It includes some great material on Neanderthals. I bet it's more interesting than the examples you heard tonight."

She cracked the hint of a smile. "I'll go. I bet you're right."

∞∞∞

Despite being angry and hurt over the men-in-the-lobby incident, Minnie didn't change her mind about where she thought her entanglement with John Dawson would lead. That conclusion left a piece of unfinished business. Saturday morning, she called his office.

"You believed me when I told you I'm usually here at this time on Saturday, didn't you?" he asked after answering his phone.

"You're generally a man of your word."

He laughed. "What do you mean' generally?'"

She matched the laugh. "No insult intended. There's something I need to ask you to do."

"Yeah?"

Minnie took a few quick breaths. "Last Sunday when you said what you wanted next was for this to become a dating relationship...."

"Yes?"

"I thought of something I should ask you, but forgot in the heat of the moment."

"Kissing and hugging took priority?"

"They did. I rather enjoyed that," she acknowledged. "An unexpected benefit of your presence on the trip."

"What did you forget?"

Minnie felt her leg and arm muscles quiver. Was she really asking him what she heard herself asking? "Whether what you called 'a dating relationship' includes being intimate?"

"You mean sex?"

"I mean sex."

She expected John would laugh and he did. When he got the laughter under control, he said, "Of course. In due time, I'm sure."

Suddenly Minnie relaxed. "Then please come by the hospital this week for a blood test."

"Are you afraid I have something?"

Her nervousness gone, she now spoke matter-of-factly. "I'm not afraid. I'm cautious. When it happens, I want spontaneity. I'm too old for awkward questions and fumbling around with condoms. I can't get pregnant, so let's get the other worry out of the way."

"I'm all for spontaneity, but rest assured, I don't have anything."

"If that's the case, you should have no problem taking the test."

"What about you? You said your husband was a closet homosexual, I think you called him."

"I also told you what he did didn't expose me to disease."

"What did he do?"

"I'll tell you at an appropriate time. This is about you and me, not him."

"Oh really?"

"Yes. Just so you know, I get tested for HIV, and other

things, every quarter. My test two weeks ago was as negative as ever."

"You've made your point. I'll come in Wednesday after five o'clock. That's your long day, isn't it?"

"It is. The lab closes at six o'clock, so make sure you're on time."

∞∞∞

Their morning conversation made the prospect of sex with John real for Minnie in a way it never had been before. If he passed a blood test, what reason existed for not jumping his bones? She could overthink this, of course, and find excuses for not doing it, but really, why not?

At first, she felt calm about it. Its inevitability eliminated worry, anxiety, or fear that bed with John might be a mistake. Then, a different realization set in. Calm wasn't the right word. As she went about that Saturday's chores, the whole idea of calm felt out of place. The word didn't belong in her vocabulary about this.

No, Minnie was excited! Breathlessness and a dry mouth told her that. She felt impatient. Assuming he passed the test, no fear of medical consequences would clutter her mind or inner feelings. The prospect of stroking and caressing his body, of feeling his thrusts, of experiencing orgasms with him, generated longing, craving, and anticipation. It was time she focused on the good side of sharing her body with him.

∞∞∞

During the next three weeks, Minnie and John had three dates. Every one increased the desire each had for the other. Each included a reminder that because of age or race or both, they were outliers in the world of male-female dating. Each time they saw each other ratcheted up the tension and their longing about sleeping together.

"I love exhibits like this," she said as they left the Perot museum. "I learn so much."

"I hung out a lot in museums in Philadelphia my third year in law school."

Her right hand flew to her chest. "You had time for hanging out in museums? I thought law students kept their noses to the grindstone 24-seven."

"That's first year. You don't know what you're doing and you're scared to death. By third year, you have the hang of it. You can't change your grade point much, so most people don't sweat it."

In a soft tone, she asked, "What kind of museums did you visit?"

"All kinds – art, natural history like today, you name it. I bought a guide to Philadelphia museums. I visited nearly all of them by the time I finished law school."

She took his arm as they strolled through the parking lot toward his car. Suddenly, three white teenagers ran past them and shouted in unison, "Old black tail! Old black tail! Wish I had some old black tail!" They ran out of view almost as fast as they'd appeared.

Minnie let go of John's arm, but he grabbed hers. They stopped, though they hadn't reached the car. "I told you we might see it every time we go out," she said.

"You won't let those clowns bother you, will you? They're just stupid kids."

They resumed walking. At the car, as he opened her door, she said, "I suppose you're right. That's one thing that makes Friday night painful. I expect more from mature, successful men than from loud-mouthed kids."

∞∞∞

A week later, they decided they'd take in *Black Panther*, a gigantic box office smash released in mid-February that neither had seen. "I can't believe we've both missed this movie," John said as they stood in line for tickets on a Saturday afternoon at a suburban theater complex. They'd nearly reached the ticket window when they heard a gasp behind them.

A young black boy blurted out in a loud voice, "Grandmomma! That white man has his hand on that black woman's behind. He shouldn't do that."

"Shush," admonished the thin, brown-skinned woman who stood beside the boy. She wore dark, neatly pressed slacks and a white blouse. John thought she looked a little older than Minnie. "Darius, be quiet. Mind your own business."

"But –"

"We don't talk about other people like that."

The boy said nothing more. John bought tickets and he and Minnie passed by the woman and the boy on their way to buy popcorn. The visibly sweating woman spoke up. "Sir, I apologize. My grandson needs work on his manners."

John said, "It's okay. I'm sure I said some impolitic things when I was his age. What is he, about 10?"

"Tell the nice man how old you are, Darius."

If Darius felt contrition, it didn't show in his loud, highpitched voice. "I'm 10."

The grandmother grimaced. "Again, sir, I'm very sorry."

Minnie looked down at the boy. "Darius, your grandmother is obviously a smart woman. You should do what she says." She grabbed John's hand and they walked toward the concession stand.

∞ ∞ ∞

Their dates left John giddy. Spending time with Minnie under no pretext provided the mental and intellectual stimulation he'd craved for so long. The interaction affected him in a way he'd not thought about before when it came to women. Being with her made him feel good inside. Really good.

John had always processed dating and relationships with women first through the prism of activities. He judged dates by what he and the woman did – talk books, hang out in museums, drink good wine, explore mutual interests, etc.

Now, with Minnie, for the first time, his feelings meant the most. When they were together, just being with her topped all else. When they parted, he felt warm and fresh inside, though he missed her as soon as she walked out the door.

They hadn't had sex yet so he couldn't say what feelings that would generate. Instinctively, John knew sex with Minnie would jump start him in a way it never had before. He just knew it.

∞ ∞ ∞

After the dinner, the museum, and the movie, John wanted an entire day with Minnie – time for walking in a park, taking a drive in the country, eating a picnic lunch, and winding up with watching a brilliant sunset from a hillside. He couldn't arrange all that – scenic hillsides are few and far between around Dallas – but on the Friday of the third week in April they got close.

John took the day off, knowing that meant a full weekend of work, given a new merger and acquisition project Ed Ward handed him the day before. Minnie didn't work most Fridays anyway, so they met at 9:45 a.m. at their usual Starbucks, sipped drinks, and swapped thoughts on *11/22/63*, Stephen King's time-travel novel about the JFK assassination.

They left her car there and took off for White Rock Lake Park where they walked for almost two hours, observing and photographing plants, birds, and waves on the lake. Beneath blue skies and in 70-degree temperatures, they sat on a blanket under trees and ate sandwiches, fresh fruit, and cookies John packed in an old-fashioned picnic basket.

Lunch done, John moved beside Minnie and wrapped his arms around her. She looked into his eyes and reached for him. Their lips met and he pulled her down beside him on the blanket. Their hands roamed each other's bodies. The embrace lasted a long moment. When it ended, they propped their heads on their elbows and just looked at each other.

Finally, he said, "We should go. I think you can imagine why."

"I agree," she replied. "Soon, John. Soon."

After the picnic, he suggested they go for a drive. On maps he'd noticed backroads north of town he thought worth exploring. They headed up the Dallas Tollway into still open spaces. Land-for-sale signs suggested things wouldn't stay that way long.

"This area is changing," Minnie said. "When I moved to Dallas in the 1980s, there was nothing out here except a few farmhouses. Now, convenience stores and gas stations have sprung up at every intersection of the old country roads. Can subdivisions and Wal-Mart be far behind?"

"Probably not," he replied. "For all I know, I'm working on a deal somebody's doing for building who-knows-what here."

After driving around a while, they headed west and reached I-35E near Lewisville before turning south toward Dallas. She looked over at him and said, "I hate seeing today end. This has been wonderful."

"It doesn't have to end. We could get dinner and spend the evening doing whatever." Especially in light of their interlude on the blanket, did 'whatever' include sleeping together that night? John's HIV test had come back negative.

"I promised Cynthia I'd go to her party tonight." Minnie's mention of Cynthia apparently put a damper on things, and John spotted it immediately.

"Who is Cynthia and why did bringing up her name make you look like you just found out you have cancer?"

She didn't hide her thoughts. "Cynthia McFadden is one of my best friends. We've known each other for 25 years. We play golf together. We're in the same clubs and organizations. We tell each other everything. I haven't told her about dating you. When I do, it won't be pretty."

John responded with a tight grimace. "Why not? She doesn't know me from Adam."

"Pure and simple, Cynthia is a snob. She thinks black women with standing in our community must have a certain kind of man. You will not make her list."

"Because I'm white? Because I'm young?"

"Those two things are just the start."

"What else could there be?"

"You don't belong to one of the black fraternities. You aren't part of the black elite."

"From what you've told me, you weren't always part of that. My impression is that you and your husband worked your way into that as the business grew."

"Your impression is correct. That doesn't keep Cynthia

from looking down on somebody who isn't part of it. What's important with Cynthia is that you can't ever be part of it."

"It still comes down to age and race, right?"

"Or race and age."

They reached the Starbucks lot where she left her car. She saw a pained expression on his face when she opened the car door. "Don't worry about Cynthia. I've thought this through. I won't let her stop me from dating you. If it doesn't work out between us, it won't be because of Cynthia."

She stepped around to the driver's side. He rolled down his window and she leaned in for a long goodbye kiss. Still, when they broke the kiss, John's troubled expression remained. "Hey, don't worry about it, I said. By the way, next Friday let me give you a treat. I'll make you dinner at my house. How about that?"

He nodded and said, "That sounds wonderful." They kissed again, she walked to her car, and they both drove away.

Chapter 26

During the days before Friday, April 27, 2018, John decided he just wouldn't think about the possibilities dinner at Minnie's house might open. He went about work as he always did, drafting documents, reviewing statutes and case law, consulting colleagues concerning problems that cropped up on his projects, and conferring with clients about options for moving their matters forward.

He worked out every day except Wednesday, his usual day off from the gym. He called Minnie Thursday and asked if he should bring wine or dessert. She said he should bring himself. John, therefore, felt little tension or anxiety when he parked in her driveway at 5:55 p.m.

She opened the front door wearing a big smile, khaki shorts, a dark blue polo shirt, low-cut white socks, and no shoes. Looking down at her feet, John asked, "Should I take mine off?"

"Would you please? Thanks for being so observant. I usually have to ask that of first-time guests. I have light-toned carpet lots of places in the house so I'm careful about what gets tracked in."

"Gladly," he said as he stepped out of his slip-ons. He'd gone casual that day at work, so he wore dark slacks and a blue button-down dress shirt, but no coat or tie. "I'll leave the shoes here in the hallway, along with my briefcase."

She laughed. "I hope you're not planning on working tonight."

"Toothbrush," he explained. "If I can, I brush my teeth after every meal, so I carry a toothbrush in my briefcase."

"Nice habit," she said, leading him through a well-lit room with overstuffed chairs and walls covered by tapestries on one side and paintings of outdoor scenes on the other. He noticed a big-screen television set, at least 60 inches, in a corner across from a leather couch. End tables and lamp stands gave the room a comfortable, yet practical, feel.

"Do you want to wash up?" she asked. "Dinner is almost ready. I'm waiting for the bread to bake."

She pointed him to a half-bath just off the kitchen. When he returned, she was putting a loaf of French bread into a straw basket. He walked through the kitchen and into a dining area, then sat down at a table with two place settings. "What're we having?"

"Salmon," she replied from the kitchen. "I'm a fish person and salmon is my favorite."

"I'm up for it."

"To go with it, we have salad and wild rice. Dessert is a surprise treat."

"This is your show. I'm just audience." When John looked up, she'd come out of the kitchen holding a big salad bowl and tongs. "Can I help?" he asked.

She set the bowl on the table. "Here's the salad. Serve both of us. I'll get the main dishes. And, oh, over there on the side table you'll find two kinds of white wine. Pick what you like and pour yourself some."

"What are my choices?" he asked as he stood up and filled the salad bowls.

"Riesling and Chardonnay. I'm not big on Chardonnay but I put out a bottle since I had no idea what you'd want. That's my glass of Riesling on the table."

"I like Riesling."

"I have two bottles of it left, the one that's out, and one in the fridge. Question for the evening: Will we finish both bottles?"

John didn't answer. He poured his wine and sat down again. She came out of the kitchen and put the main dishes on the table. He stood up. "Hey," he said in a loud voice. "I forgot something."

"What?" she asked, seeming startled.

"You deserve a better greeting than I gave you. We haven't seen each other in a week. I can do better than coming into your house, taking off my shoes, and plopping down my briefcase."

He embraced her. They kissed on the lips and held the embrace. He smiled as she turned and began serving the food.

"I agree, that was better," she said, as they sat down. "Thank you. But wasn't I the one who should have given you a better greeting? I'm the hostess this evening."

"It's okay. All's well that ends well."

She held up her wine glass. "Fair enough, but right now let's toast the possibility of a great evening."

They clicked their glasses and he said, "To a great evening."

She unfolded her napkin and placed it in her lap. "I don't make a big deal of saying grace before meals. It's a personal choice. I sometimes say a short, silent prayer of thanks before I eat. Whatever you want to do is fine."

"Please, Minnie, do what makes you comfortable."

She bowed her head for a few seconds while he sat silently. She lifted her fork and declared, "I'm ready for food."

They ate slowly. Conversation and savoring the meal and the wine took precedence over all else. Topics ranged from the state of Minnie's golf game to the fall mid-term elections and the possibility Democrats might take control of the House of Representatives.

At some point, John asked how she cooked the salmon. "It's so good," he said.

"It's about the spices," she replied between bites and sips of wine. "I use garlic powder, onion powder, sage, black pepper, and paprika. I bake it at 325 for 30 to 35 minutes. The key is seasoning it in the morning, so it marinates all day."

She asked about the deals he worked on at the law firm. He told her she didn't want to know as much as she thought she did, but still gave her a basic primer on what he did for 55 to 65 hours each week. "You're right," she said at the end of his soliloquy. "I could have done without a lot of that."

They finished the first bottle of Riesling. She got up, retrieved, and opened the second. He stopped her after she poured him half a glass. "I'll fall asleep if I have more than this."

"We can't have that. I don't think I'll have that problem," she said as she filled her glass.

"Any books worth talking about?" he asked when they'd both finished eating.

"Yes, but let's talk about them in the family room – the room you came in through. We can do that as soon as we finish dessert."

They took their plates into the kitchen. "No pots and pans to clean?" he asked, noticing the tidy range top and sink.

"I clean as I go. I hate having that left after a nice dinner. Here, hand me your plate. I'll scrape it and put it in the dishwasher right now. After dessert, I'll turn it on and I'm done. How about that?"

"I'm impressed. You're amazing."

She broke out the surprise dessert, strawberry cheesecake that he swore, "is as good as what we had at Sutton's a few weeks ago."

"I hoped you'd like it. I buy it at a little bakery that's close by. They say it's their most popular item."

After an hour of book discussion and more wine, John

announced he needed a restroom break. He scurried off to the outer hallway and returned with his briefcase in hand. He put it down on the couch, grabbed his toothbrush, and said, "I'll be right back. I know where the little bathroom is."

∞ ∞ ∞

When 27 – year old John Dawson emerged from that bathroom and ambled back through the kitchen, he would never have imagined the sight that greeted him. There in the subdued light of her family room, beside the chair in which she'd been sitting through their exploration of *Faces at the Bottom of the Well*, Derrick Bell's fanciful missive about race in America, 55 – year old Minnie Donaldson stood, wearing only a bright yellow bra and matching panties.

The bra had lace cups and little flowers sewn along the edges. The hipster panties set off her brown skin, creating a glow. As John entered the room, she put down her wine glass and held out both arms. "Have I made myself clear about what we should do with the rest of the evening?" she asked.

He embraced her and ran his hands up and down her back. Before long, he slid his hands down, under the waistband of her panties, and onto the cheeks of her butt. She responded with soft moans. They kissed for a long moment, their tongues probing each other's mouths. She must have brushed her teeth while he did, because she tasted fresh. When they finally broke the kiss, his hands still inside her panties, he said, "You have made yourself perfectly clear. I do think, however, I'm overdressed."

"You are. If you'll come with me, we can rectify that." She pulled out of the embrace, took his hand, and led him down a hallway. Her fingers felt smooth and welcoming in his hand. She opened the door of her bedroom and he followed her inside.

The bedroom light, what there was of it, came from floor-level plug-ins. It wasn't dark, but it wasn't bright either. He didn't pay the furniture much attention aside from locating the queen-sized bed. As they stood beside it, they resumed the embrace and had an even longer kiss. Her soft skin made him think of how much lotion she must use, given her time in the sun.

"John, your clothes."

"Oh, yes." He unbuttoned and shed his shirt. She unbuckled his belt and pulled it out of the loops of his slacks. He stepped out of them, leaving a pile on the floor. His socks and black briefs, which together they pushed down, topped off the pile. That left him naked and with a pronounced erection. His anticipation grew by the second.

"Now, you have too many clothes," he teased.

"Not for long." She reached behind her, unhooked the bra, and slipped the straps off her shoulders. Her panties hit the floor next. "There," she said. "We're even." They resumed their kiss, but soon fell together onto the bed. Again he relished the fresh taste of her mouth and the gentleness of her touch.

From their first moments in bed, John understood this wouldn't be like any other sexual event he'd had. He didn't believe it was only because she was more experienced by decades than any woman he'd been with before. He also knew it wasn't because of some demeaning racial stereotype. This was different because this woman had something rare, something she must have had for years. Perhaps it had been hidden, shrouded, bottled up in a deteriorating marriage. Minnie Donaldson – as a sexual being – was extraordinary.

After wondering for months what she looked like without clothes, John found himself taken not so much with the sight of her nakedness, as with her sexual energy. He couldn't imagine a woman more alive. Her rounded bottom, the one he'd kneaded under those yellow panties while they kissed in the family room and standing by the bed, fascinated him. So did her firm breasts, which filled his hands. Black nipples and areole punctuated their size and shape.

Her bottom and breasts were great assets. They weren't, however, what confirmed he could accept the slings and arrows he might suffer from family, friends, or the public for being with a woman of her age and hue. Aside from her other qualities, possible aspersions were worth it because this woman loved lovemaking. Besides that, it became clear she liked to fuck.

Minnie possessed the bed. She didn't stay in one spot, waiting on his moves. She thrashed around in his arms. She caressed his bottom and fondled his genitals. He gave thanks she wasn't shy about that. She moved behind him and rubbed his shoulders and neck. She rolled him over and pushed him down on his back, then climbed atop him and pulled his erection inside her. "Ahah," she gasped at that first penetration.

John had had sex in the cowgirl position a time or two, but it wasn't memorable. The experience left him asking what the fuss was about. Now he understood the position wasn't the story. The story was who was in the position with him.

Minnie's undulating hips, deep kisses, and hands that wandered across his chest made him ecstatic this was finally happening between them. She leaned over so her nipples grazed his chest. Moments later, she moved forward enough that those nipples, extended and stiff, reached his mouth. He lifted his head and nibbled on them. She sped up her hips and rubbed his chest harder. She pinched his nipples. Her kisses made him grow firmer inside her.

Was she like this because she'd lived so much longer than he had? Was it all about experience? Did pure lust drive her? Could her energy stem from real feelings for him? All of the above, he hoped.

Was it the frustration of having done without during the waning years of her collapsing marriage? When they sat under the trees and ate the picnic lunch, she'd hinted a sexual drought set in well before her husband died.

Was it her fitness level? Tonight, she showed she didn't reserve her athleticism for the golf course and the weight room. Perhaps an erotic gene generated her sexual energy.

John got so lost in her movements it took a while before he noticed the way her mouth had dropped open and that the sound of her shallow breathing and low moans now filled the room. Something was happening. Her hips moved faster. She held onto his arms, again reminding him of the smoothness of her hands. Suddenly, she shuddered. He felt a spasm inside her. It went on and on, before she finally relaxed and leaned back. That move, in the dim light, pasted an image of her breasts on his brain. This woman knew how to have an orgasm!

He wasn't done. He turned them over and moved atop her. Now John pushed into her. She wrapped her powerful legs around him. He felt captured. He gave silent thanks for the leg lifts she did. It was okay she could do more than he could. She whispered in his ear. "John, please! Fuck me hard. It's been so long."

He complied with her wish. Now his youth energized their lovemaking. He pushed harder and harder. She climaxed again, though he remained a distance from his. She held him tighter. Her embrace spurred him on. Finally, he felt his climax building. He erupted inside her.

Minnie and John fell asleep in each other's arms and stayed

that way until the early hours of Saturday morning. She awakened and, after a bathroom trip, snuggled up against him from behind. A few minutes later, he turned over and embraced her.

They made love again. This time they were quieter. They took longer. They experimented with different positions. Again, her multiple orgasms amazed him. He delayed his release until he became convinced of her satisfaction. Finally, she implored that he, "Finish me, please. I need one more." When he exploded inside her, she shuddered and her body went limp. He rolled off her and they slept again.

When daylight awoke them both, she turned over and looked into his young, blue eyes. She whispered, "Thank you for showing me I can still live this life – a life in which I join with someone I care about and express myself in the way we did last night and this morning. I had started questioning whether I still could. Whatever happens between us, you gave me that and I am grateful."

He said nothing. He kissed her again and smiled.

She touched his lips with her index finger. "There's nothing you need to say, John. Nothing at all."

Chapter 27

L utheran Memorial Hospital hosted three major social
events each year. Two – the Harvest Moon Dinner Dance
in October and the Memorial Day Picnic – were heavily
advertised fundraisers for the hospital's community outreach
programs. The annual employees-only Christmas party
rewarded the staff for the year's work. Even in retirement,
Minnie attended two of the three, missing only the dance
while on her trip after Bradley's death. Each presented an
opportunity for hanging out with friends and catching up on
hospital gossip.

Cynthia McFadden always attended the dance and the
picnic. Though not a Lutheran Memorial employee, she
counted a long list of friends and real estate clients on
the nursing and administrative staffs. Her husband served
numerous legal clients among the hospital's physician corps.
Between them, they bought over two dozen tickets to each
event every year.

Knowing Cynthia would show up at the picnic, Minnie
faced her first public dilemma about her involvement with
John. Not going wasn't an option. She could show up with him
and endure a confrontation with Cynthia during or after the
event. She could leave John behind and hate herself for hiding
a relationship that was becoming increasingly important in
her life.

She discovered how important the week before the picnic.
John took a business trip in advance of the Memorial Day
weekend. She felt empty during his absence. They'd fallen
into the habit of his staying at her house on Thursdays,
Fridays, Saturdays, and Sundays – nights before her days off.

"John, you can't use this against me, but I seem lost in

this house without you here," she told him on the phone Friday afternoon when he called with his Saturday flight information. She'd dropped him at the airport Tuesday night and promised she'd pick him up when his flight arrived from Chicago. "Isn't that the silliest thing you ever heard?"

"No. My hotel room has felt pretty empty."

She clenched her jaw. "I've lived in this house 23 years. Three children grew up and left the nest. My husband croaked. I didn't feel lonely here after any of that. I might have been lonely in my life, but the feeling wasn't about being by myself in this house. This is crazy."

"Don't sweat it," he said. "I'm coming home tomorrow afternoon. We'll make up for lost time."

"You can say that at 27 a lot easier than I can at 55. I don't know how much time I have left with you."

"Age doesn't mean everything. I might get run over by a bus on the way to the airport tomorrow. Hell, the plane might crash. I don't know how much time I have with you."

Minnie swallowed hard. "I'm just lonely, that's all."

He laughed and said he'd see her late Saturday afternoon.

∞∞∞

Still anxious about how she'd deal with Cynthia at the picnic, Minnie learned that fate had brought the issue to a head. Cynthia discovered Minnie's involvement with John and phoned her about it the day before the picnic.

"What are you doing?" Cynthia asked when Minnie answered at 5:15 p.m. Sunday. John had gone to his office to tidy up a few documents, leaving Monday clear for a morning in bed and the picnic in the afternoon. He said he'd return before eight o'clock. "Who is that young white boy I saw you with today?"

Minnie's heart raced. She knew what was coming. "You saw me today? Where?"

"Not that it matters, but at Starbucks on Northwest Highway. You haven't answered the question. Who is he?"

Wishing she was somewhere else, Minnie said, "I don't appreciate your tone. John is a friend. What business is it of yours who he is? It's like you were spying on me." Minnie wondered why she said that. She knew Cynthia had run across them by accident.

"I wasn't spying on you. I went there for the same reason you did – drinks. Today, I got mine to go. You didn't. You sat in the back doing kissy-face with whoever he is. You were so busy you couldn't see me."

"No, I didn't see you."

"You're stalling. Tell me who he is and why you were draped all over each other, playing patty-cake games with your hands, and whispering in each other's ears."

Minnie felt her fingers turn cold. Talking about this with Cynthia wasn't fun. "Yes, I'm dating somebody new. He is young and he is white. His name is John Dawson.

"I have no idea what will happen between us. We enjoy each other's company. For the moment, we've decided we'll spend time with each other." Minnie thought she sounded defensive.

Cynthia leaped to the bottom line. "Are you sleeping with him? And no bullshit about that being none of my business. You and I have told each other all kinds of things about our sex lives for a long time. You even said Bradley wouldn't screw you for three years before he died. Tell me if you're opening your legs for that white boy. How old is he, anyway? He looks 15."

"John isn't 15. He's 27, a summa cum laude graduate of

Brown University and ranked number one in his class at the University of Pennsylvania Law School."

"Well, la-de-da. Good for him. You didn't answer my question. Are you screwing him?"

Minnie's stomach felt heavy. She hesitated. Was she ashamed about having slept with John or disappointed in herself that she hadn't told Cynthia she could go to hell? Finally, she said, "John and I have been intimate."

Cynthia's voice grew louder. "Don't give me that 'been intimate' bullshit. Come out and say it like it is. You're letting that little white boy stick his dick between your legs, aren't you?"

"I've said what I'm going to say."

Minnie reflected for a second on the conversation. She'd heard real hostility from her friend. It wasn't just the shrill, outraged tone or the aggressive cross-examination. It was also the crude language. She didn't use vulgarities except when really upset. As Minnie had feared, her involvement with John bothered Cynthia.

"Well, I'll be goddamned," she continued. "You are fucking a little white child. Why are you doing this? What could you possibly see in a 27-year old white boy? You're old enough to be his mother. Have you lost your mind?"

"I haven't lost my mind. I've given this lots of thought, including how friends like you might react. Unfortunately, my prediction about you has come true. You can't help being petty."

Minnie spoke on the edge between hurt and hope. She fought back tears as she said, "I fantasized you might show compassion and interest in my happiness and emotional wellbeing. I thought maybe you could look beyond race and age and ask what this means for me. Dating John has made a big difference in my life. I'm a new person. Things I wondered if I could ever feel again, I feel. My outlook on life is better than since long before Bradley died. I wish you could be happy for me."

If Minnie's words or her tone made any difference for Cynthia, it didn't show when she responded. "Don't think you can make me see this differently with high and mighty talk or that I'll have sympathy for you because you claim you're lonely. This is beyond the pale. I'd say something if you were dating a 27-year old black guy. That'd be bad enough. But a 27-year old white boy?"

"You didn't object when Dorothy Hindman and Juanita Wherry divorced their black husbands and married white men."

Cynthia snapped back, "I objected all right. I raised hell with both of them. But they at least had enough sense that they got with men their own age. In Dorothy's case, she tried hard to find a black man and kept striking out. How hard did you try?"

"Hard enough. But that's beside the point. When John asked me out, I decided I'd say yes. That's all that matters."

Cynthia asked, "How'd you meet this boy, anyway?" She didn't turn down the volume.

Minnie's neck stiffened. Cynthia's attack has been longer and more intense than she'd expected. "Please quit calling him a boy. He's not a boy. He's an accomplished young man who has a bright future as a corporate lawyer."

Cynthia remained undeterred. "I asked how you met him."

"He was a patient in the hospital last year. He had a serious automobile accident near Tyler and was flown in by helicopter."

A big sigh came through the phone. "That makes this worse. You know you shouldn't do that."

"I didn't do anything wrong. John and I did nothing while he was in the hospital except talk. We didn't date until months later – long after he got out."

Minnie felt Cynthia's disbelief through the phone. "If you

say so."

"That's the truth. You know me better than that."

"I thought I knew you. It looks like I don't know you at all. I sure didn't think you'd do something this stupid."

Minnie's body tensed and she ground her teeth together. "I don't appreciate being called stupid."

"I'm sorry. I didn't say you are stupid. This is a really stupid thing you're doing. There's a difference, you know."

"I've had enough from you, Cynthia. I assume I'll see you at the picnic tomorrow?"

"You may see me, but I have nothing to say to you. Don't bother me. I'll have better things to do than waste my time talking to you. Good bye."

∞∞∞

When John returned from his office, as promised at eight o'clock, he noticed Minnie's vacant stare and downturned mouth. "Again, you look like you got that cancer diagnosis. I'm guessing you had a conversation with somebody who's not happy about our seeing each other."

She tugged on her hair, tonight partially covered by a light blue scarf. "How'd you know?"

"Nothing else bothers you much."

They stood by the kitchen table. She'd poured them tea and set out bowls filled with blueberries, blackberries, strawberries, and sliced bananas. She added side plates of baked chicken fingers. Minnie seldom ate anything this late except such light fare. Before they sat down, they embraced and enjoyed a long kiss.

When they pulled back from each other, John asked, "Isn't that worth whatever tacky things somebody said about the old woman and the kid? And, they threw in that we aren't the same color, right?"

"Of course. It was my friend Cynthia. The way she talked at the end of the conversation she's now my ex-friend."

He blinked his eyes. "Did you tell her about us? How did she know?"

"She saw us at Starbucks today. She found inappropriate our public displays of affection."

"We laid it on thick. Did you see her?"

Minnie threw back her shoulders and grinned. "I focused all my attention on you, Mr. Dawson. The Queen of England could have come in and I'm not sure I'd have realized it."

"What did Cynthia say?"

"She had a litany of questions about who you are, how we met, and what in the world I could possibly see in a 27-year old 'white boy', as she kept calling you. She said dating you is really 'stupid'. That's a quote."

He twisted his nose and mouth. "What did you say?"

"She was angry and vulgar in a way Cynthia usually isn't, so I said a lot, especially that dating you has made a big difference in my life. I said I feel better than I have since long before Bradley died. I mean that. I really do."

"You hadn't told me that."

"Not in those words. Her attack made me focus. I feel a difference. It's related to what I said after the first time we made love. I'd begun to wonder if I could feel and express myself in a relationship – experience and share my emotions, give and receive with my body. Because of you, I know I can."

They ate the fruit and chicken, drank the tea, and caught up on each other's worlds. He described his work in Chicago. She reported on her Saturday golf round and her frustrating airport trip, complete with fear she wouldn't get there on time because of construction delays. As they relaxed, they said less. Mostly they exchanged smiles and squeezes of hands. Just before ten o'clock, when they'd put their dishes into the dishwasher, Minnie said, "I didn't answer one question you asked a little while ago."

"And that was?"

"If the kiss we shared was worth the tacky things people say?"

"And?"

"It damned sure is."

They headed for the bedroom and stayed there until after 10 o'clock the next morning. Minnie remembered that they made love three times in that 12 hour span. She wasn't sure, however, it wasn't more than three times.

Chapter 28

Cynthia kept her word that she wanted no interaction with Minnie at the Monday picnic. Twice Minnie approached her, but Cynthia waved her away each time. Minnie decided not to chase her anymore.

"I guess she meant it," Minnie told John as they sat at a long, cloth-covered table enjoying barbecue, potato salad, and slaw. Slices of carrot cake waited on the dessert table. Lutheran Memorial held the picnic at the Dallas Arboretum, not far from White Oak Lake Park, where John and Minnie spent that Friday the month before.

Organizers set up tables under a clump of trees, providing shade from the warmer-than-normal sun, but a discrete distance from the flowers and shrubs that made the arboretum one of the city's top attractions. Several restaurants catered the event, meaning a choice of food that included Tex-Mex, burgers, and barbecue. A country-rock band played familiar tunes as background. Hundreds of people went through the serving lines during the six hours they remained open.

"She'll get over it," John responded. He sipped iced tea and nibbled on beef brisket. "You should stop worrying about it. It is what it is."

"I now hate that expression," she said as she shook her head.

He nodded. "I get it. People overuse it."

Minnie crossed her arms over her chest. "Do they have barbecue in Wilmington?" she asked. By now, they were sitting side-by-side. They'd started out across from each other, but he moved beside her and rubbed his leg against hers. They both wore shorts, highlighting the contrast between her dark thigh and his light one.

"Yes, but it's not cooked like this. It has a different flavor. I can't really describe it."

At that instant, Dawn Brooks and a tall, lanky black man who looked about 50 approached their table. Both carried full plates of Tex-Mex. "Minnie!" she exclaimed. "Can we join you? This is Bob Carter."

Carter extended his free hand. Minnie didn't get up, but put down her fork and shook vigorously. "Of course you can. Bob, I'm Minnie Donaldson. This is John Dawson," she said, tapping John on the shoulder.

Seeing that their bare thighs touched, Dawn pointed at Minnie, then John, and asked, "Are you two together?" She stopped her jaw from dropping as far as it first seemed headed.

Minnie laughed loudly. "Yes, we are."

Dawn set her plate on the table, but kept her gaze fixed on John. Then she looked at Minnie and asked, "Where have you been hiding him? I didn't know you'd found somebody young and handsome you could hang out with."

"You learn something new every day, don't you?" Minnie asked and laughed again. She felt relieved dating John hadn't cost her another friend. "We're new at this, but we're having a great time."

If an older black woman/younger white man couple bothered Bob Carter, he didn't let on. "What's your thing man, aside from good–looking women?" He directed the question at John, but tipped his straw hat to Minnie. She appreciated he didn't say besides good looking old women.

John pushed his Philadelphia Phillies baseball cap back on his head. "I'm a corporate lawyer. I work at a firm downtown."

"Nice. Let's talk before we leave here. Maybe you can steer me in the right direction about something I'm working on."

"I'll give you a card. Call me at the office."

"That's cool," Carter said. He took the card after John pulled one from the back pocket of his blue shorts.

"Thank you, John," Dawn said, "for nipping that in the bud. Talking business wasn't in my plan for this picnic." She poked Bob's ribs.

"Sorry, Miss Dawn," Carter said. "I get the message. Got to move when I can, though. John here might make a difference with some things I'm doing."

The four of them cleaned their plates while making small talk about how hot the summer might get, Dallas-Ft. Worth traffic, and people they knew. During dessert, Minnie and Dawn exchanged broadsides at hospital administrators. John and Bob talked NBA playoffs.

With the meal over, Dawn asked Minnie if she and John would pose for a picture. "I want one of you with your new man. I tried so hard at fixing you up." Through a grin she added, "I see you can take care of business on your own."

Minnie cleared her throat. "You certainly tried. I'm so sorry about Clifford's plane crash."

"It was sad, wasn't it? I planned on attending his service, but work got in the way that weekend."

"John and I went. It was nice and respectful."

Dawn took four pictures of Minnie and John together, then coaxed a woman sitting at the next table into snapping a group shot of the four of them. Before they scattered, John leaned over, wrapped an arm around Minnie's middle, and kissed her. The woman snapped that too.

The picnic reassured Minnie. John handled meeting Dawn Brooks and her date with ease. There'd been no squirming, no uneasy looks, no scanning the crowd out of fear of who might see them together, thighs touching and hands wandering over each other's arms and faces.

Being photographed with her in a way that showed their affection hadn't bothered John one bit. By hugging and kissing her, he'd made it likely anyone who saw the photos would think of them as a couple.

She'd feared he might be content with letting people think they were just casual acquaintances, friends who knew each other through work or some social or civic organization. Perhaps they harbored nothing more than pleasant plutonic vibes for each other.

No, John took that off the table. At the picnic, as on their dates, he'd acted like a man out with his woman, nothing more, nothing less. Ordinarily, Minnie thought, that's not such a big deal. When there's a 28-year age gap and a color imbalance, maybe it is a big deal – a really big deal.

∞ ∞ ∞

On a Friday night, almost two weeks after the picnic, Minnie asked John if he'd do her a favor. They were lying in bed at her house after making love and had been talking about where they might go for the July Fourth holiday.

"What favor would you like, my love?" he asked, his head propped on his elbow.

She lay on her back, looking up at the ceiling. After a deep breath, she responded, "I'd like you to go to church with me."

His breath caught for a second in surprise. "That doesn't seem like an onerous request, but why?"

"So I can share it with you, at least once, maybe from time to time if you can stand it."

He leaned over and kissed her nipple. "Tell me about that."

Still on her back, she said, "It's a part of my life, part of who I am. It seems important right now that I share it with you." She turned toward him and continued, "You're becoming such a big part of my life that I want to make you a part of that, at least sometimes."

"You go to what church?"

"Dodge United Church of Christ. It's not far from here."

"Is that the denomination you grew up in?"

"No. Finding it took years and painful battles with my husband."

John nudged her in the ribs, below her left breast. "Tell me about that."

She described her long history with the Baptist Church, including childhood. She covered the years she and Bradley spent at Rock of Ages, her decision that she couldn't remain there, and her protracted search for a church she could attend. She told him how she believed they would find Dodge a welcoming, safe place for them as a couple. She finished by relating Bradley's plan for disinheriting her and their daughters and leaving the church his fortune.

"That's awful," he said, then raised his eyebrows. "Is this the time you tell me the details of his being a closet homosexual, as you put it?"

She nodded and grimaced. "It's as good a time as any." After a brief pause, during which she noticed that green numbers on the bedside clock read 10:35 p.m., she continued. "Bradley hired young boys – teenagers – who gave him blow jobs, often in his car in public places."

John's mouth slackened and his eyes widened. "How'd you find out?"

"After Bradley died, my son Jerry told me."

"How did he find out?"

She gritted her teeth. "Jerry saw him one night and confronted him about it. He confessed. He said it started in college, though he didn't pay for it then."

John licked his lips. "You said he never exposed you to

disease?"

"Apparently he only received oral sex. The research says that generally won't give the recipient HIV. I told you, I've been tested regularly for years – always negative."

By now, both had propped their heads on their elbows and looked into each other's eyes. "Back to going to church with you. Tell me why that's important."

She hugged him as they remained beneath the covers from the waist down. "It's clear I'm falling in love with you. I want the comfort of you by my side when I experience the comfort church gives me. Explaining that is hard. It's just something I need."

John leaned back and looked into her eyes in the subdued light. "I can give you my presence, but I should tell you I've been unchurched since high school. I don't know if I'll ever have the feelings about church you have."

"I'm not asking that of you. Just go with me from time to time. Can you do that for me?"

"I can," he said, reaching for her.

"That's good enough." Her passion stirred. She returned his embrace. They made love again before falling into sleep that took them past 7:15 a.m. Saturday.

∞∞∞∞

It was about the time in late June Minnie and John finalized plans for spending the July Fourth holiday on the Oregon coast, when John's mother called him on a Wednesday evening. He'd left the office an hour and half earlier than usual so he could catch up on paying bills and organize clothes for four nights at Minnie's house.

Only a few words came out of Marion's mouth before the

pleasant feelings John had about seeing her number flash on his phone disappeared. "What in the world are you doing?" she asked, practically shouting. "I'm disgusted with you."

"We haven't talked in three weeks. What could I possibly have done that would make you disgusted with me?"

"Running around kissing and hugging on an old black woman, that's what. For all the world to see, that's what."

John recoiled. How could she possibly know about Minnie other than that she worked at the hospital where he spent all that time? He remembered that his parents met Minnie while visiting him in Dallas. He could only ask, "What are you talking about, Mama?"

"Don't play dumb. You know perfectly well what I'm talking about. I told you when I was there at the hospital you paid her too much attention, but I never imagined this. This is outrageous!"

What am I hearing, John asked himself? How could she know? What did she know? He still couldn't figure out what he should say. This attack came from so far out in left field, any response he thought of seemed off the mark.

Then it hit him. Somebody must have sent her a picture from the picnic. But who? Why? How would anyone who'd been there connect Marion Dawson in Wilmington, Delaware with him? "What is it you think you know, Mama? And how do you know it?"

"You ever hear of something called Facebook? I thought your generation cornered the market on social media!"

Facebook? Facebook? Really? "Yes, I've heard of Facebook. I'm on Facebook. I wasn't aware you are."

"I'm not. I have friends on it. They tell me about things they see there. That's what happened today. Someone I know well is a Facebook friend of somebody who was at a picnic you and that woman went to. My friend told me today she'd seen

262

photos of you, kissing her. She sent me the pictures. I was revolted."

His mother's reference to Minnie as "that woman" irked John. It turned him from wondering whether he could in some way finesse this to a full throated defense of his lover. "She's not 'that woman'. She has a name – Minnie Donaldson. And yes, she has become special to me."

"Your saying that is as disgusting as seeing you plastered all over the internet kissing and hugging her. Have you lost your mind?"

"My mind has never been in better shape. If you want to hear about Minnie and me, I'll tell you. But you must sit down, stop shouting, and listen. Can you do that?"

"I'm sitting down. And I don't need lectures from you about – well, about anything."

"Then there's nothing we can talk about."

Silence came through the phone. John sensed that his mother hadn't anticipated he'd defend his involvement with an older black woman. She probably thought he'd never admit it.

"Okay, you win," Marion finally said. "I'm sitting down and I'm all ears. This better be good."

"You met Minnie when you and Dad were in Dallas after the accident last fall. While I was in the hospital, she and I discovered we enjoyed talking with each other and liked many of the same things. After I got out, she gave me advice that helped get my rehab on track. Eventually, I asked her out to dinner and she said yes. We've been dating since. That's the whole story. Nothing more."

Now, some of the sting left Marion's voice. "What in the world do you see in her?"

John found himself smiling. He couldn't sway his mother, he knew, but he could make a case for Minnie and he liked doing that. "She's wonderful. We have this mutual affinity for books of all kinds – fiction, politics, memoir, you name it. We both like museums, the outdoors, and sports.

"She's a terrific golfer. She stays in great shape. I can't keep up with her in the gym, at least not yet. We talk so easily and enjoy talking with each other so much. It's like nothing I've experienced before."

"Anything else?"

John checked himself so he didn't say something about how great Minnie was in bed. "There's lots more, but I'll leave it at the fact she's a marvelous companion."

"How old is she?"

He'd dreaded this since the conversation began. Should he lie and say she was in her 40s? Marion would research Minnie and discover her real age. It was out there on the internet, no doubt. Should he say he wasn't sure, that he'd never asked because a gentleman shouldn't ask a lady her age? John had never lied to his mother. He couldn't make himself start now. "She's 55."

A long pause followed. Finally, Marion asked, "Did you say 55?"

"Yes, I did."

"Fifty-five?"

"She's 55." He didn't mention that Minnie would turn 56 in August, a few days after his 28th birthday.

John decided people as far away as Dover probably heard the explosion that came next. "This is impossible! John, what in the world is wrong with you? Are you sleeping with that old woman? I know you must be."

"I've never discussed my sex life with you, Mama. I'm not starting now."

"I'll take that as a yes."

"Take it however you want. I'm not talking about it with you."

Marion turned down the volume when she spoke next.

John heard sadness in her voice. For a short moment he even sympathized with his mother, despite this cruel and unfair tirade and her pot shots at Minnie. "I will never have grandchildren. Never. My life is over."

"We're not getting married. We've been dating a few months. Who knows what'll happen?"

"No. This is it. I hear it in your voice. I feel it. You've found your woman, your soulmate. You will marry that old woman, or at least live with her so long, I'll be gone. This is the worst day of my life."

John knew his mother was laying on a thick guilt trip, even if at some level he understood her hurt. Many parents of a 27-year old adult child who learned he or she was involved with someone in their mid-50s wouldn't have a positive reaction. John decided he'd show his mother some kindness.

"I'm sure this comes as a shock. I was surprised myself when I realized in the hospital how attracted I was to her. At some point I took a chance she'd say yes when I asked her out. It's just one of those things that happens in life."

Marion told him he faced a "bleak future" if he cast his lot with a woman so much his senior. She then made a less-than-subtle reference to Minnie's color. "She's so different from you. I don't see how this can work."

He warned her, "Don't go there. You don't know her, so you don't know what's different." Marion went silent.

Their conversation didn't end with a dramatic flourish, but died a slow, anguished death. They agreed they'd disagree. She repeated her feeling that "this is a really bad idea." He said he'd keep seeing Minnie no matter what she thought.

$$\infty\infty\infty$$

John didn't tell Minnie of the verbal tussle with his mother until the afternoon of July Fourth as they drove through western Oregon toward the Bandon Dunes Golf Resort. Since Independence Day fell on a Wednesday, John moved heaven and earth during the previous week and finished three major projects. Minnie covered three shifts the weekend before the Fourth, setting them up for four days of sex and playing golf out of the Dallas heat and humidity.

He related his mother's age gap complaints and her concern about how "different" they were. He acknowledged that was probably a racial reference. Minnie shook her head and asked, "Does that stuff never stop?"

John didn't mention one of Marion's objections. He said nothing about his mother's whining that his involvement with Minnie would mean she'd never have grandchildren. He decided he wouldn't lay that on her. That was his mother's fixation. He saw no reason for making it a factor in why they should or shouldn't stay together. Coping with all the other things people said was enough.

Chapter 29

In early July 2018, 36 holes of golf with Minnie in a single day exceeded John's capabilities. Still working his way back into shape after the accident, he couldn't yet match her stamina. He had trouble sustaining, over that many holes, the mental concentration and focus she kept on golf fundamentals.

On Thursday, their first day at Bandon Dunes, they played the Pacific Dunes course in the morning. John managed a respectable nine over par 81. She settled for what she called a "mediocre" four over 75.

He admitted that by the eleventh hole of the afternoon round on the tough Bandon Trails course his swing had "gone to hell." Meanwhile, Minnie consistently drove the ball straight, hit accurate iron shots, and employed her deft short game in recording a one over par score of 72. As in the morning, she lipped out putts that prevented an under par round. John didn't break 85.

They played both rounds from the middle tees, 6,065 yards in the morning and 6,207 yards in the afternoon. That left John amazed. "I knew you were good, but I had no idea you could score like that from men's tees. Hell, you shot 75 this morning and it should have been even par but for four putts you lipped out."

As Minnie stood just off the practice green and leaned on a putter, she looked up at John and explained, "I'm straight with the driver, so I nearly always play approach shots from the fairway. Because of my fitness level, I generate enough club head speed that I hit the ball far enough so even on 400-yard par four holes I'm near the green in two. My short game lets me consistently get up and down. As you saw, I reach par fives and par threes in regulation nearly all the time. I seldom three putt. That's the formula."

"I saw how you hit the ball on the driving range, so I wasn't surprised by that. What I didn't get since we hadn't played a round together was your short game."

Mischief appeared on her face. "It's what I practice nearly every day. You should try it."

"Fat chance of that," he snorted. "You know my work schedule."

∞ ∞ ∞

They spent Friday morning making love and played golf in the afternoon. They tried out Bandon Dunes, the resort's first course, the one someone in the pro shop claimed was its most forgiving. She could handle its length – 6,595 yards from the middle tees – as her one over par 73 showed. He shot 86.

She was primed for 36 holes Saturday, their final golf day. They'd reserved Sunday morning for bed before they headed home. He joined her for a morning round Saturday, a second go at Pacific Dunes. She improved to even par 71, while he matched his first-day 81.

John decided he'd rest in the afternoon. For her second round of the day, the pro shop paired Minnie with an Asian-American man from Denver who looked about 40 and a young white couple from California. Playing from the middle tees at 6,350 yards, she shot a two under par 69 on the Old Macdonald course, her best round of the trip. While she played, John sat in the grill sipping South Australian cabernet and reading Mary Karr's infamous 1995 memoir, *The Liars Club*.

When he hugged Minnie after the round, with the sun setting over the Pacific Ocean and a cool, gentle breeze blowing off the water, she whispered, "Except being in bed with you, this is as good as life gets for me."

Mesmerized by her gentle facial features, toned body, and mature presence, he kissed her and said, "For me too, and I didn't even play golf this afternoon."

∞∞∞

Before falling asleep Saturday night, Minnie reflected on Marion Dawson's "tirade," as John called it. She wasn't surprised. She hadn't expected his parents would endorse their romance. She'd found Martin and Marion nice people when she met them while he was in the hospital. That, of course, meant nothing now. There she'd been just another health care worker serving John.

Things had changed in nine months. He now asked that they accept a long-term relationship between Minnie, a 55-year-old black woman, and their precious 27-year old son. How would she feel about the prospect of Jerry spending the best years of his life in the clutches of a woman over 50? Yes, Jerry now dated someone eight years older, but eight years and 28 were different. Weren't they? That's where in her musings sleep overtook her.

She awakened with those thoughts, but John put them out of her head with his caresses. As his hands roamed her body, behind her she felt the tell-tale firmness of his erection. She grinned in the early morning light. The man's member was huge! And it was all hers.

Minnie tossed the covers off them, turned over and around and curled herself into a ball with her head facing the foot of the bed. That signaled that she wanted him from behind. She lifted her top leg and, with her help, he entered her.

Immediately, her soft moans and his urgent grunts filled the room. She'd learned this position from a college boyfriend.

Bradley never liked it, so the way John embraced it made for a refreshing treat. His staying power and deep penetration allowed her several orgasms before he finished inside her.

When it was over, she crawled back to the head of the bed into his embrace. She salivated at what she knew would come next. They'd doze a while, then start Round Two, likely with her astride him in the cowgirl position. After he recharged, they'd have Round Three. Probably he'd take her from above. Her insides fluttered. She grinned and licked her lips in anticipation. Business was good!

They had until noon before their two-hour drive to Eugene and an hour-long flight to Portland. A 5:50 p.m. departure would get them home around midnight.

Monday, John would dive back into work and she'd use the day for house keeping.

When the Dallas humidity slammed them as they got off the plane, she'd regret the adventure's end. But, it had been so much fun. She never got her fill of this trip's two indulgences – golf and sex. She could say, however, that she'd temporarily satisfied her appetite.

∞∞∞

Marion Dawson's attack on John crept into Minnie's mind as she did her household chores Monday. What she said bothered Minnie less than how Marion learned of their involvement. If Marion heard about it in Wilmington, Sandra, Crystal, and Jerry certainly could hear about it in Winston-Salem, Alexandria, or Norman. Social media revealed everyone's secrets now.

How would her children react? As she'd thought during the winter before she and John began dating, the two involved with white partners could have no racial complaints. Minnie smiled in the solitude of her laundry room and mused about pots calling kettles black.

Sandra's and Jerry's interracial liaisons probably nixed an objection from Crystal. Would she call out everyone in the family for dating across the color line? Hardly, Minnie thought. Sandra would rake her over the coals for that kind of narrow-mindedness. Crystal would want no part in such a battle with Sandra.

Any pushback, therefore, would concern age. Did the eight-year gap between Jerry and Rachel sideline him for criticism of his mother on that issue? Eight years was just enough that their gap wasn't irrelevant. Jerry told Minnie in a pre-July Fourth call that questions about how he and Rachel could forge a life together remained unresolved. Some of those questions originated in their age difference.

Both Crystal and Sandra loved men only a few years older than they were, so neither had experience with the age-gap issue. Minnie had difficulty imagining Sandra objecting once she understood Minnie's feelings for John. That was how things worked between them. They heard and respected each other's wishes and desires.

But was 28 years too much, even for Sandra? Minnie didn't think so, given the confidence she had in her youngest daughter's intellect and the trust between them. Still, she crossed her fingers and hoped this wouldn't turn into a nightmare. That brought her to Crystal.

She didn't have now, and hadn't had in a long time, a trusting relationship with her middle child. Things began going off the rails during her daughter's "bad actor" phase in high school. That started with Crystal's early excellence in track. She got her first college recruitment letter during her freshman season in which she ranked as the nation's tenth best high school hurdler, an astounding accomplishment for a ninth grader. More letters arrived in May and June. The trickle became an avalanche in the fall after she recorded spectacular times during summer meets.

Minnie's mother would have said the attention Crystal got for her track prowess gave her "the big head." Her grades slipped. She stayed out past curfew. Living with her ego became a headache for everyone in the family except Bradley who made the problem worse by doting on her and hinting she could stop living by the rules her siblings did. It was an awful time. Minnie could barely stand Crystal, and Crystal could barely stand Minnie. Eventually, they just stayed away from each other.

We repaired our relationship, Minnie thought as she folded and hung clothes she'd washed after the trip. Crystal lost her prestigious college scholarship chance at Kansas, where she'd committed, because her grades plummeted so much. But, she found a junior college in Oklahoma where she got her track career and academic life in order. At Louisiana Tech she realized her potential. She became the nation's top-ranked 100-meter hurdler and reached number three in the world by the time of the 2012 U.S. Olympic Trials.

Still, the years of mother-daughter conflict took a toll. Minnie and Sandra grew close before Sandra left for college. Minnie and Crystal, however, seldom spoke until after Crystal enrolled at Louisiana Tech. While they no longer sniped at each other, they'd lost the opportunity for closeness. The result was a mostly transactional relationship.

These days, when Minnie visited Crystal, much of their interaction concerned her grand-daughter, Sarah Alexis. Minnie, in fact, found herself having deeper, more thought provoking conversations with Crystal's husband, Michael. Minnie feared she could never convey the depth of her feelings for John in a way that let Crystal get past whatever problems she might have with their age and race differences.

Right then, as she put away the last of the laundry, Minnie

decided she'd hold a family summit meeting. She would tell them about John herself so they didn't learn about the relationship on social media or through gossip spread by children of her friends like Cynthia and Dawn. They could meet him and draw their own conclusions.

She'd ask that all three come to Dallas on a Saturday morning. They'd talk about it, eat lunch with John, then talk more after he left the house. They could stay overnight and go home Sunday. This needed doing and soon.

∞∞∞

It took cajoling and haggling, but at 9:45 a.m. Saturday, July 21, Minnie arrived at Dallas-Ft. Worth International Airport and picked up Sandra and Crystal from flights that landed within 10 minutes of each other. Jerry told Minnie he'd drive in from Norman for what Minnie described as an "important" family meeting. He was in place when Minnie and her daughters walked into the family room just before eleven o'clock. Pleas for information followed greetings and hugs.

"What's this about, Mom?" Sandra asked, sitting in a chair beside the couch across from the television set. "I rearranged my schedule so I could get here."

"Flying from Alexandria anywhere is a major league pain," Crystal added. She leaned on the door between the family room and the dining area.

Jerry, sitting in another big chair, shrugged his shoulders. "No problem for me. Rachel and I got in the car about seven o'clock this morning and drove down here. I dropped her at a mall where she's meeting a grad school chum for a day of shopping. It's a treat for us."

Minnie stood in the center of the room, looking at her offspring. Inside, the love she felt for each battled her anxiety.

How would they take this news? She took a deep breath. Her limbs tingled and her stomach churned.

Crystal spurred Minnie into action with a simple, direct question. "Are you getting married?"

"No," she replied. "But this does involve a man."

"Then you must have a boyfriend," Sandra said. "That hardly seems worth flying us all here for a big to-do."

Minnie took another deep breath. "I brought you here because of who he is. You're right. My having a boyfriend isn't that big a deal."

"Is he the future King of England or something?" Crystal asked.

Minnie began, "He's white and –"

"That's not a big deal," Jerry chimed in.

"Sure isn't," Sandra said. "I resemble that remark."

"He's young," Minnie continued. "Very young compared to me."

Now, Crystal spoke. "So you're a cradle robber? That's the big deal? How young is he?"

"Twenty-eight in August." Sandra and Jerry offered only blank stares. Crystal gasped and covered her mouth.

"You said he's white?" Crystal asked when she let her hand drop.

"Yes."

Minnie looked again at Sandra and Jerry. Their faces remained blank. Crystal, however, clutched her chest and let out another gasp. She asked, "Do I have this straight? You're dating a 27-year old white guy?"

"I am."

From his seat, Jerry looked up at Minnie, then at Crystal, who remained standing by the door. He said, "As someone who's dating an older white woman, I suppose I can't say much about this. It's your business, Mom. How did this start? I am curious about that."

"We met last fall when he was a patient at the hospital," Minnie replied. "He was in an automobile accident and stayed for weeks. We enjoyed talking so much that after he got out we kept in touch. Eventually – months after he left the hospital – he asked me out. We started dating. That's the sum of it."

"What do you see in him, especially since he's so much younger?" Jerry asked, intertwining his fingers and flexing them.

"Despite our age difference, we like many of the same things – books, golf, ideas, travel -- "

"Sex?" Crystal asked.

Minnie didn't hesitate. She knew this was coming and had thought it through. "John and I have a mutually satisfying physical relationship. That's all I'll say about it, so don't ask for details."

Jerry looked at Crystal, shook his head, and muttered, "Please. That wasn't necessary."

"It's okay," Minnie said. "I knew I'd get the question. It's out in the open now. The only other thing I'll say about John is that he's very kind and considerate. He's old school. He attends to my needs. He takes me seriously. You can draw your own conclusions about him. He'll be here at one o'clock for lunch."

"That'll be wild," Jerry said. "He's younger than I am."

"Yeah, than I am too by a few months or so," Crystal added.

Minnie looked at Sandra, still sitting in the chair beside the couch. "You're quiet."

"I don't see what I can or should say," she replied. "Who you date is your business. I assume you've made a decision, as the rational person you are, that he's who you're dating for now. I assume, since this hasn't been going on long, you aren't saying it's permanent. If you want a relationship with – what's his name?"

"John. John Dawson."

"With John, if that's what you want, I hope you have it and get as much out of it as possible."

Minnie blew Sandra a kiss. "Thank you, youngest daughter. Thank you."

∞∞∞

They talked another half hour, then Jerry and Sandra helped Minnie put lunch on the table. John arrived at 12:55 p.m. With good humor, he endured interrogation about his childhood, education, and work life. Minnie filled in details about his honors and awards, since he left them out. As she'd asked him in advance, at half past two he excused himself. Minnie knew he had a golf lesson scheduled with her pro that afternoon.

"Guys, what do you think?" Minnie asked after they'd cleaned the kitchen and again taken up places in the family room.

"Nothing different from what I thought this morning," Sandra said. "I trust you. I like him. I'd be friends with him if he lived near me or I went to school with him. It is weird thinking of him as my mother's boyfriend, but that's my problem, not yours."

"I'm in the same place," Jerry said. "Nothing makes me think I should tell my mother she shouldn't do what she wants. This is your call."

All eyes turned toward Crystal. The shock and apparent disgust she reacted with earlier now seemed gone. In a calm voice, she said, "Jerry and Sandra are right. It's your business. What we think doesn't matter."

Minnie breathed a sigh of relief, then realized Crystal wasn't done.

"There are two things you should think about. The first may not amount to much. Based on what little I know about big law firms, it's likely he'll make plenty of money. I assume he's not after your money, even if he knows how rich you are."

"He knows and doesn't care. He might end up with more than I have."

"The second thing is sensitive and I hope you won't take offense. You're an attractive, nearly 56-year old woman. Given how you take care of yourself, you'll be an attractive 65-year old woman, and an attractive 70-year old woman.

"But no matter how hard you work at it, eventually gravity and the passage of time will make you sag certain places. You'll have wrinkles. Other things will happen that make you not what you are now.

"John may find you appealing at the moment. Perhaps you titillate him. Maybe just the idea of you does. What I worry about is that you'll put five, 10, 15 years into this relationship and everything's fine. Then, the aging process takes over. He's 50 and you're pushing 80. What so attracted him in 2018 is gone and he doesn't find what's there in 2040 nearly as captivating."

Minnie stopped her. "John and I live day-to-day. We're not thinking much about the future. We know we must face it at some point, but we're not looking ahead now."

It had become a two-person conversation. Jerry and Sandra listened as Crystal continued. "That's good, but don't think in terms of the relationship failing. Think about what happens if it succeeds, at least for a time.

"I hope you don't give him your whole life for X number of years, then have him leave you high and dry because he finds someone else more attractive."

"John and I are together for much more than our looks."

"I'm sure you are. For reasons many people likely have difficulty understanding, you now find each other physically, mentally, and emotionally attractive. But, you will lose your physical attractiveness before he loses his.

"And I haven't even mentioned dementia. What will he think when your boobs sag and you can't remember the names of your children, much less who wrote War and Peace? Think about it, Mom. That's all I'm saying, and it's all I will say."

PART V

Chapter 30

August 2018

O ne Tuesday morning in mid-August, Ed Ward summoned
John to his office for "an assignment and something fun."
When he arrived, he found Ward and Kevin Monroe chatting
about completing their Westover project.

"John. Come in," Ward said, beckoning him with his right
hand. "Kevin and I were just finishing up something he's
working on for me."

"Hey John," Kevin said from his chair across from Ward's
desk. "You look fully recovered. Haven't seen you since March,
I guess. You were still a little out of it then."

"I've been rehabbed," John replied with a playful grin as he
sat in a chair on the other side of Ward's desk. "I'm good to go.
I even spent a few days playing golf in Oregon over the Fourth
of July holiday. Walked every round."

"That's one reason I asked you up here," Ward said. He
rocked back in his chair. "You know Tim Patrick, don't you?"

"Assistant general counsel at Betters Industries. Sure, I
know him. Remember I worked on the Markham matter in
February and March. We talked a lot. Don't think I've seen him
since."

"There's a strong chance he gets promoted and becomes GC
at Betters. Carl Davidson is retiring. Tim has the inside track,
so I'm working at staying in his good graces. I've invited him
for a golf outing at Burnham Country Club Labor Day weekend.
Can you join us?"

"Which day?"

"Saturday. He's available because his wife has some big
social event he's not part of, so they aren't doing family stuff

until Sunday and Monday. He can play golf with me and whoever else I ask that Saturday."

John looked up, his eyes blinking. "Who else are you asking?"

"Kevin."

John realized the likely reason for Kevin's inclusion. Ordinarily, a partner in Ward's shoes would have invited another firm lawyer for such an event, not an outsider like Kevin. But Tim Patrick was black and VWM had only two black lawyers in its corporate section, both women who didn't play golf. Black lawyers in other VWM sections must not have fit the bill for one reason or another. John knew Ward would have thought through all the possibilities.

Probably Ward believed he shouldn't invite Patrick to an all-white gathering. Bringing along his black personal right hand man would show an inclination toward inclusivity and perhaps make Patrick more comfortable. John could play the role of up and coming, heavy hitting young corporate associate, especially since he'd worked with Patrick in the past.

"I see no reason I can't do it," John said. "I should make sure I don't have another obligation," an oblique acknowledgement that he should check with Minnie. "How about if I call you this afternoon?"

"That's fine," Ward said. "Now, we should talk about the next thing you can work on for me."

Kevin recognized his departure cue. "I'm out of here, guys," he said, as he stood up. "Ed, I'll be in touch about Westover and timing on the golf thing." He pointed at John.

"Good seeing you, man. Glad you're doing so well."

∞∞∞

Back at his desk, John called Minnie. She was on her way out the door for work. "Hey," he asked, "are you doing anything special the Saturday before Labor Day?"

"I'm in Shreveport that weekend," she replied. "I'm playing in that tournament I won last year. You know, defending my title." The pride in her voice came through loud and clear. "I hoped you might go with me. I'd like having support in the gallery."

"When do you leave?"

"Friday. The tournament is 54 holes and runs Saturday, Sunday, and Monday. I should get there Friday afternoon so I can walk the course and practice, even if it's only putting."

"I'm sorry. I can't get away Friday because of a closing scheduled that day. I've now been invited on a client entertainment assignment Saturday. Could I fly over when I'm done, be there for Sunday's play, and ride home with you after the round Monday?"

In her response, John heard suppressed disappointment. "We could do that. I wish you could come for the whole thing, but I understand about work. I'll take what I can get."

"I'll look into a Saturday afternoon or early evening flight."

It turned out John didn't need a flight. At the hospital that afternoon, Minnie ran into Judy Shields who mentioned she was spending the Labor Day weekend with relatives in Mansfield, Louisiana, a small town 30 miles south of Shreveport. She and her husband, Dick, planned a Friday morning departure. Minnie asked if she could ride with them, "as long as you have room for my golf clubs." Judy said they did, so Minnie told John he could drive over after his Saturday event.

The Dallas-Shreveport ride gave Minnie time for reflecting on her increasingly close and intense relationship with John. She'd later conclude she overthought things and, in the process, created turmoil that threatened the bliss she'd felt since the spring.

Dick drove, so Judy sat beside him in the front seat of their blue, six-year old Honda Pilot. Minnie sat behind Dick, so that the women could talk more easily. The two of them spent the first 45 minutes swapping nursing stories and hospital gossip. When Dick turned on the radio, Judy said she knew she should give him some attention. Minnie said she'd nap a while.

The nap lasted 15 minutes. Minnie awoke distressed. As for Dick and Judy, as much as Minnie heard of their conversation, they could have been speaking Russian or discussing differential equations.

That morning, as the drab northeast Texas landscape rolled by, Minnie heard Crystal's pointed words about the dangers in her entanglement with John. "But you should think about what happens if the relationship succeeds, at least for a time," her daughter had said. Then she added the killer.

"I hope you don't give him your whole life for X number of years, then have him leave you high and dry because he finds somebody else more attractive. You will lose your looks before he loses his. What will he think when your boobs sag and you can't remember the names of your children, much less who wrote War and Peace?"

Encouraged by it's-up-to-you-Mom reassurances from Sandra and Jerry, Minnie didn't feel the full impact of Crystal's reservations during her children's visit. Now, alone and unsure whether John realized how much different they might become as she aged, Minnie felt terror. Her thoughts crept to the worst possible outcome – the one Crystal suggested. She'd invest years in John Dawson and he'd leave her for someone younger and better looking. Ruth Popper, Sonny Crawford, and Jacy Farrow flashed through her mind from The Last Picture Show.

Minnie pressed her face against the car window and fought back tears. Despite her intense feelings for John and how much the relationship did for her now, didn't a good chance exist Crystal was right? What if she was?

With a man five years younger or five years older, in 25 years she'd be 81 and he'd be 75 or 85. They'd worry about arranging senior care and planning funerals.

But with John, in 25 years she'd certainly be 81, but he'd be 52, younger by four years than she was now. How would she look? Would he find her the least bit attractive? Wouldn't he flee as soon as he could make anything like a graceful exit? Would he even care about doing that? Maybe he'd leave without letting the doorknob hit him on the way out.

Minnie's pulse raced and she felt weakness in her legs. How was she supposed to play in a golf tournament feeling like this? When they crossed the Texas–Louisiana border, she asked herself why she'd even made this trip. This had disaster written all over it.

"Didn't you say you were staying at a Marriott?" Judy asked from the front seat. "I saw a sign back there that said we're two exits from a Marriott."

"Yes," Minnie replied. "I stayed in the same place last year, so I know it's not far." She didn't say how much she wished for a return to Dallas.

∞∞∞

John felt the chill of Minnie's sour mood when he arrived at the hotel Saturday evening. In the lobby, she greeted him with a tepid kiss and no hug. In their room, she begged off making love. "I should focus on tomorrow," she said.

"Since when did sex keep you from focusing on golf?" he asked, startled by the mere idea. "That's sure not what I saw in Oregon."

"I'm just not up to it," she said as she retreated from his embrace.

He didn't press further that evening and didn't pursue her Sunday night. She seemed distracted and disinterested. At breakfast Monday, he asked how she felt going into the tournament's final round. She gave him a strange answer. "I've won this once. If I don't get a second one, it's no big deal."

John had a hard time believing he'd heard those words come out of Minnie Donaldson's mouth. "I haven't known you that long," he said. "But I've known you long enough that I'm sure your competitive spirit never lets you think that way. What's going on?"

She shook her head. "Nothing's going on. I decided I wouldn't obsess about this tournament." She jumped up from the table and ran for the elevator, leaving her breakfast half eaten and his jaw on the floor.

As they headed for the golf course, she kept quiet and resisted his attempts at engaging her. "What's wrong, Minnie?" he pleaded. "This isn't like you."

"Just leave well enough alone. I don't need a scene before the round starts."

He backed off. When they reached the course, before she got out of the car, he told her, "I'll just watch and be there for you. Talk to me when you feel like it, okay?"

"Fine, John. That's fine."

Though she began the day with a two stroke lead over the second place golfer, her playing partner in the final pairing, Minnie's game fell apart in ways John couldn't imagine after what he'd seen in Oregon. She managed pars on the first two holes and kept her lead only because her pursuer missed two makable birdie putts.

At the par four No. 3 hole, she flubbed a chip and turned a likely par into a double bogey. She regained a one stroke lead by the time they reached No. 7, a short par three with deep bunkers on each side of the green. Minnie pushed an eight iron into the right bunker and miss hit her sand shot, leaving an almost impossible downhill par putt.

Watching from beside the green, John said under his breath as she lined up the putt, "Don't hit this too hard." Minnie did exactly that, leaving a ten-footer back up the hill. She didn't make that one either, meaning her second double bogey of the day.

And so things went the rest of the round. Each time it appeared she'd rallied and gotten her game on track, she made another mistake. Her chance at repeating as champion ended on No. 17 when she three putted from twelve feet, leaving her three strokes back with one hole remaining.

∞ ∞ ∞

John found the drive home excruciating. Minnie said almost nothing the entire 175 miles. When they arrived at her house he suggested he go home instead of staying with her overnight. She said, "That's the best idea I've heard all day."

They had a couple of tense calls over the next few days, but no in-person visits and certainly no time in bed. Her standoffishness got under his skin by mid-week. He phoned her only because of a promise he'd made. "Minnie, this is John. I need a favor."

He heard her skepticism through the phone. "And that is?"

"Before leaving for Shreveport last Saturday, I played golf with Ed Ward, one of the partners in the firm you've heard me mention, Tim Patrick, who's a client, and Kevin Monroe, a friend who runs his own business and manages Ed's rental properties.

"Kevin took up golf last year and now hits the ball pretty well. But he has no course management skills. I told him I'd ask my girlfriend if she'd give him a playing lesson sometime. Could you do that? I promised I'd ask."

"Given the way I played in Shreveport, he wouldn't learn much from me."

"That was an outlier and you know it. You were out of sorts for some reason and that got in your way."

Her tone remained frosty but she said, "I'll take your friend out for nine holes at North Central and show him some things. Have him call me."

∞ ∞ ∞

Though she knew she wasn't being fair and had, in fact, grown tired of her anger at John that stemmed from the terror created by Crystal's fears, Minnie still provoked a fight with him the weekend after Shreveport. As he headed for a football game and client entertainment outing in Austin, she called him Friday night. Without evidence, she accused him of seeing other women while she'd been on the outs with him. "I'm sure you must have taken advantage of this little break we've been having from each other and hooked up with some 25-year-old blonde bombshell."

He ignored the age and race references and focused on the fact it wasn't clear what her beef with him was. "What are you saying?" he asked. "I don't really know why we're having this 'break' as you call it. I won't dignify that with a response."

She wasn't direct with him about what was bothering her. "It makes sense. After four, five months with, as your boys in the restaurant lobby would say, this 'old colored woman,' aren't you catching up with what we can call age-and race-appropriate females?"

Despite how much the reference to the men in the restaurant pained him, he thought he should ignore it beyond asking, "What in the world has gotten into you?"

"I'm just steeling myself for what I know is coming. I'm sure the thrill of fooling around with me is gone. It's a matter of time, isn't it?"

John reset his mind. She was telling him something. A real fear lurked amidst the invective. But he doubted she'd let go of that in favor of constructive dialogue, at least for the time being. "We should have a rational conversation about something that's obviously bothering you. Are you ready to tell me what it is?"

"Figure it out, John. You're the number-one-in-your class genius."

That annoyed him. She'd pulled his chain with that line before and he wasn't having it. "Since you won't tell me what's really going on, since you insist on saying crazy things and playing games, I'll stop this now and wait until you regain your senses. Then maybe I can talk with the Minnie Donaldson I know. The person on the other end of this phone call isn't her." He hung up.

Crystal's warning wouldn't leave Minnie's mind, but she missed John. She'd grown accustomed to his laughter, to her sereneness when she was around him, and most of all, to their lovemaking.

John's absence from her life created a deep, hurtful void. When he stayed over, she felt an ease as he puttered around the kitchen. When he plopped down in front of the television set and watched a sporting event or a news show, she loved looking in on him so she could make sure he really was still there. She most missed pulling him away from whatever he was watching for an interlude in the bedroom. Not having those things created a painful sadness.

Despite this hurt, she couldn't put aside her angst about the future. Would he do what Crystal feared – stay with her for years, then ditch her for that blonde bombshell or a mature woman with raven hair, a beguiling face, and no negative effects from gravity? Might he even replace her with a younger black woman who in 25 years looked like she did now? For a second, Minnie heard that "once you go black you can't go back" nonsense rattling around in her brain.

∞ ∞ ∞

Minnie decided she needed advice about the situation. Cynthia McFadden, of course, wasn't an option since she led the not-only-no-but-hell-no chorus when it came to Minnie's involvement with John. She thought about calling Dawn Brooks, but feared whatever she told her would work its way back to almost everyone she knew, especially in black women circles. Telling Dawn could have the same effect as putting whatever she said on the front page of the *Dallas Morning News*.

On the Shreveport trip, she'd considered confiding in Judy Shields, someone who might well give her good advice and would stay quiet. Dick's presence, however, nixed that idea. He was a nice man, but opinionated and judgmental. Unlike Judy, he wasn't compassionate about things that happened in male-female relationships. He reached conclusions and ran with them, no matter the facts.

The person who'd most likely understand this conundrum was Carol Robbins. Despite the Mark Gibson fiasco, details of which Minnie hadn't shared with her, Carol remained perhaps the smartest, wisest person Minnie knew. Nobody had been more sensitive or considerate or expressed more empathy with her loneliness, before or after Bradley died.

Would Carol see Crystal's dire predictions as worth worrying about? Would she say 'live for today and let the future take care of itself?' Or would she feel Minnie should protect herself from a heart-breaking outcome by getting out now when the hurt might not hurt as much? Minnie wasn't sure.

What she was sure of was that Carol would listen, respect her feelings, and help her think through the problem. In that instant, as she reached for her phone so she could call Carol, a smile broke out on Minnie's face right there in her family room. As much as she hated admitting it, Carol would approach the problem the way John would.

∞∞∞

Carol accepted Minnie's invitation for a round of golf at North Central Country Club on the Friday two weeks after Shreveport. Minnie remained cool toward John. She shunned his attempt at staying over the Thursday night before the round with Carol.

John's overture tempted Minnie, but she stuck with her plan that she should talk with Carol before re-engaging with him. That didn't prevent her from tossing and turning all night while she craved having his long, sleek body in her bed. She woke for good at 5:10 a.m., dressed in a white polo shirt and red shorts (North Central didn't frown on shorts for women), and headed for some early practice.

Carol, wearing a white skort, a burnt orange University of Texas polo shirt, and her customary straw hat, arrived at 6:30

a.m. for their tee time 55 minutes later. On the range, Carol noted something different. She slapped her hands against her cheeks. "A golf cart? What's gotten into you? You always walk. Is the heat bothering you?"

Minnie frowned. "It's not about the heat. Today is more about talk than golf. A cart makes that easier."

"Fair enough. I wondered if you're slipping in your old age. You did just have a birthday."

Minnie ignored that. "Let's get warmed up, so we can start."

After 30 minutes of hitting balls and chipping, 10 minutes on the putting green, and a restroom stop, Minnie and Carol checked in at the starter's hut, a small building painted in the club's red, white, and blue colors that sat 50 yards from the first tee. The starter was a pleasant, middle-aged man with graying blonde hair that was getting grayer by the day. He wore shorts and a red North Central polo shirt. Gavin Henson immediately recognized Minnie.

"Good morning, Mrs. Donaldson. Nice to have you with us today. Who's your guest?" After Minnie introduced Carol, he asked her, "How'd you get Mrs. Donaldson to use a cart? I'm not sure I've ever seen her ride before."

"We've got serious talking on the program today," Minnie interjected.

Gavin checked Minnie's receipt, handed them the day's pin placement list, and warned of two wet "cart path only" spots on the course where they couldn't drive the cart onto fairways.

"Thanks, Gavin. We're off," Minnie told him as they headed for the tee.

After they hit their drives, as they walked back to the cart, Carol asked, "What are we talking about today that means we're not focusing on golf?"

While adjusting her baseball cap, Minnie replied, "My man issues."

Carol seemed perplexed for an instant. "I know it didn't work out with Mark Gibson. I'd appreciate hearing that story sometime. I suppose that means there's someone else giving you a hard time."

"He's not giving me a hard time. If anything, I'm giving him one. The problem is I'm scared."

"Scared of what?"

They'd reached their drives and selected clubs for approach shots. Carol hit a high, floating seven iron that settled a few feet shy of the cup. Minnie sent her ball well past the flag and could tell, even from the fairway, a difficult downhill putt remained. "I knew that was an eight iron," she muttered on the way back to the cart.

"Go on. Tell me what you're scared of," Carol urged.

As they climbed into the cart, Minnie explained, "I'm dating a young guy – a very young, very white guy. We hear nasty comments from people in public and get admonished by family and friends. I can put up with most of it, nearly all of it, in fact. But one thing freaks me out."

"What's that?" Carol asked, as they sped down the cart path.

"That we'll stay together, maybe a long time, then he'll ditch me for somebody younger, somebody more attractive."

At the green, Carol got out of the cart and grabbed her putter. "Lots there, Minnie. Tell me about it on the next tee."

When they got back into the cart, Carol offered a puzzled look. "This really is bothering you, isn't it? I haven't seen you three putt from that distance in ages."

Minnie nodded before they drove off. "It has done a number on my golf game. I barely finished second in that tournament in Shreveport two weeks ago. I won it by three strokes over a better field last year."

Now riding toward No. 2 as Minnie drove, Carol said, "Go back to the beginning. How'd you hook up with a 'very young, very white guy?' And, how old is he?"

"Former hospital patient. He turned 28 last month."

Carol shook her head. "That sounds perilous."

"His age or the fact we met while I was his nurse?"

"Both, although I'd worry more about what might have happened in the hospital. His age is what it is."

"We started dating a while after he left the hospital."

"That's good. What's the attraction?"

A deep breath preceded Minnie's response. "We talk. We relate. We invigorate. And yes, we have the hots for each other. At least we did until I started acting weird and pushed him away. Right now, he might not care for getting within ten feet of me, much less into my pants."

Carol pushed her hat higher. "How long have you been seeing him?"

"Really dating since April. We had what you could call dates in February and March. He asked me for advice about his rehab from the injuries that put him in the hospital. And I did help him with that.

"Before long, though, rehab became an excuse for seeing each other. We'd spend a few minutes talking about rehab and hours on everything else. I could call those meetings dates."

Carol offered an understanding nod. "No law against that. Helped you get to know him, right?"

That statement startled Minnie. She let out a huge breath. "I'm glad you said that. My feelings for him grew during that time. I craved exploring him. As I think back on it, I regret that I thought of that phase of our relationship as almost dirty. It was a time of learning for both of us, even if we were sort of cheating so we could see each other."

"At some point you acknowledged, including to yourselves, you were dating?"

Minnie nodded when they pulled up at the next tee. As they played the following three holes, she described the Houston trip for Clifford Nguyen's memorial service and how things unfolded at the end of that. She recalled the scene on the street in front of his office building when John said they should begin what he called a dating relationship that stirred her inside. She suspected she'd later find her panties damp.

At the turn, Carol asked Minnie how things had gone since she and John admitted to themselves they were dating and made the relationship public. "We upset some people who see us doing what couples do in romances. We hold hands, we kiss, we whisper into each other's ears. The fact we're as different as we are doesn't change that. It bothers some people. Others ignore us."

After teeing off on No. 13, a par five, and the longest hole on the course, Carol asked about the reaction of family and friends.

Minnie replied, "Cynthia McFadden won't speak to me because I'm with John." She held up a hand. "Before you ask, its all snobbery. John's not part of the black elite and never will be, so I'm persona non grata for being with him.

"John's mother has given him a hard time. I'm not part of the conversations, of course, so I know only what he tells me. I think she can't get her head around the idea her baby is with someone who looks like me. That's a race and age thing."

"Or is it age and race?" Carol wondered.

"John and I ask that all the time, and not just about his mother."

By No. 16, they'd exhausted the objections of Minnie's friends, John's mother, and the general public. Carol had one more question. "What do your kids think?"

"Sandra and Jerry are both dating – living with – white partners. In Jerry's case, the woman is older. The gap is smaller than between John and me, but there's a gap. As John the lawyer says, neither of them has clean hands for complaining about me."

Only a brief smile escaped Carol's lips. "What about Crystal? Is this another thing you and she just don't see eye-to-eye on?"

"You know our history, don't you?"

Carol shook her head up and down. "I sure do. I got plenty of those distressed phone calls back in the day when you couldn't figure out what you'd ever do with your middle daughter."

"Crystal is the fly in the ointment. But it's weird. She admits this is my call and says she's not interested in interfering. But, she warns how risky this is for me. She wonders if John will ditch me 10, 15, or 20 years from now when, as she puts it, gravity makes my boobs sag, I have wrinkles, and I can't remember which end is up."

"And that's what you're scared of, right?"

"Yes."

"Why?"

"Because it could happen."

They had reached No. 17, a 161-yard par three with a green guarded on the left by deep bunkers and a pond on the right. The slick, undulating green and the back right pin placement near the water made going for the flag foolish. The only sensible play was a middle-of-the green approach that preserved the chance of a two-putt par.

"I could make a hole-in-one here," Carol said while setting up her shot. "That could happen. I'd bet every dollar my family makes in the stock market this year that I won't."

She completed her pre-shot routine, then struck a high arcing shot with a hybrid club that turned ever-so-slightly right while in the air. It hit the green and rolled a short distance forward before stopping 20 feet from the flag.

Knowledgeable as she was about golf, Minnie knew pros – women and men – who couldn't regularly hit a better shot. Many wouldn't try getting closer.

Carol was right. Crystal's expressed fears could happen. But, could didn't mean would. Worrying about what could happen might jeopardize the good times Minnie knew in her bones a life with John would bring.

Chapter 31

During Minnie's "pullback" from him, John dealt with one brutal reality. He missed her terribly. Without the overnight stays at her house he so craved, long days in the office became grinding ordeals. Solitary nights in his apartment piled up, lonely reminders of the drought her absence from his life created.

John read less because he couldn't talk books with her. One night he picked up a new novel he'd bought on line and caught himself asking out loud, "What's the point?"

He didn't frequent the driving range because golf reminded him of her. He didn't stop at Starbucks for coffee because the tea selection she wasn't there to make left him feeling something important was missing. Life seemed flat. It lacked inspiration.

He tried "working the problem," figuring out a strategy that would bring her back. Nothing had crystalized by the day before Kevin's scheduled golf lesson with Minnie. John wondered if something about that might break the log jam. Any hope was better than no hope.

He wondered whom he could talk with about her absence, the reasons for it, and what it was doing to him. John hadn't told his friends much about Minnie. Several knew he was dating "an older woman," but not that she was black and not how much older she was. Unlike what had happened with Minnie's friends, Dawn Brooks and Cynthia McFadden, none of his pals accidentally discovered them.

John ran through his list of friends, first asking himself how each would react once they learned the basics of the relationship. Second, what advice would each give about the current break in the action?

John saw Don Young as a wild card. Would his political conservatism – indeed what John viewed as his reactionary opinions – produce outrage or disdain when he learned John had taken an older black lover? Don opposed most equity initiatives and programs that promoted a more inclusive, progressive society. Hell, the man endorsed voter suppression legislation, found little or no fault with police in high profile shootings of black men, and opposed anything that sounded like affirmative action in hiring and college admissions.

Yet, few in John's circle treated individual black people as well. Don went out of his way, for example, in helping orient Nicole Robinson, a black associate who transferred into VWM's corporate section after flaming out as a litigator. Mostly because of Don's teaching efforts, she now understood the ins and outs of corporate practice and it appeared she had a fighting chance of surviving in the firm, a doubtful proposition if she'd remained in litigation.

Then, there was his actual experience with Minnie. John could only smile when he remembered how Don swooned over her while she cared for him in the hospital. Something made him see black individuals and black people as a group much differently.

Inside, though, John suspected Don would keep whatever problem he had with Minnie's color, if he had one, to himself. He might or might not have a thought on age. Because John so valued Don as a friend, he decided involving him in his current messy situation with Minnie didn't promote the long-term welfare of their friendship.

Don one day would know about John's love affair with Minnie. He wouldn't criticize the relationship just because it existed. Civility meant too much to him for that. But seeking his advice on the issues John suspected lay behind Minnie's disappearance invited a response that might not help anyone.

Smith Davies, an accountant John played golf with, and

Ralph Martindale, a real estate lawyer in a small suburban firm and the only other Penn law graduate John knew in Dallas, had become drinking buddies. Smith was a confirmed bachelor who'd apparently endured some kind of trauma with women years ago. Ralph was happily married and had been for a dozen years.

Nothing in either man's relationship history, or in John's friendship with them, suggested they could help. Both were casual acquaintances. That left his two women friends in the VWM corporate section, Kate Hart and Margaret Brandt.

Two things dissuaded him from seeking advice from Kate. First, his crush on her from a year ago left him leery of discussing personal matters with her. It felt creepy for some reason. Second, he'd blown her off about her friend Jody Lawrence. If she'd brought up that idea a year ago he'd have welcomed the gesture. But she suggested it during the months he spent plotting how he could spend more time with Minnie. John suspected it best he keep his love life out of what was otherwise a positive professional relationship with Kate.

Margaret Brandt was a different story. Despite her full head of jet black hair, smoky brown eyes, beguiling smile, and svelte figure complete with long, shapely legs she seldom hid under slacks or pant suits, John had never been attracted to her. He had a hard time saying why – he just hadn't been.

Maggie definitely wasn't gay. She'd appeared at numerous functions during John's two years at the firm with at least three different male escorts. And, she'd never once tried fixing him up.

Aside from the fact Maggie didn't have Kate's negatives as a confidant, she had some definite positives. When John arrived at VWM in 2016, no one did more that made him feel welcome. No other partner, associate, or support staff person expressed greater interest in him as a person. Maggie stopped by his office in those early days and asked how he was settling into

Dallas, not just how work was proceeding at the law firm.

When he returned from his hospital stay, Maggie took the lead in the corporate section in smoothing his way. She helped him retrieve materials from the library and documents he needed from files. She encouraged partners about going to John's office when they gave him assignments instead of demanding he come to them. John guessed she saved him at least two trips a day during that time when getting around had been so difficult. Maybe that kind of care and compassion could help in dealing with this crisis with Minnie.

∞∞∞

It was 4:35 p.m. Friday when John decided he'd go see Maggie. He suspected he'd find her at her desk, grinding out shareholder agreements or reviewing memos. Because she'd been an English major at Duke and articles editor on the *Texas Law Review*, partners often asked her to check legal memos written by associates for content, writing clarity, and production errors. Litigators even consulted her about appellate and trial briefs.

"You are still here," John said when he stuck his head into her 42nd floor office.

"Where else would you find me on a late summer Friday afternoon?" she asked, looking up from the work on her desk. "You know me. There's always one more thing I can do."

As a seventh year associate who'd been a star from day one, Maggie's office reflected her success at VWM. As she neared partnership, she already owned expensive art she'd hung on the walls. Plaques and awards decorated her shelves. Personal mementos from client victories sat on her credenza. John looked straight into her eyes. "Have you got a few minutes for a personal conversation?"

"Yes, but I warn you. We don't have long. I'm taken for the night. One of my on-again-off-again suitors is feeding me a late dinner this evening."

"What time?" John asked, pulling her office door closed.

"I'm meeting him at seven thirty at a place downtown, so I don't have far to go."

"This won't take until then."

Rocking back in her chair, she said, "Sit down. What's on your mind?"

"I've never told you about the 56-year old black woman I'm involved with."

Maggie didn't try hiding her shock. Her hands rushed toward her mouth. She rubbed her throat and drew in an audible breath. "Boy! That came out of left field," she said finally. "Did I hear right? You're involved with a 56-year old black woman?"

John smiled quickly. "You aren't going to say something like, 'not that there's anything wrong with being black?'"

"No, but I imagine I'm one of the few people in this law firm who wouldn't say that or something like that."

John showed his gratitude for Maggie's sensitivity by laying his left hand on his heart and gesturing to her with his right. "I'm dating a 56-year old black woman, and it's serious."

"Marriage serious?"

"I don't know. It's never come up, but until about a week ago, I don't think either of us would have dismissed the idea without thought."

"Do you have a picture of this woman? Let's see what capturing the great John Dawson requires. Perhaps we should all take lessons from her."

John grinned. "Stop, Maggie. You can't help it can you? But, yes, I have a picture." He punched up one of the picnic photos on his phone and passed it to her. "This got me into all kinds of trouble with my mother. That's a subject for another day. This is what Minnie looks like."

"A very fit, attractive woman," Maggie said while she examined the photo. Then she handed John his phone back. "She doesn't look 56. I would have guessed maybe 44 or 45. You've done well for yourself, my young Jedi."

"She has done a number on me, I'll grant you that."

"Something happened in the last week that derailed this adventure for a time? That's why you're here, right?"

He sat back in the chair in front of her desk. "In a nutshell, yes. That's why I'm here."

"So, let's go back to the beginning. How did this start and why have things gone off the tracks?"

With as little embellishment and hyperbole as possible, John told Margaret Brandt the story of his romance with Minnie Donaldson. He spent half his soliloquy offering his suspicions about why she'd backed off. He wasn't sure, of course, but he assumed this was all rooted in their twin dilemmas of age and race. Or race and age.

Maggie listened intently. When he stopped, she leaned toward him and said, "That's quite a story. I'm amazed it's worked as well as it has. Suggests to me there's something there."

John felt a sudden lightness. This didn't strike someone with Maggie's logic-driven internal compass as crazy? "It has been wonderful," he told her, then described the Oregon trip. He left out only the bawdiest details.

She raised her eyebrows. "What happened? Why did bliss turn into trauma?"

John tapped his fingers on the table beside his chair. "Hell if I know. We were doing great. Then in Shreveport, she went crazy on me. It's like something happened on the trip over there. She was fine before she left. She rode over with a friend the day before I got there."

"Do you know the friend?"

With a shake of his head, John said, "Not sure I've ever met her. Whatever she knows about me, Minnie told her. That assumes she even talked with her about me. For all I know, this might have all been in Minnie's head."

"Is she like that – somebody who stays in her own head?"

"Not more than anybody else with a college education who's had a successful thirty-plus year professional career."

For the next fifteen minutes, Maggie cross-examined John about Minnie's every word and action during and after the Shreveport trip. At the end she said, "You're just going to have to hear from her what's going on."

John let out a heavy sigh. "I was afraid you'd say that."

Maggie seemed to gather herself. She parted her lips slightly and shifted in her chair. "I will say one thing. Don't give up on this, John. I see it in your eyes. I hear it in your voice. You care about this woman. You love her.

"Your feelings are what matters. Don't give them up until you know there's no chance. Big deal that she's old, that she's a different color. Hold on to this if you can."

∞ ∞ ∞

Alone at home, Minnie wished she hadn't agreed she'd give John's friend that golf lesson Saturday. A cross current of emotions raged through her that Friday night. She wanted to see John as early as possible Saturday, eat breakfast with him, and entice him into bed for the day. Despite that desire and Carol's proffered wisdom, she couldn't shake the idea she should call off the relationship. Finally, something – she wasn't sure what – told her she shouldn't decide yet.

So, early that evening Minnie stewed, alternately warming to Carol's advice yet, from time to time, hearing Crystal's words of caution. She hoped sleeping on the matter would help her decide if trying to reclaim her life with John was right or whether the whole thing was too crazy.

As she readied herself for bed, she relaxed and a revelation struck. Suddenly, she understood the problem. Seeking certainty about the future with John hadn't worked. This was a problem amenable only to an imperfect solution. Tolerating ambiguity would ease her troubled mind, not a quest for an unreachable holy grail. No guarantee existed that Crystal was right, and none existed that she wasn't.

That conclusion, and fatigue, ended the turmoil at 12:30 a. m. when Minnie fell asleep. Her alarm would go off in five hours. Saturday morning Kevin Monroe would get nine holes and some words of wisdom. After that, she had other fish to fry.

Chapter 32

Coincidence, or fate, put Minnie back at North Central Country Club for Kevin Monroe's playing lesson the day after her round with Carol. She asked him to meet her in the club parking lot at seven o'clock. She'd booked a 7:50 a.m. tee time on North Central's nine-hole course.

When she saw a young black man dressed in khaki shorts and a green shirt get out of a late model Toyota Camry and look right past her, she suspected it was him and that John hadn't described her. She waved and shouted, "Kevin?"

He turned around, appearing unsure where the voice had come from. Then he spotted her and rushed her way. She laughed at the astonished look on his face. Out of breath, he asked, "You aren't Minnie Donaldson, are you?"

"I am," she replied. She shook his hand and worked hard at keeping a straight face. She barely succeeded. "I suppose John didn't tell you much about me, especially what I look like."

"He just said you were his girlfriend, you play golf really well, and you're a little older than he is."

"Well, he's right about one and three. How good I am at golf is debatable. Maybe I can give you a few pointers. Get your clubs and wait here. I'll pick you up as soon as I can get a cart. I usually walk, but I have no idea what kind of shape you're in for this heat. I hear it could get to 90 degrees before we finish, over 100 later today. I hope you can get something out of this without fatigue becoming the issue that gets in our way." They began on the driving range.

She told him, "I won't fool with your swing. John said you're taking lessons. I won't confuse you by telling you things that might contradict your instructor. I'll check ball flight, tendencies with various clubs, and how you manage the course."

After 15 minutes on the range, they spent 10 minutes in the chipping area, and finished the warm up with 10 minutes of putting. Gavin Henson greeted them at the starter's hut. "Back again today, Mrs. Donaldson? Glad you're here." He looked at his clipboard. "You're playing our nine-hole course, correct?"

"Right," Minnie said. "Things to do today. I'm giving Kevin here some pointers. Nine holes should exhaust my knowledge." In truth, Minnie's mind had turned to John and making contact with him after golf.

Henson chuckled. "I doubt that." He turned toward Kevin. "Watch and listen carefully. She knows her stuff. Have a nice time."

When they drove toward the first hole, Minnie pointed at a wooded area on their right and explained, "The club wants that land so it can build another nine holes. We'd have two full championship courses. The nine we're playing today would become the back nine for that new course and they'd run the front through that area. It's a perfect piece of land for a golf course."

"Looks that way to me," Kevin agreed.

"Apparently the owner is an old guy who isn't interested in selling, no matter the price. The club is waiting for him to die because his children will sell. In the meantime, we live with having 27 championship holes, not 36. I think you'll find this nine plenty challenging."

At the first tee, Minnie asked Kevin what he saw as they looked down the fairway.

"Not sure what you mean," he replied. "The flag is 375 yards from this tee, if that's what you're talking about."

"What's in between?"

"Fairway."

She ignored his lack of awareness. "I noticed on the range

you hit your driver between 220 and 240 yards, usually left to right. What's at that distance?"

He scanned the area again. "Oh, yeah. Looks like deep rough on the right."

"That's it. Given that, stay left or consider hitting a shorter club, like a three wood or five wood so that heavy rough doesn't come into play."

Kevin still used his driver and barely kept his 240-yard tee shot out of the rough. Minnie hit left with a three wood and wound up behind him, but with an easier angle to the hole.

She played first and dropped her approach shot on the green, 15 feet from the pin. Standing behind Kevin's ball, Minnie told him, "Go through your pre-shot routine, hit the shot, and we'll talk on the ride up." He pushed his ball right, barely staying out of a greenside bunker.

"Two things," she told him on the ride. "First, get with your pro and work out a pre-shot routine you use before every shot. You did totally different things before you hit off the tee and before your approach shot.

"Second, the next time you play this hole, or one like it, you'll know that coming in from the left is much better than from where you were. I had a longer shot, but a better angle. That bunker you're behind, and now must pitch over, wasn't in play for me. Yes, I was 20 yards behind you, but compare where I am now with where you are."

"I see what John meant about you. I never think about things like that. I just hit the ball."

"Not uncommon for beginners. You've been playing a year, right?"

"Yeah," he said, as they reached the green and he moved toward his ball. "I started last August."

"You're doing fine," she said after he pitched over the bunker and onto the green. "Let's see what else you can learn today. Course management can save you five strokes a round, sometimes more, once you get the fundamentals of the game down."

On the two par-five holes she told him, "Resist the temptation – which you will have when you play with big hitters – to try reaching the green in two, especially if a hazard comes into play at all. Pros reach par fives in two all the time, of course, but not many amateurs can. Find a spot that's comfortable – 75, 85, 100 yards out. Play to that distance on your second shot and work on your short game so you get on the green in regulation and two putt for par, or sometimes make a birdie."

They continued through the holes. She advised him he should "think about how you take the big number out of play. That kills scores for inexperienced players. They make three or four pars, maybe even a birdie, then take an eight on a par four hole. Lots of times that results from course management errors, like trying to hit shots over hazards they can't hit and may never hit."

As they drove back to the clubhouse after their final hole, he asked her, "How did you learn all this?"

"Three things: I practice. I play. I watch."

With eyes as wide as an open prairie, he said, "Tell me about that."

"Practice not only helps improve your game but also tells you what you can and can't do. On the course, I don't try shots my practice says I can't hit.

"I play a lot, both for fun and competitively, so I have a feel for situations that come up. Not much I haven't seen on a golf course.

"I watch tournaments on television and attend tournaments locally and elsewhere. I've been to four U.S. Opens, two for women and two for men, one Ryder Cup, and one Solheim Cup. I've been to the Masters twice – try getting those tickets – and a British Women's Open at Royal Birkdale. I played the Old Course at St. Andrews on that trip. By the way, watching includes reading books and magazine articles about course management and course design."

She declined his invitation for a post-round drink given the early hour – 10:35 a.m. when they pulled up at the pro shop – and her fixation on getting cleaned up so she could connect with John.

As they parted, Kevin shared a thought with her. " I see why you and John are together, despite your superficial differences."

His words surprised her. "Tell me what you mean."

"You're just alike. You think the same way. You both size things up, then figure out what you have to do to make something work. You study whatever problem you come across. You work at that solution once you figure it out. You both seem very patient. You're well matched, even if you do look like the odd couple."

$$\infty\infty\infty$$

Following a shower at North Central, Minnie jumped into her car, but sat in the parking lot, reflecting on Friday with Carol and hearing Kevin Monroe's morning observations ring in her head. Reaching John became her number one priority. She figured he was in his office so she dialed that number.

He picked up on the first ring. "To what do I owe this treat?" he asked playfully.

"Meet me at our Starbucks in 20 minutes. I'd suggest my house, but we'd get distracted there, or at least I would. We need to talk. Now."

"Are you over your malaise, or whatever has kept you out of

sorts – not to mention kept us apart?"

"I think so. But, there are things you must understand. Can you meet me?"

He laughed. "I imagine this buy-sell agreement I was working on will be here this afternoon."

"Or tomorrow. Or Monday."

"Yes, but I need it finished by Monday."

"Just get to the place, John."

∞ ∞ ∞

She arrived first, but by only a few minutes since they were coming from equidistant locations. By the time she'd taken the customary seat in the back, he was in line ordering his drink.

She stood up as he approached the table. My how she wanted to hug and kiss the man! She restrained herself, offering him a peck on the cheek.

"It's good to see you," he said. "What's it been? Two weeks since we laid eyes on each other?"

"The phone calls haven't been especially satisfying either," she added.

"Purely transactional. Is all that gone at last?"

"I hope so. I owe you an explanation and an apology. But, I had to do what I did."

He shrugged his shoulders and threw open his palms. "You needed space?"

She swatted at the air. "That's trite, John. And maybe even condescending. But I won't let a small indignity get in the way of what's important."

"I'm sorry. I was trying to be funny. I shouldn't have said

that."

She held her hands together under her chin. "I backed away from you because of something my daughter Crystal said at the July family summit meeting. It started nagging at me on the Shreveport trip."

He nodded his head. "You sure seemed different as soon as I got there."

"On the ride over, I reflected on Crystal's comments. They got to me. I shouldn't have let that happen. At least, I should have told you about it. Maybe we could have worked through it. That's what I hope we can do now."

"What did she say?"

"Crystal said she was okay with our being together, but she warned me about what could happen in 10, 15, or 20 years. She said I'll lose my looks before you do. She suggested there's a good chance after I put all those years into a relationship with you that you'll trade me in for somebody prettier – somebody whose boobs don't sag, who has no wrinkles, and who isn't a forgetful old fool."

He stared at her, then folded his arms across his chest. "You're right about one thing. You should have told me you were thinking about that."

"I was scared."

"Of what?"

"That she might be right."

He pulled her hand from her paper tea cup and held it. "My attraction to you doesn't start or end with your looks. I like how you look, but I'd love and care for you no matter how you looked if you were the same person inside. Why deal in hypotheticals about what we'd do if you looked different or what either of us might be like 20 years from now?"

"Carol Robbins helped me see that yesterday."

"Carol Robbins?"

With an elbow on the table, Minnie propped her chin in her right hand. "She's a very rich woman I play golf with. I'm well off, but I'm not in Carol's league. That doesn't keep her from being a great friend, which she's been for years. I played with her yesterday."

"What'd she say?"

"We were on the tee for this really difficult par three hole. She said she could make a hole-in-one there but could didn't mean would. She hit a great shot, a truly great shot, but she didn't make a hole-in-one – not even close. That told me expecting perfection from my significant other and predicting what might happen far in the future is silly. I love what we have now. I should enjoy it. Finding it was hard enough. I'm sorry I messed with it. That wasn't fair.

"And one more thing. Your friend Kevin Monroe helped me see something that's important."

He frowned and narrowed his eyes. "You told Kevin about our troubles?"

"No, I didn't. As we parted, he volunteered that he thought we belong together because we're so much alike, even if we are the 'odd couple', his exact words. He said we both think things through and approach problems in the same way. Having that in common with your main squeeze is rare. I sure didn't have it with Bradley, at least not in the later years. I'll have a hard time finding that with anyone else. Since I have it, I should work on keeping it."

He leaned across the table and kissed her. "Tell me what you'd like now."

"I want three things. You can start doing one of them next week. You can do one tomorrow, Sunday. You must do the other today."

He leaned back in his chair. "Tell me what they are."

"Next week, you can move in with me. I want you around all the time. Can you do that?"

"I could say I should think about it. If I did, I'd have the same answer I have now, which is yes."

Her eyes lit up. "Tomorrow – Sunday – I want you to go to church with me. As for that, you said you could be present for me or something similar. Remember?"

"I made that promise and I'll keep it. What's the third one, the thing I must do today?"

Minnie grabbed her car keys from the table. She held them up. "Follow me to my house. If you can't figure that one out, I take back everything I said."

About The Author

I G Cummings

Besides writing, enjoys reading, sports, and learning about the world.

I G Cummings writes novels and short stories about relationships.

These works involve people who look to their inner feelings and put aside superficial differences in the quest for love.

Sign up for I G Cummings newsletter at website

igcummings.com.

Please leave a review

Amazon

Good Reads

Public Library

Facebook & Instagram

Other social media

Website igcummings.com

Or email author@igcummings.com

More Books By This Author

Weeks In May - A Novel

Jo Ann Davis and Robert Hart are lonely, middle-aged people, putting up with the cards life has dealt them. At 51, she is tired of the shortage of black men suitable for an upwardly mobile professional, black woman. A 63-year old white man, he's been widowed and alone for eight years, but he's far from done with love or career.

A chance meeting between Jo Ann and Robert one day in May brings them together for a year-long, head-spinning adventure.

By the time, it's all said and done, she'll be set up to run a Fortune 1000 company, he'll be on his way to becoming a multi-millionaire, and they'll have a set of twins together – after foiling a plot that would have destroyed their family and business lives.

That's Different - A Novel

Jennifer and Gavin McCain, after thirty plus years of marriage, divorced for many of the same reasons hundreds of thousands of other Americans divorce each year -- neglect, infidelity, out growing each other, etc. Both Jennifer and Gavin wound up with new, much younger partners. While the age gap between Gavin and his new girlfriend and Jennifer and her new beau may have been identical, the reaction of the three adult McCain children wasn't.

That's Different is about what can happen in a family when one parent's new relationship gets viewed one way and the other parent's new relationship receives an entirely different look. Age gap relationships happen in America. Sometimes the man is older, the woman younger. Sometimes the woman is older, the man younger. As *That's Different* shows, which is which can be a big deal, a very big deal.

Bonus

WEEKS IN MAY - A Novel By I. G. Cummings
Chapter I

J o Ann Davis sat in the night club, nursing a glass of wine. The old school rhythm and blues band finished Al Green's "Let's Stay Together" and took a break. Her date stood up and said, "I'm going to the restroom."

Soon Jo Ann was shifting in her seat, wondering where he was. She sipped her wine and noticed him standing at a table across the room, carrying on an animated conversation with two women. Giddy smiles, wandering fingers snaking up one woman's arm, and the firm grasp of the other's hand said he didn't want to leave. Frank Wilson was making a little time, even as he made his way toward Jo Ann.

Jo Ann long ago tired of black men's wandering ways. She hated thinking of it in racial terms, but she only dated black men, and so many behaved that way, that's how she saw it.

She'd had high hopes for Frank Wilson, a tall, brown skinned, medium build man with short hair and a round face. A 48-year old bank lawyer, he claimed he worked all the time and went out sparingly. She saw through that story after he put her off or stood her up three times.

"Who were you talking to?" Jo Ann asked when he returned. "You said you didn't know anybody here."

"I don't, baby. I was just being friendly."

Jo Ann sneered. "That wasn't being 'friendly.' You were hitting on those two. I know it when I see it."

"I just said hello."

"Your hands were all over them. At least have enough class not to hit on somebody else – two somebody else's, in fact – when you're out with me."

"We're not a thing. I can be friendly with whoever I damn well please. You don't own me, --"

Jo Ann gritted her teeth. "You were going to call me a bitch, weren't you? You were going to say, 'You don't own me, bitch.' That's what men like you call any woman who dares call out their low-life behavior."

"Quit acting a fool, Jo Ann."

"I'm tired of being made a fool, Frank." She shook her fist. "I need a man who at least pretends he respects me. I don't have any say over what you do when you're not with me. But, when we're together? Please. That was insulting."

"I've had --"

"Take me home. You're not staying over. I'm not seeing you anymore."

He sat up. "Fine. I don't need this. I don't care if you are a big time

320

corporate executive with a six figure salary. I didn't do anything except talk to a few folks here at the place."

"You did more than that. You've told me blatant lies about where you were, like the time you claimed you were playing tennis with your buddies, but my girlfriends saw you with some woman at a sports bar. You've stood me up time after time."

He put down his drink. "The woman at the sports bar was an old friend from school."

"Then why lie about it?"

"My tennis match was later that day."

"Sure it was. I've heard your hushed phone conversations while we're driving. I've seen you shut off your phone when it rings. I've seen little smiles when you get a text, I ask you what it was, and you say, 'nothing.' Once upon a time I would've put up with that, but not now. I'm done with you."

The next day, Jo Ann and her friend Betty Martin ate dinner at an Italian place near Betty's house in southwest Houston. The setting sun provided a comforting backdrop as they sat on the restaurant patio.

"Did you go out with Frank last night?" Betty asked toward the end of the meal. "You've been seeing him for what, two months now? Must be something to it." A thin, brown-skinned woman of 47, Betty's bright eyes and ready smile hid the pain of family life troubled by a wayward son who kept getting into trouble.

Jo Ann, wearing a blue top and white shorts, put down her fork and leaned back. "I'm done with him."

"What?"

"He's like all the other black men I've been out with recently. If it has tits and indoor plumbing, he gets on its trail."

"What'd he do?"

Jo Ann tugged at her left ear and wrinkled her nose. "He hit on two women at a table across from us on his way back from the restroom. It was blatant."

"You couldn't hear him, could you?"

"No, but I saw. It wasn't the first thing he's done that showed me what he's like. Kendra and Tiffany saw him with some woman when he'd told me he was playing tennis with friends. He got phone calls he'd hang up on when he realized I was listening. It was as bad as with James."

"James was bad, wasn't he?" Betty said, chuckling at the mention of Jo Ann's ex-husband. "I'd just met you. You'd call and tell me about his philandering."

"I'm not going through that again."

Betty sighed. "There must be a good brother out there somewhere. I found one."

"Charles is a good man," Jo Ann agreed. "You've been great for each other."

Betty nodded. "Our marriage has been good. What're you gonna do now that this one's over?"

"Hope the next guy is different, that he wants something real, that he wants more than adding to his conquest list."

Betty leaned closer. In a low voice, she said, "You still have friends."

"Yes, I'll hang out with you and Kendra and Tiffany." Jo Ann stopped and grinned. "My vibrator will get more work. That's the only thing I'll miss about Frank. He may be a no good s.o.b., but he knows how to use his dick. It's long and thick. He must be on Viagra or something. I think he could stay hard that four hours they talk about in the commercials."

Betty giggled. Jo Ann sometimes said things like that, having fun at her friend's expense. Betty was kind and compassionate, but her prudish streak set her up for embarrassment when Jo Ann flaunted her open attitudes about sex.

"I don't need it as much as you," Betty said, now controlling the giggling. "Once every few weeks seems enough."

Jo Ann frowned. "I need more than that, but I'm not staying with a shit just so I can get laid."

"You'll find someone. Maybe not where you expect him, but you'll find him."

"I hope so. I'm tired, tired, tired of being alone. And did I mention I'm tired of being alone?"

"You did." Betty picked up the check.

"Let me get that. I cried on your shoulder. At least I can buy dinner."

Betty kept the check. "You reminded me how good my life is compared with what it could be. Buying dinner is a small price for knowing how good I have it."

When Robert Hart woke up he felt lost. He rubbed his eyes. Red numbers on the end table clock said 8:33 p.m. As he ran his hands through his brown hair and noticed the contrast between his tanned arms and the pale of his wrist where he wore his watch, Robert realized the big screen television across the room was on.

Fifth inning said the box in the corner. Didn't the game just start?

Robert stretched his long arms. He blinked. "Oh, the Astros are playing the Mets," he said out loud. "It's 8:30. I fell asleep. I know why."

Yes, he did, Robert said silently, thinking of the old pattern. He stood up, walked to the window, and looked into the darkness of the warm May evening.

Robert turned from the window, moved to the desk in the corner, and reached for the phone. He still had a land line, even if hardly anyone else did. The "real phone" he picked up and cradled between his ear and chin gave him a comfortable feeling, a sense of connection with things he knew. Darla always called him from this white phone or the yellow one in the kitchen.

Oh, he had a Smartphone with all the bells and whistles. There wasn't much it couldn't do. Neither the youngsters at work nor his adult children outdid him on technology. He kept the land line because it made him feel the world hadn't careened out of control.

After four rings, he heard the familiar voice say, "This is Terry. Leave a message. I'll call you back."

Robert thought about calling Jon Weinstein, one of his few guy friends who was single, but remembered he was busy with a client meeting.

As he put down the phone, Robert heard the flap of the dog door in the utility room being pushed open. Moments later, Rufus, his nine-year old golden lab, ambled into the family room. Rufus stood just inside the doorway that led from the kitchen wearing his 'feed me,' expression.

"It's coming," Robert said, starting toward the laundry room where he kept the dog food. "It's just you and me again, big guy. We watch the game together?"

Rufus whimpered and turned his head slightly upward, emphasizing that eating meant more than any baseball game. Robert retrieved the food, filled the hungry dog's bowl, and watched him eat for a few moments before going back into the family room and sitting down.

Tonight resembled nights eight years ago, right after Darla died. Watch a game for a short while, fall asleep, wake up after a couple of hours, the television blaring, go to bed when the game ended, lie awake for an hour, play around on the computer until 2:30 or so, crawl back into bed, and fall into fitful sleep until 6:30.

Being single in the couples world Robert and Darla inhabited made things hard. At first, friends like Joyce and Terry Peters and Harry and Jeri Morris regularly invited him over for dinner, card games, or watching television. Their hospitality helped, but couldn't continue indefinitely.

Robert felt himself wearing out his welcome, even if they insisted he wasn't. Soon he spent most nights at home with Rufus.

Robert tried changing the pattern. He tried reading, and crossword puzzles. He tried drinking a glass of wine or beer before bed. He tried delaying his daily workout until evening. He tried eating dinner early and he tried eating dinner late. He tried skipping dinner or eating light. Nothing worked for long.

Two years after Darla died, things started getting better. Still, every once in a while the pattern, and its misery, returned. Friends offered advice he resisted or only sort of took. A doctor prescribed sleeping pills. Robert, fearful of getting hooked, balked at taking them, but briefly relented. They worked for a while, but left him feeling hollowed out. He stopped taking them.

Two good friends, after what they called the "decent interlude" of two years, suggested he work at getting laid. Even now, with Darla gone eight years, Robert couldn't stomach pursuing another woman. His wife's memory burned so brightly he couldn't think about sharing a bed, much less his life, with someone else.

So, here he was, watching a baseball game with Rufus curled up beside him, wondering if he again must endure sleepless nights, drowsy days, and the blah feelings that went with being alone.

When the game, a 7-3 Astros victory, ended, Robert turned off the television and invited Rufus outside for his evening romp around the yard. The dog comfortably in for the night, Robert headed for bed, knowing he'd likely end up at his computer, surfing internet sports sites in the wee hours. He arrived at work the next day, far from wide awake, but current on the projected college football top ten.

Chapter 2

R obert went to his JAX Oil Company office assuming he had the place to himself. It was 4:30 p.m. Friday, May 24. It appeared everyone had cleared out for the Memorial Day weekend.

As he walked down the executive suite hallway, Robert noticed a muffled voice. He couldn't make out the words, but he sensed distress. He heard a phone receiver slammed into its cradle, then sobs. He realized they came from Jo Ann Davis's office.

Robert barely knew her. Her job involved data gathering. When he needed a fact or figure, he sought her help. They'd been in a few meetings together and smiled at each other in the hall.

When he looked into her office, Robert saw an attractive black woman with dark, medium length hair and a small scar on her chin. She appeared upset, working at holding back tears and not succeeding. Her chair faced sideways. Robert noticed mascara streaks. She turned and shifted her reddened eyes in his direction.

"I'm sorry, Jo Ann. I didn't mean to intrude. I just –"

"Robert! I should have closed the door before I took that call."

He studied her face. She had round, brown eyes, long lashes, thick eyebrows, a flat nose, and full lips. She wore a green and blue scarf over a tan sweater top. A blue suit jacket hung in the corner. "Is everything all right?"

"I could claim I'm fine," she said, looking down, then up at him. "But you can tell that'd be a lie. I'm sorry. Can I help you with something?"

"I was headed for my office and heard you. I felt I should look in and see if you were okay. I heard someone in pain."

She forced a smile. "You got that right."

"I'm intruding here," Robert said, backing away. "Let me know if I can do anything."

"No. I wish you'd stay. Being alone isn't what I need right now. Sit down. Let's talk for a few minutes."

She motioned him to a chair in the corner. He sat down, hands clasped between his long legs. He wore dress khaki slacks and a blue polo shirt.

"I heard you sobbing," he said. "You seem like a strong person. You wouldn't be crying in your office unless something was wrong. If you're up for telling me about it, I'll listen."

"That's very kind. I'm not sure I want to talk about it. But, I'd like to talk with you. I'd like knowing who you are. I'd like knowing all the people I work with."

"Well, what can I tell you?"

"Whatever you'd like."

"We'll start with the easy stuff. I'm 63 years old. I retired from JeVon Oil last year after 39 years in the industry. When I retired, my old friend, David Marks, asked me if I'd work for him. I said no. He begged. We finally agreed on this consulting arrangement."

"I didn't know all that. I looked around one day and you were here."

"I pick my projects. I work on strategic planning, people management, that kind of thing. I set my schedule. They pay me well, with no hassles. It's good."

"Do you have a family?"

"Three children – two sons and a daughter. My wife died eight years ago. The kids are grown, so I live alone except for Rufus, a nine-year old golden lab. And no, I don't have a girlfriend." He wasn't sure where the last line came from.

Jo Ann sat up. "How tall are you?"

"The years have cut me down. I'm 6-7, but in college I was 6-9. And yes, I played basketball, at Drury, a small college in Springfield, Missouri."

"That's always the next question, isn't it?"

"I expect it."

She had stopped sniffling. "Where did you grow up?"

"Suburban Kansas City. I matured late. I was a 6-6 high school center too small for major college basketball. I picked Drury partly because of its church affiliation. Before starting college, I grew three inches. Coaches at bigtime schools like Missouri and Iowa State who'd ignored me, started calling. I told them they could go to hell."

"Were you good in college?"

"I made small-college All-America twice. My junior year we lost by three points in the finals of the national tournament. I was tournament MVP, but not winning that championship still galls me. My senior year, two of our other top players got hurt and we lost in the semi-finals."

"Did you have a chance at the pros?"

"At only 200 pounds, I couldn't play center in the NBA. I didn't have the outside shot for playing forward. I got a graduate school scholarship and took the sure thing."

"Where?"

"Harvard."

"MBA?"

"Yes."

"I got one too, finally. Nothing so elegant as Harvard. I did night school at the University of Houston."

"Don't knock it. It seems you do your job well. When I've asked you for something, you've given me what I needed."

"Thank you. Being appreciated is nice. Tell me about your wife."

He took a deep breath. "We met at Gulf Oil, my first job after school. We got married three years later and stayed married 28 years, until she died. She was kind, smart, and dedicated to the kids and to me."

Jo Ann leaned forward. He thought her calm now. "Your kids?"

Before responding, he looked around her office, noticing pictures of her with children at sporting events. He saw no man in any of the photos. "We had two boys, Bill and Al, and a daughter named Sandra. The boys attended Stanford, then got MBAs from other, different schools. Both now work for big companies. Sandy graduated from Central Missouri State."

"Grandchildren?"

"Bill and Marcia have a four-year-old daughter. None yet for Al and Deena or Sandy. She was married briefly, but divorced her husband last year."

"Where do they live?"

"Bill and Marcia in Cleveland, Al and Deena in Memphis, and Sandy stayed in Florida, where her husband grew up."

"I have a granddaughter too," Jo Ann said, looking out the window, before turning back toward Robert. "She's four and delightful. Her name is Shonda, my son's child. They live in Denver. But let me ask you, why no girlfriend? I can't imagine such a handsome gentleman wanting for female company."

He grinned at the compliment, but turned serious. "Thanks. I still can't imagine being with anybody but Darla."

"I get that, but eight years is a long time."

"Seems like it, sometimes. Other times it seems like yesterday."

"Do you still grieve her?"

"I guess so. I still think about her."

"It's great you had her in your life. It doesn't happen for everyone."

"I guess not. But wait," he added after a pause. "Why are we talking about me? You were the one crying."

Her face lightened. "I was crying because I'm so lonely sometimes. The woman who called works in accounting. I've tried cultivating a friendship with her, expanding my circle. We planned a Fourth of July trip to San Diego. She backed out. She's going with other people to Las Vegas."

"Sounds like she's just rude, 'mean' as my older son's wife would say."

"And as my youngest daughter would say," Jo Ann added, chuckling.

"She wouldn't be much of a friend," Robert continued. "How long was the trip planned?

"Two months."

"I take it you weren't invited on her trip?"

"I wasn't."

Robert turned calm and made a rare impulsive suggestion. "I doubt you feel like working anymore. What I came in for can wait. Why don't we head out for one of the places nearby? We could have a drink, maybe eat something. You can tell me about yourself. I'll buy."

"Deal," Jo Ann replied.

....

To read more go to Amazon to get your copy...

Acknowledgement

A lot of people helped with *A Love for the Ages*, I start with my readers:

* Monica Harris
* Henry Jones
* Verleria Jones
* Carla Moore
* Hallie Moore
* Pat O'Connell

Each provided unique insight that improved the end product.

Whatever shortcomings remain fall on me.

Others helped in big and small ways anyone doing this kind of thing must have:

~ Kelly Hooper and Raven Cole, who cleaned up the manuscript time after time.

~ Karyl Paige, an incredibly meticulous proofreader.

~ Karen Soane, who assisted with the last effort to get this book onto Kindle and Amazon, ready for print.

~ Shaun Wiley, my daughter, who taught me most of what little I know about how one does this.

www.ingramcontent.com/pod-product-compliance
Lightning Source LLC
Chambersburg PA
CBHW021453240626
47154CB00002B/347